I0787168

Don't Ask, Ghosts Tell

Don't Ask, Ghosts Tell

AN LGBTQ+ HORROR ANTHOLOGY

Edited by

Vince A. Liaguno and Sirrah Medeiros

TUNDRA SWAN
PRESS

Stafford, Virginia

DON'T ASK, GHOSTS TELL
Copyright © 2025 Tundra Swan Press, LLC. All rights reserved.

Foreword © 2025 Rachel Branaman
Shellshocked Stars, Piece by Piece © 2025 Maxwell I. Gold
All Souls © 2025 Michael Thomas Ford
A Haunted Alcoholic © 2025 Eric David Roman
Water Rites © 2025 Rook Riley
Smolder © 2025 Christina Bergling
My Lover, The Muck © 2025 Benjamin Larned
Gänger © 2025 G.B. Lindsey
Imposter © 2025 Toshiya Kamei
The Carers © 2025 Sean Eads
When We Laid Down Our Arms © 2025 Sumiko Saulson
The Elixir © 2025 May Walker
Devil's Tree © 2025 Amanda Dier
Bloom House © 2025 John Grover
The Elevator in FKD Mall is a Hungry Sukebe © 2025 R.J.K. Lee
Like Velvet on His Neck © 2025 Ryan Cole
The Abyss and The Apex © 2025 J. Daniel Stone
Phantom Limbs © 2025 M. Edusa
The Scold's Bridle © 2025 Amanda Nevada DeMel
Need to Know © 2025 Darrell Z. Grizzle
The Bitter Unthreading © 2025 Sara Tantlinger

This is a work of fiction. Names, characters, places, and incidents are products of the authors' imaginations or are used fictitiously and are not to be construed as real. Any resemblance to actual events, locales, organizations, or persons, living or dead, are entirely coincidental.

No part of this book may be used or reproduced in any manner whatsoever, stored in a retrieval system, or transmitted in any form or by any means, without written permission by the publisher except in the case of brief quotations embodied in critical articles and reviews. No part of this publication may be otherwise circulated in any form of binding or cover than that in which it is published and without a similar condition, including this condition being imposed on the subsequent purchaser.

Editors: Vince A. Liaguno and Sirrah Medeiros

Cover Design: Ruth Anna Evans Designs

Original Interior Illustrations: Nemanja Designs (pages 20, 106, 182, and 220)

Interior Design Layout: Sirrah Medeiros, Tundra Swan Press

Hardcover ISBN: 978-1-965712-02-3

Paperback ISBN: 978-1-965712-01-6

eBook ISBN: 978-1-965712-00-9

Library of Congress Control Number: 2024927501

Published by
Tundra Swan Press
TundraSwanPress.com
Printed in the United States of America

RJK
LEE

Benjamin Larned

Christina Bergling

May Walker

Ryan Cole

M. Edusa

A. N. DeMel

Toshiya Kamei

"The aim of art is to represent not the outward appearance of things, but their inward significance."

— Aristotle

Proceeds from your purchase of this book will be donated to the
Modern Military Association of America
a 501(c)(3) charitable organization.
For more information, visit
www.modernmilitary.org

Content Warning

The stories that follow may contain content that is concerning to some readers.

Please go to page 311 for more detailed content warnings.

Table of Contents

Foreword

RACHEL BRANAMAN

In 1993, the Clinton administration issued Defense Directive 1304.26, known as Don't Ask, Don't Tell (DADT); a legislative compromise that prohibited qualified gay, lesbian, and bisexual Americans from serving openly in the Armed Forces. Modern Military's founding organization, Servicemembers Legal Defense Network (SLDN), was created that same year in direct response. For 17 years, DADT sent a message that discrimination was acceptable and led to the discharge of over 13,000 qualified service members.

The military is known for building deep, enduring bonds due to the shared experiences and mutual dependence soldiers have on one another. But you can't build authentic bonds when you can't share your life, reveal your true self, or talk about your family with those serving alongside you. LGB service members lived in fear and secrecy, and while some who were investigated were fortunate enough to receive honorable discharges, many did not — robbing them of benefits and opportunities simply due to their identity.

In 2010, DADT was overturned by the Obama administration, followed by the repeals of the Defense of Marriage Act in 2013 and the ban on transgender military service in 2016. Even after its repeal, DADT's ghosts continue to haunt the LGBTQ+ military community. The enduring impact of these policies continues to reverberate in the lives of service members, veterans, and their loved ones.

Living under the shadow of DADT meant many LGBTQ+ service members and their loved ones had to hide their true identities, relationships, and families. Some pretended to be their children's nanny in order to access military housing, some hid sexual assaults for fear of being outed, and countless others endured discrimination and bullying. Forced inauthenticity and the toxicity of silence can become an internalized poison that persists within a person long after a policy is repealed.

For those directly targeted while serving under DADT, the consequences were devastating. The trauma of being betrayed, the loss of community, stigmatization by the military, and lost opportunities continue to torment service members and their families. We are still dealing with the aftermath, including:

- Economic consequences of job loss, a loss of pension, access to healthcare, housing, and other military benefits.
- Mental health consequences associated with living in secrecy, facing discrimination, and the trauma of discharge lead to higher rates of post-traumatic stress, anxiety, depression, substance abuse, and thoughts of suicide.
- Increased risk of becoming unhoused due to difficulty finding stable employment with a less than honorable

discharge, legal housing discrimination against LGBTQ+ people, and the compounding effects of economic and mental health consequences.

• Social isolation and family strain, which may follow from the stigma associated with being discharged under DADT and exacerbated by feelings of guilt, shame, and resentment.

The ghosts of DADT may never be fully exorcised, but by acknowledging the policy's harmful legacy and working to create a more inclusive and accepting environment, we can rebuild hope by ensuring that DADT's impact on future generations is minimized.

We invite you to confront these truths, recognize your own biases, and acknowledge the pain inflicted upon those who were marginalized and silenced. The ghosts that linger in these pages are not mere specters of the past, but fallen soldiers, best friends, and lovers whose memories were silenced by bigotry and fear. Their stories, ranging from the deserts of Kuwait and the stone buildings in Baghdad to the cattle ranches of East Texas and the downtown streets of Detroit, can no longer be escaped. Once buried beneath layers of prejudice and shame, these ghosts now rise to the surface, haunting the living with their unacknowledged pain.

The horrors depicted in these tales range from fantastical creatures to the chilling realities faced by service members and LGBTQ+ community members—realities that individuals outside of these communities may never imagine or think possible. These are stories of trauma, loss, and the enduring power of the human spirit, told with raw honesty and unflinching intensity. They force you to see the realities of military life, the struggles of reintegration, and the parts that we keep hidden even from those closest to us.

Step into the shadows and let the terrors unfold. Once you enter this realm, there is no turning back from the understanding that these tales are not merely fiction. They are a stark reflection of the challenges, triumphs, and sacrifices endured by these authors while navigating the complexities of their own identities.

We thank the authors for sharing their stories, the reader for opening their minds to horrors they may never have known existed, and the editors for making this anthology possible. We are honored to receive your support through the purchase of this book. You can learn more about the work we do to repair the harmful legacy of DADT and build a brighter future for LGBTQ+ and HIV+ service members, veterans, and their families at modernmilitary.org.

Rachel Branaman
Executive Director
Modern Military Association of America

Shellshocked Stars, Piece by Piece

MAXWELL I. GOLD

Displaced were the body-bags and shell-ghosts ripped apart by plastic traumas whose corpses, which once were stars; now nothing but wrinkled and empty relics. Shaken by thunderclaps, there was nowhere to hide from noiseless flashes, the silent crashes that haunted me like tatters of raggedy shadows who begged the boom-blasphemies to cease. A prayer to take back the orders which escaped my lips, and step back across desert and glassed memories until the embrace of oblivion warmed my heart.

Piece by piece, bits of skin and senility fell off like flecks of ash and gold, one day at a time until little remained of what used to be. Old eyes that used to see in the shadows hugged the dim and dreary walls of my pathetic house, begging for a shred of light, like monsters that used to play strange songs longing for familiar melodies. Rattling inside the rickety skull-shack that was my head, my tired eyes sagged and swayed, falling towards the inevitable darkness until piece by piece I lost that which was bright and bold, my soul.

Now, forever bathed in fog and light, the walls of my casket-closet were blended in grayness and sorrow. A house built in blood, muscle, and commands, consumed with phantom graces – the shades of tomorrow – pulled me closer to the ledge, shapeless and thoughtless, my body floating into the starless vacuum of the unknown whereupon I welcomed that precious oblivion until what used to be dreams cradled me lovingly in the arms of a waking dawn, gnawed at the remnant pieces of myself collected at the feet of gods. Too familiar, became the body-bags and shell-ghosts whose corpses which once were stars; the remnant ghosts of old rainbows and faded lights.

All Souls

MICHAEL THOMAS FORD

"In the center of the chamber, there's a dais."

"A what?" said Brad.

"A platform," Morris explained. "Made out of stone. There are three steps at the front and a statue on top. The statue is carved out of black rock of some kind."

"A statue of what?" Brad asked impatiently.

"Who's the dungeon master here?" said Morris.

Brad huffed and shook a handful of Bottle Caps from the box straight into his mouth. He chewed loudly while Morris, ignoring him, continued. "The statue is about four feet tall," he said. "Humanoid, but not quite."

"So, a dwarf," said Brad.

"Short horns protrude from the figure's forehead," said Morris.

"A *horned* dwarf," Brad said. "Or maybe some kind of faun. Does it have hooves or feet?"

"Shh," Charlie admonished. He liked Brad well enough, but the constant eruptions were taking him out of the game.

"Hooves," said Morris. "And its eyes are gems. Red ones."

"Rubies," Brad said excitedly. "Now you're talking. Finally, some treasure."

"What do you want to do?" Morris asked.

"I take my knife and pry out one of the eyes," Brad said.

"It's not your turn," said Morris. "Todd goes first."

Brad groaned. "Todd is going to write a song about it. Or a poem. Fucking bards, man."

Charlie looked at Todd, who was seated across the table from him. Unlike Brad, who was every bit the stereotypical high school football jock, Todd was more of a quiet observer. Where Brad rushed into every situation, ready to act first and think later, Todd asked questions and worked through every possibility before making a choice.

"This temple is where the cult of the sea demon made sacrifices," Todd said. "We know that from the story the barkeep at the inn told us. But that statue isn't big enough to be the demon. They would have made that bigger and more impressive. My guess is this one's a distraction and the real statue is going to be in a hidden chamber. We need to figure out where the entrance to that is and—"

"Blah, blah, blah," Brad interrupted. "Stop talking and do something." He took a swig from his can of Dr. Pepper.

"I think I want to search for—"

"Dooooo something," Brad belched.

Todd leaned back in his chair. "Okay," he said. "I'm going to stand and watch while Brad—sorry, while Stonenads the fighter over there—pries a gem out of the statue and gets himself killed, probably by poison gas that comes out of the eye socket."

Brad raised a fist in triumph. "You heard the bard," he said.

"Which eye do you take first?" Morris asked him.

"Does it matter?"

Morris nodded.

"Fine. The right one. I pry it out. That'll buy me some nice new armor when we head back to town. Or maybe a night with a halfling wench at the Crowing Cock."

Morris winced, and not at the crude joke. "Moments after you remove the right eye, a huge block of stone falls from the vaulted ceiling. It lands on"—he looked at Todd— "Sweetsong the bard. Sorry, man."

"Shit," said Brad. "Is he dead?"

"The block weighs half a ton," Morris said. "Yeah, he's dead."

Todd closed his eyes but said nothing.

"Wait a minute," Charlie said. "Can't I heal him?"

"Right!" said Brad. "He can use a resurrection spell. I saw it in the booklet."

"That's a fifth-level spell," Morris said. "He's only a third-level cleric."

"Just let him do the healing thing," Brad argued.

Morris shook his head. "If we don't play by the rules, we might as well just make up anything."

"Why'd the trap kill Todd and not me?" asked Brad. "That's not fair."

"Because the sea demon is all about sacrifices," Morris explained. "And chaos. The trap is meant to kill one of the companions of anyone dumb enough to fall for it. To teach them a lesson. If you'd picked the left eye, Charlie would be dead."

"You're the dungeon master," Brad said. "It's *your* story, so this is *your* fault."

"I thought Todd would talk some sense into you!" Morris objected. "And he tried. Even you should know a statue with gems for eyes is obviously a trigger for a trap!"

The two of them argued about who was to blame for Todd's death. Charlie blocked them out, focusing his attention on Todd. Todd still hadn't moved or looked at any of them. Watching him, Charlie felt his heartbeat accelerate. His breath caught in his chest, and the sound of Morris and Brad's voices became a roar in his ears.

Don't think about Ed, he told himself. *Don't think about that.*

But now all he could think about *was* Ed. His brother. Ed and the story he'd told Charlie about finding his best friend, Ham, wounded on the ground following an ambush by the Viet Cong. Ed had done his best to save Ham, but there was nothing he could do.

Charlie had heard the story so many times that he could see it play in his head like a movie. In the year Ed was home after being discharged, he'd spent time with almost nobody but Charlie. Holed up in the cabin their family owned out at the lake, he'd tried to piece his life back together, first with the pills the doctors gave him and then with ones he bought himself from guys downtown. Each time Charlie went to see him, he looked less and less like a living man and more and more like the ghost of one.

On New Year's Eve of 1973, he finally became a ghost himself, wading into the lake and swimming out until he sank beneath the surface. Charlie, there when the divers pulled the body out a few days later, would never forget the paleness of his brother's skin or the deadness of his eyes.

Many times, he'd tried to put himself in Ed's position, imagined himself in a jungle thousands of miles from home and safety, holding a friend while the life drained out of him and into the dirt of Vietnam. Now, in a small way, he understood. Todd's bard was fictional, and Todd himself still sat across the table from Charlie, his heart beating, very much alive. But the feeling of helplessness in Charlie's soul was very real. And if what he felt was even a tiny fragment of what Ed had felt, he understood a little better the choices his brother made.

He stood up. "I have to go."

He pounded up the basement stairs. Behind him, Brad called out, "It's just a stupid game, man!"

Charlie nodded brusquely at Morris's mother as he passed through her kitchen and went out the side door into the carport. He hopped on his bike, which was leaning against the wall, and pedaled away. The cool October air brushed his face as he rode, calming him a little. But only a little. His heart still rattled in his chest, and not just from the effort of riding.

The truth, which he'd revealed to no one, including himself, was that Todd was more to him than a traveling companion in an adventure game, more than just one of his group of friends. Although he had yet to put a name to these feelings, he nevertheless knew something inside of him had changed during the time they'd been playing. Unlike Brad, who acted without thinking, Todd reacted thoughtfully to every encounter, considered the consequences of his actions, treated even fictional characters and creatures as if these interactions had real-world implications. Watching this had stirred something inside of Charlie. Todd possessed an awareness of others, a kindness, that Charlie longed for, particularly now that Ed was gone.

His friends knew about Ed, of course, at least about his death. That it was self-inflicted remained a secret that Charlie shared with no one. Not even his parents talked about it, preferring to let people believe Ed had simply drowned, that it was all an accident. When conversation around them touched on the topic of the increasingly common issue of returning soldiers taking their own lives, his parents only shook their heads and said what a shame it was. Charlie was fairly certain that they had convinced even themselves that Ed hadn't chosen to leave them voluntarily.

When he reached his house, he stowed his bike in the garage and went inside, where he discovered that the telephone on the table in the front hall was ringing. He picked up the receiver.

"Hello?"

"Hey," said Todd's voice.

"Hey," Charlie said. "Sorry about before. I don't know why I got so upset. Brad's right, it's just a game."

"It's okay," Todd assured him. "I get it. Sweetsong was a great character. But I'll make a new one. And Brad feels really bad about causing my untimely demise, so he's paying for all of us to go see *Jaws* tonight. Dinner at Mickey D's first too. You coming?"

Charlie almost said no. He was still embarrassed by how he'd overreacted, especially since explaining *why* he had done so would make things so much worse. Besides, they'd seen *Jaws* at least three times since it came out. But not going would make his friends think he was still upset. And going would mean spending time with Todd.

"Sure," he said. "See you in a couple hours."

"YOU GUYS BETTER PUT out after all the money I'm spending on you tonight," Brad said, as he settled into his seat at the Razzle-Dazzle. "I had to spend every bit of gold that ruby eye got me at the market."

He chuckled at his own joke while the other three shook their heads.

Brad was seated on the aisle, with Morris beside him, then Todd, and finally Charlie. Charlie had a tub of buttered popcorn on his lap and held a Coke in his right hand. His left hand rested awkwardly on the shared armrest, and when he felt Todd's arm brush against his, he quickly grabbed the popcorn bucket and hugged it to his chest.

He relaxed a bit when the lights went down and the movie started, at least as much as he could relax knowing what was to come. After his first viewing of *Jaws,* he'd been reluctant to go swimming, even in the community pool. Like millions of other people, he now feared sharks were lurking in every body of water, waiting for him to venture in. He sensed his friends felt the same way, as none of them had suggested going swimming in the lake even once during the summer. This was a relief to him for more than one reason, as there was something more frightening than even a Great White lurking in those waters.

Given that the movie had been out for months, and the inescapable discussion about it, he was certain that there wasn't anyone in America who hadn't seen it. Yet judging from the startled screams and audible gasps of surprise that erupted around him as the shark claimed each new victim, there were apparently people for whom it was a new experience. Charlie felt a little jealous of them, seeing it for the first time.

As the story played out, Charlie lost himself in it, so that by the time police chief Brody, marine biologist Hooper, and grizzled fisherman Quint were engaged in their final hunt for the massive shark, he'd forgotten that he wasn't there on the boat with them. Then he felt something touch his hand. It was Todd's little finger, resting gently alongside his own. Realizing this, Charlie experienced a tingle of excitement—electric and dangerous—course through him. His stomach fluttered and, to his horror, he stiffened inside his pants.

He sat in the dark, terrified to move, waiting for *Todd* to move, for him to realize that they were touching and be disgusted by that fact. When Todd *didn't* move, let his finger lay alongside Charlie's without pulling away, Charlie then started worrying about why. Did Todd not realize what was happening? Was this all accidental? Or was there meaning behind it? Had Todd put his hand there—just there, like that—on purpose?

The hardness in Charlie's pants grew unbearable, and not just because of the physical discomfort. It was proof that something was very wrong with the way he felt, a betrayal by his body that was both inexcusable and impossible to ignore. It terrified him how a few inches of bare flesh, pressed together, could ignite a fire so bright and hot that it threated to set the entire theater ablaze.

He wanted very much to press his finger more firmly against Todd's, as a test. Would he press back? Or would the increased pressure make him realize what was happening and finally pull away? Charlie didn't think he could bear either answer and so he sat there, frozen, watching the movie but incapable of thinking about anything other than the thoughts that raced through his head, more thrilling than any on-screen action, more terrifying than a shark a million times the size of the one that was devouring the *Orca*.

Too soon, the movie ended, and the lights came up. Todd, stretching, broke his connection to Charlie. "That was the best," he said and Charlie—knowing he meant the movie but hoping he meant much more than that—could only say, "Yeah."

Outside the theater, before they went separate ways, Morris said, "Halloween is on a Friday this year. We're 16 now, which is kind of old to go trick-or-treating. Brad and I were thinking we should have a party." He looked at Charlie. "And we were thinking your cabin at the lake would be the best place to do it."

"The *only* place," said Brad. "If we do it at any of our houses, our parents will hang around and we won't be able to do anything fun."

"We won't invite *too* many people," Morris assured Charlie. "And we'll help clean up, so your parents won't even have to know there *was* a party."

"We can get beer," Brad said. "And I can score some weed from my sister's boyfriend. It will be a blast."

Charlie didn't know what to say. The last thing he wanted to do was hang out at the cabin. But Morris and Brad seemed so excited about the idea, and were staring at him, waiting for an answer.

"Don't worry," Todd said. "I won't let Brad do anything stupid this time."

Todd's assurance was all Charlie needed to decide. "Sure," he said.

"Cool," Brad said, like he was already sitting by the fire with a beer in one hand and a joint in the other.

"Are we doing costumes?" Morris asked.

"Definitely," Todd said. "It's Halloween."

Brad started to protest, but Todd cut him off. "Cindy Brimmer will be way more into kissing a werewolf football player than a plain old human one. She'll probably let you score a touchdown."

Brad grinned. "Arooooooo!" he said.

Brad and Morris went in one direction while Charlie and Todd walked in the other, as they lived only a few blocks apart.

"I hope you didn't feel like you had to say yes about the party," Todd said. "If you think it might be a problem, we can tell the guys it's off."

"It's okay," said Charlie. "My folks never go there anyway. They won't even know. I'll just say I'm spending the night with you guys. They won't ask where."

"I think it will be fun," Todd said. "I just have to think of a costume. What are you going as?"

"I haven't even thought about it," said Charlie.

"Well, we've got two weeks," Todd said. "We'll come up with something."

They parted when they reached Todd's street and Charlie continued on alone. As he approached his house, he saw that someone was sitting on the front steps, illuminated by the porchlight. It was a man, but no one Charlie recognized. His parents' station wagon was parked in the driveway, and he wondered why the man hadn't rung the bell if he was there to see them. It was like he was waiting for Charlie.

As he drew nearer, he saw that the man was young, probably no more than 20. On the thin side, his dark hair was cut short, and he was clean-shaven. He wore jeans and a plain white t-shirt, which seemed to Charlie to be inadequate for the chill fall night. An unlit cigarette was tucked behind his ear.

"Hi," Charlie said. "Can I help you with something?"

"Maybe," the man said. His accent was unlike any Charlie had ever heard, sounding both Southern and foreign at the same time. "I'm looking for Eddie Comstock. He live around here? Pretty sure he told me Poplar Street, but I can't remember if he said number 32 or 34. Figured I'd try 32 first."

"You got it right," Charlie told him. "Number 32. You're a friend of Ed's?" No one he knew called Ed Eddie.

The man nodded. "We were in Vietnam together. You must be Charlie."

Charlie nodded.

"Eddie talked about you all the time," the man said. "Said you were the best brother a guy could ask for."

Charlie felt his throat catch.

"I'm James Bonne," the man said. "Bonne as in *good*, not like the spy fella. So, is Eddie around?"

Charlie shook his head. "No," he said. He didn't know how to continue.

James was watching him with dark eyes, waiting for Charlie to tell him where Ed was.

"He's dead," Charlie blurted, immediately feeling awful. "I'm sorry. I didn't know how to say it."

James took the cigarette from behind his ear, put it in his mouth. "How?" he said.

Charlie didn't want to talk about his brother's death. He wanted to run up the steps of the porch, open the door, and retreat into the golden light that glowed behind the windows. He wanted to be where it was safe, not standing outside in the cold, telling his brother's friend that Ed was not here. Not anywhere.

"He drowned," Charlie said. "In the lake."

"When?" James asked.

"Last December," Charlie said. "New Year's Eve."

James thought for a moment. "Swimming in a lake in December isn't the best idea," he said, looking at Charlie intently.

"No," Charlie agreed. "Not the best idea."

James Bonne nodded, then stood up. "It was nice to meet you, Charlie," he said as he came down the steps. He walked past Charlie and headed down the street. Charlie watched him go, then went into the house. His parents were sitting in the living room, watching *The Mary Tyler Moore Show*.

"Did you have fun at the movies?" his mother asked.

Charlie nodded. Again, he wondered why James Bonne hadn't rung the doorbell. Surely, he could tell there were people inside. And yet, he'd waited on the steps. Something wasn't making sense about his visit. And if he and Ed were such good friends, why had Ed never mentioned him?

Charlie went upstairs to his room. Sitting on his bed, he pulled open the drawer on his nightstand and took out a photograph. It was the last one taken of him and Ed, almost exactly a year ago. They were standing in front of the house, each of them holding a jack-o'-lantern they'd just carved. Charlie was smiling widely, but Ed was staring straight at the camera with eyes deadened by the drugs he was taking. He'd let his hair grow, refusing to cut it after he returned home, and it hung past his shoulders. He'd also grown out his beard, which formed a bush around his face and added to his wildman appearance.

It was not a pleasant photo. But Charlie loved it because it was of him and his brother. While other people had grown fearful of Ed after his return home and the changes began in him, or he just made them uncomfortable, to Charlie he was always the big brother he knew would take care of him if he needed help.

He just wished he could have taken care of Ed when he needed it.

He put the photo away and got ready for bed. As he passed by his window, he glanced out. Across the street, standing in a cone of hazy yellow light, was a figure that very much resembled James Bonne. He stood looking at the house, his hands in his pockets. Then the streetlight flickered, and when it came back on, the figure was gone.

Charlie decided he must have imagined seeing someone there. Probably he was thinking so hard about who James Bonne was to Ed that he'd projected an image of him onto the street. He wished now that he'd asked more questions. This was the first time he'd met anyone who had spent time with Ed in Vietnam. He regretted not taking advantage of the opportunity to find out more about what his brother had experienced there.

Then he remembered Ed had attended a few meetings of a support group for returning soldiers that met at the community center. Maybe if James Bonne was hanging around town, he would end up there, looking to connect with other soldiers. Or maybe someone there would know him. As Charlie recalled, there was a meeting every Sunday morning. He would go and see.

THE MEETING ROOM AT the community center was small and airless thanks to the ancient radiator that hissed hot breath and the windows, painted shut, that could not be opened. A circle of metal folding chairs took up the center of the space. Three of them were filled with men sitting, arms folded over their chests, not speaking to one another. All of them were young or had been before their tours of Vietnam. Now they looked haunted, their eyes unfocused and their faces hard.

One, a black man wearing a faded green field jacket with the name Ronson stitched over the right front pocket, looked up. "Think you in the wrong room, little man."

The other two now looked at Charlie as well. With three sets of eyes on him, he found his courage fading rapidly, and almost left. James Bonne wasn't there anyway, and Charlie suddenly felt foolish for thinking this was a good idea.

"I know you," one of the men said. "You're Ed's brother, right?"

Charlie looked more closely at the man. "Greg," he said. "Greg Small, right? You went to school with my brother."

The man nodded. Then he stood up and came over to Charlie, opening his arms. Before Charlie knew what was happening, Greg engulfed him in a hug. "Sorry about Ed," he said.

When Greg released him, Charlie saw that the other two men had stood up and come over as well, as if he was suddenly someone important. Each held out a hand. Charlie shook one and then the other.

"Ed was good people," the man in the field jacket said, his eyes wet.

The third man didn't speak, returning to his chair and sitting down. Once again, his arms crossed over his chest.

"What can we do for you?" Greg asked Charlie.

Charlie had almost forgotten about his reason for coming to the center. "Someone came to the house yesterday looking for Ed," he said. "A guy named James Bonne. Said he knew Ed from—from over there. I thought he might be here today, or that you might know him."

Greg shook his head. "Ed and I weren't in the same unit," he said. "None of us were. And I've never heard of anyone with that name. Sorry. If he shows up, though, we'll tell him you're looking for him."

"Thanks," Charlie said.

He didn't know what to say next. Part of him wanted to stay with these men, who were probably his brother's last friends before his death. Maybe talking to them would help him understand more about what Ed was feeling. But maybe he never could understand. Maybe what happened to them was a story only they could know. Charlie guessed that's why they got together like this. Perhaps it was something he wasn't meant to understand.

Fortunately for him, a man walked in. "You guys ready to start?" he asked. Then he noticed Charlie. "Hi," he said. "I'm Peter, the facilitator."

"This is Ed's little brother," Greg said.

"Oh," Peter said. Then he seemed unsure what to say next. "We all miss Ed," he concluded.

"Me too," said Charlie. "I should go."

Not knowing what else to do, he waved awkwardly, then left the room and walked back outside. He hung around in front of the community center for a few minutes, still hoping James Bonne might show up, then got on his bike and rode home.

He spent the rest of the day thinking about his costume for the Halloween party. He considered and discarded any number of things, until eventually his thoughts drifted to Todd and how their hands had touched during the movie. Remembering this, his body responded, and he found himself imagining what might have happened if he'd been brave enough to take things further. His mind, caught up in the fantasy, unspooled a movie of its own, and after making sure his bedroom door was shut and locked in case anyone came looking for him, Charlie let it play out. When the inevitable climax arrived, his body shivered, and he held his breath until he stopped shaking.

He was surprised to find that he felt no shame for what he'd done, what he'd imagined. Instead, he felt only joy, as if the idea of being with Todd had freed him to be who he really was. He was surprised too to discover that his brain—perhaps having released the tension that had kept it from thinking clearly—had arrived at an idea for a costume.

Getting up, he went downstairs to look for some cardboard.

"THE BEER IS HERE!"

Brad popped the trunk of the car, revealing three cases of Pabst Blue Ribbon. "Just call me Boozo the Clown," he said. "Get it? Like Bozo, but—"

"We get it," Morris said, lifting out a case. He was dressed as Dracula, with plastic fangs and a black cape. "But I thought you were going to be a werewolf."

"Turns out Cindy Brimmer is afraid of dogs," Brad said. "But she loves the circus so . . . honk honk!" There was a large plastic daisy on the front of his costume. He reached into his pocket, squeezed something, and water shot out of the flower. "I'm planning on getting her all wet later."

Charlie, standing on the porch of the cabin, tried to relax. He was still anxious about being there, not just because he worried what would happen if his parents found out about the party, but because of the memories that were crowding around as if they'd been lurking in the surrounding trees for him to return. He tried to keep them at bay, but every so often one tapped him on the shoulder, startling him.

"Get a load of Jaws," Brad said, approaching with a case of beer.

"Technically, the shark's name is Bruce," Charlie said. "I read an article about it in *People.*"

He'd worked on his costume for a week. Constructed of cardboard and painted gray and white, his shark body had holes for his arms to go through. A gray sweatshirt transformed his arms into fins. His face peered out from the gaping mouth. Pointed teeth, some stained with red, framed his head. He was delighted with how it had turned out, even if wearing it was a little uncomfortable.

"You'd better watch out," Brad said, setting the beer down on the picnic table in front of the cabin. "Todd might harpoon you."

Charlie didn't understand. Then Todd's little red Gremlin pulled in, and when he got out Charlie laughed. He was dressed as Quint, the fisherman from *Jaws,* complete with sideburns and a mustache made of cotton stuffing glued to his face.

"Hey, Quint," Brad said. "I think you're going to need a bigger car."

Todd joined them. Eyeing the cases of Pabst he growled, "What, you couldn't find any Narragansett Lager?"

For the next hour they got the place ready for the party. This consisted primarily of starting a fire in the stone circle, opening bags of chips and candy, and setting the beer and cans of soda in a cooler filled with ice. By the time dark was settling over the cabin, the people they'd invited began to arrive.

Finally, Charlie began to relax a little. This was helped by the can of beer he opened and nursed as he stood by the fire. He didn't particularly enjoy the taste of the beer, but it was exciting to be doing something he knew his parents would probably disapprove of. And when someone in a Scooby-Doo mask handed him a lit joint, he took a puff on that too. He was familiar with the smell of pot, as Ed had used it, but he'd never tried it himself. When a few minutes later, he started feeling like he was on a carnival ride, he decided to take a walk.

Shortly, he found himself by the lake. There was no dock, just a short stretch of beach and then the water. But there was a large boulder, and seated on this was a figure. Charlie almost didn't see it, but then a face turned towards him, and he was looking at a skull. For a moment, the beer and pot combined to make him think he was seeing a skeleton. But it was only black and white greasepaint.

The skeleton beckoned him closer, and he obeyed. Drawing nearer to the rock, he saw that the person on it was wearing a black top hat, initially indistinguishable in the gloom. Apart from that, they were wearing jeans and a white t-shirt.

"Hello, Charlie Comstock," said a familiar voice.

"James?" Charlie said.

"Not tonight," the voice said. "Tonight, I am Baron Samedi."

"I don't know who that is," said Charlie. "Is he from a comic book?"

The Baron laughed. "Baron Samedi is the father of the spirits of the dead. He digs their graves and then leads them to the underworld. Where I come from, in the bayous, we know him well."

"How did you find out about the party?" Charlie asked.

"Am I not welcome here?" Baron Samedi asked.

"No," Charlie said. "I mean yes, you're welcome here. I just wondered how you even knew it was happening."

The Baron didn't answer him. He sat looking out over the lake. Charlie wondered if he would say anything else. He had so many questions he wanted to ask James himself, but he found he couldn't. It was as if James really was Baron Samedi, and he doubted the Baron would answer him in anything other than riddles. His head still swam with ever-shifting dreams, and he wondered if perhaps he was imagining meeting his brother's friend here, at the place where Ed had ended his life.

"It's easy to die," Baron Samedi said, breaking the silence. "Easy enough, anyway. The harder thing to do is to live, at least if you live as the person you're meant to be." He turned his head, the skull face looking directly at Charlie with eyes that glittered. "Do you understand what I'm telling you, Charlie Comstock?"

Charlie wasn't sure that he did, but nodded anyway.

The Baron grinned, his skeleton mouth growing impossibly wide. "Live, Charlie Comstock," he said. "Live as hard as you can, so that when we meet again you will have many stories to tell me."

The Baron stood up from the rock and walked toward the lake. He kept going, wading into the water. Charlie tried to call out for him to stop, but found he couldn't speak. The feeling in his head enveloped him, and he saw everything through a cloud. He could only watch as Baron Samedi disappeared into the lake until just his top hat remained above water. Then it, too, sank beneath the surface.

"You okay?"

Charlie's head cleared somewhat as he heard someone speak. Todd came to stand beside him. "I noticed you hadn't come back for a while," he said. "I thought maybe I should come look for you."

"I'm okay," Charlie said. "But thanks. How's the party going? Has Brad hooked up with Cindy Brimmer yet?"

"Last time I saw her, she was making out with a mummy," Todd said. "But Brad's so high he probably doesn't notice."

Charlie laughed. "I'm glad people are having fun," he said. "I guess parties just aren't really my thing."

"Me neither," Todd said. "It's nicer down here. I mean, I'd rather be hanging out with you."

Charlie felt the now-familiar stirring inside. Had Todd meant what it sounded like he meant? Or was Charlie reading too much into it? "Me too," he said.

They stood together without saying anything. For Charlie it was like being back in the theater. He longed to reach out and take Todd's hand. But he found he couldn't. Even though only a few inches separated them, it might as well have been a universe. He feared what Todd would do. What he wouldn't do. What he might do. Most of all Charlie feared what he himself *wanted* to do.

Then he saw Baron Samedi, heard his words. *Live as hard as you can.*

He reached out, found Todd's hand, closed his fingers around Todd's. Everything stopped as he waited, his heart pounding wildly in his chest. And then Todd squeezed his hand back. "Do you think Quint and the shark fought so much because they were in love with each other?" he said.

Charlie laughed. "Maybe," he said. "It would have been a very different movie, that's for sure."

They continued to stand on the beach, holding hands, not talking. But now Charlie wasn't afraid. He was happy.

"We should get back," Todd said after a while. "But I was thinking. Maybe we could share a bedroom tonight. You and me. Would that be okay with you?"

"Yeah," Charlie said. "That would be okay."

The party seemed to take forever to end. But eventually, well after midnight, people began to leave, until it was only the four friends who remained. It was easy to get Brad, who had drunk enough beer to get an entire car full of clowns tipsy, to fall asleep on the couch. And Morris was more than happy to take the bedroom with the large bed for himself. That left the second bedroom and its twin beds for Charlie and Todd.

This was the room that Charlie and Ed had always shared when the whole family was at the cabin. It was also the room that Ed had chosen to stay in when he lived there alone, even though the larger room was available to him. He said it was more familiar to him, reminded him of better times, and felt safer.

Charlie shut the door. It had no lock, but he knew neither Brad nor Morris would come in. He started to remove his shark costume, but found his arms were stuck.

"Here," Todd said. "Let me help you."

He lifted the cardboard body over Charlie's head and set it in a corner. Then the two of them stood looking at each other. A moment later, Todd's mouth was pressed against Charlie's.

"Your beard tickles," Charlie said when they parted.

Todd laughed. He took Charlie's hand and guided him to one of the beds. Then he started to undress. Charlie followed suit.

When they were naked, Todd knelt in front of him. "Let's see if this tickles," he said.

Later, lying together on the bed as they took a break from discovering what they could do with each other, Todd picked up a book that was sitting on the bedside table. It was a battered copy of *The Lord of the Rings*.

"That was Ed's favorite book," Charlie said.

Todd opened it and flipped through the pages. As he did, a photograph fluttered out and landed on his stomach. He picked it up and he and Charlie looked at it. It showed two men at what was clearly a Halloween party. One of them was Ed. He was wearing his beloved Baltimore Orioles baseball hat, which he'd taken to Vietnam as a good luck charm and had smeared eye black under each eye. The other man was James Bonne. And he was dressed as Baron Samedi. Ed had his arm around James and was caught in mid-laugh. James stared directly at the camera.

"It's him," Charlie said.

"Him?" said Todd.

"James Bonne," Charlie said. "He came to the house looking for Ed. And he was here tonight."

"You said his name is James Bonne?" said Todd. "That's funny."

"Why?" Charlie asked.

"James Bonne," Todd repeated, but with an accent similar to the one the real James Bonne had. "When you say it like that it sounds like *jambon*, the French word for ham."

Charlie's heart skipped.

"You okay?" Todd asked. "You just shivered like someone walked over your grave."

Charlie took the photo from him and turned it over. On the back, in Ed's familiar scrawl, was penciled ME AND HAM HALLOWEEN '72.

"It was him," Charlie whispered. "Ham."

"Ham?" said Todd.

"Ham was Ed's best friend," Charlie explained. "It was a nickname. I never asked where it came from."

"Didn't you tell me once that Ed's best friend was killed in Vietnam?"

"Yeah," Charlie said. "Ham. James Bonne. This guy in the picture."

"But you said he came to your house? And he was here tonight?"

Charlie knew it all sounded ridiculous. "Yeah," he said again.

"Maybe it was someone dressed like him?" Todd suggested. "Playing a weird practical joke? But that would be really messed up."

"It would be," Charlie agreed. "But I don't think it was someone playing a joke."

He waited for Todd to tell him he was crazy, that he was imagining things because he missed his brother. Instead, Todd put an arm around him, leaned over, and kissed him on the cheek. "Then again, it is Halloween," he said. "Maybe you saw a ghost."

Charlie looked at the photo again. He *had* seen a ghost. Or a spirit. Or whatever Ham was now. He thought about what Baron Samedi had said about coming to lead the dead to the underworld. Had he come for Ed?

Charlie turned off the light and lay in the darkness with Todd's arm slung over his chest. Not long after, he heard Todd snore lightly. He waited another few minutes, then gently got out of bed and pulled on his pants and a t-shirt. Todd murmured something and rolled onto his back. Charlie left him sleeping and quietly opened the bedroom door. He crept through the living room, where Brad was passed out on the sofa, dead to the world, and went outside.

The night air was cold and refreshing, filled with the lingering scent of the fire and of leaves becoming earth. Charlie had forgotten to put on shoes, but the path to the lake was worn smooth by years of other feet passing over it and he walked without trouble, his way lighted by the waning moon overhead. Then he was at the big rock.

Resting atop it was a Baltimore Orioles baseball cap. Picking it up, Charlie looked inside. Written on the band in faded black marker was COMSTOCK. Charlie placed the hat on his head and looked out at the water. The lake was still, but he suspected that beneath the surface a whole other world existed. Just as one existed inside of every person. Inside of him. Waiting to be explored.

"I'm going to live," he declared to the lake. "I promise. I'm going to live as hard as I can."

Then he turned and walked back to the cabin, where Todd was waiting.

A Haunted Alcoholic

ERIC DAVID ROMAN

"Hello.

"My name is Ryan…and I'm an alcoholic.

"I'm usually at the 7:45 Tuesday meetings. That's where my crew is. Been a while since I've addressed a *whole* room full of new faces. Hi everyone. Even in my early days of recovery, I never wandered into one of these late meetings. But we walk through those doors when we have to, no matter the time.

"I can't sleep. Mind is so noisy. House too noisy. I needed to get out…get some quiet, but I found myself in front of the old bar I used to frequent. I don't know how I got there. I don't know why I was parked in front. But there I was.

"I wasn't going to go in…at least I'm pretty sure I wasn't. I came here instead.

"I feel like I can say the things I need to at this midnight meeting that I couldn't in my normal one. Which is okay. As long as I'm here, sharing my fears and pain, and not internalizing it, then I'm still doing what I need to hold on. Shit. I can't even imagine what I must look like; some deranged lumberjack who hasn't tamed his hair or his beard in days, in the same fucking clothes for the past three.

"I probably don't look like I took my Ten-year chip a couple of months ago. Ten whole years of sobriety. At first, I thought that would be an unreachable goal 'ya know. In those first few months in these meetings, you don't think you'll make it, but here I am.

"So, some backstory…one year ago, I lost my husband and daughter in an accident. We'd been out at a friend's birthday party. I wasn't in the mood to go. I'd wanted to stay home. You ever been to a nine-year-old's birthday party? Kids running amok, the parents getting tipsy, happy their kids are occupied. Sugary food, greasy pizza. It's exhausting. Even more so sober.

"It was a good day, a really good day until some asshole came out of nowhere. Hit us at a red light. I woke up in the hospital two days later—they were gone.

"A year now.

"Doesn't feel like it, though. Feels like no time has passed. I recovered, shattered both the fibula and tibia in my left leg, fractured hip, broken ribs, and some internal bleeding. Time didn't register in the hospital, laying in that bed, every day blurred together, plus they were really generous with the painkillers. I mean, the wildest thing I've had in my system for the past ten years is ibuprofen. Nothing mattered, not my sobriety, not my own life. I cried all day and woke up every night calling out for them in fits so severe, I had to be sedated.

"Rinse and repeat for nearly two months. The whole time, refusing to believe they were gone, somehow convincing myself I'd see them the minute I got back home. As soon as I got home, I wanted to go right back to the hospital. There were no emotional landmines in that hospital room. Her purple and pink sneakers weren't by the door. His in-progress Lego project wasn't still in a mess on the table. Walls filled with our pictures. A sock. I saw her sock on the couch, and it caused a meltdown because it smelled like her. That blank, white room in the hospital didn't have any visceral reminders.

"I go to a grief counseling group three times a week. Not helping. I'd bail on that sadness circle jerk if I could, but I promised my sister I'd stick with it. And our sobriety rests on us keeping our promises. I see a lot of them in that group numbing themselves with booze and drugs, and I know it's wrong, but I've placed silent bets on which ones will end up in one of these meetings first. I know…it's not the right attitude to have. I should care more, care about them, like I do all of you in this meeting, even not having met you. I still feel, to a degree, I know you and your story. I've sat in those chairs, listening to Shares, finding my way into being a part of something bigger.

"I don't find the same thing in that group, though, and it's been months. And I don't know whether it's wrong of me, or if I am being an asshole—or is this some other symptom of grief blocking me? And honestly, I don't care. Nothing much worth caring about lately. I've tried…well, I think I've tried anyway. I go to those meetings, and I try, so I don't understand why I have a hard time finding my way out of this darkness. I think, maybe, it's because they're not really going through what I'm going through. In these meetings, we may not hear our exact story, but we hear enough things that resonate with us to make shit click. But I've been going to that grief group for nine months now and I've not related to anyone. Not one story, not one person.

"None of the people who've come through in those nine months have had a double whammy upend their life like I did. Not one share in that group has made me feel like someone knows what I'm going through, that there's some hope—a light at the end of the tunnel. Three times a week, I sit there, expecting to find some comfort. Expecting—I dunno—to find some bridge back to myself, back to the world. All that happens is that I leave feeling worse. Then, feeling like shit, I have to go back to that empty house and face the emotional landmines I'm still not strong enough to overpower.

"Everyone in that group cries and whines and I know this doesn't make me look good, but I can't find an ounce of compassion for any of those people. Maybe their crying over one person bothers me when I'm missing two. Maybe I'm jealous that their grief is less than mine and that makes me zone out when they're talking. Maybe I am bitter. That's not the kind of person I want to be, but I feel nothing. The people in that group, yes, they've lost someone they loved, and yes, it's hard that Sheila doesn't know how to pay her electric bill and Sam doesn't know who's going to feed the kids. And I want to scream at them to shut the fuck up. I want to slap the goddamn Styrofoam cups out of their hands and scold them for not only fucking up my life, but polluting the planet, too.

"I don't want to be like this. This isn't the person I strive to be—but they don't understand how exhausting it is mourning two people at once. Two-thirds of my heart—gone, and all that's left is the empty space I have to find a way to build a bridge over. Except, I can't.

"I can't move forward. I'll be in bed at night, trying not to focus on the emptiness and silence of the house. Trying to let the TV soothe me to sleep, but then an episode of *Golden Girls* plays, and I think about Nathan. Our nights in bed with those ladies in the background, our talks, our kisses, our passionate sex, and then I'm plunged deeper into my sorrow; the kind wrenched from the very depths of our soul.

"And if that—if all that—isn't enough to make someone spiral out, midway through, I'm reminded my daughter's dead too. And then it's what kind of sonofabitch am I, forgetting that for even a moment?

"My sadness doesn't matter after that intrusive thought bullies its way in, because guilt is all I feel. How could I not be thinking about her? How could I have stopped grieving her for even a second when she was my life? And then I realize, I put mourning Nathan on hold to mourn her, and then feel like a shitty husband. We were together long before she came. Doesn't he deserve a higher level of mourning? Does she, since I saw her grow from a baby?

"These feelings don't make sense. Don't have to. *That's grief,* so they tell me in their high-pitched voices. What a goddamn lie.

"Back and forth. Sorrow and guilt. Until I'm so paralyzed I can't do anything but curl up wherever I'm stuck in the house, and I cry. I know *it's okay to cry—okay to feel.* But I'm tired. It's been a year of feeling like it's still day one. It's not supposed to.

"And that group, who are the ones to help me find comfort, help me find the light at the end of the tunnel, don't. I see other people feeling better, having more good days than bad when I can still barely function. I know…I know, it's not their fault, they're all going through their own hells. But nothing shared in those meetings helps dull the pain of losing the two most important people in my life. Nor do the constant, prepackaged, trite platitudes they love doling out afterward. Like us, they have a saying for everything, but all of them piss me off. I'm stuck and I can't move on to the next stage of this grief bullshit.

"I think it's why I've been wanting a drink.

"I *know* it's why.

"And I also know it won't solve anything; it'll make everything worse. It's always made everything worse. We're all in this room because that's our truth. And really, all you newbies out there, this is why we keep coming back. You can go ten years never thinking about a drink and then suddenly like me one—

"Sorry…but did anyone hear that?

"I thought I heard…doesn't matter, um…what was I saying? Yeah, like me, years of not even thinking about a drink, and then wham, you're parked outside a ba—I'm sorry…seriously, no one heard that?

"Wow, what I must look like to y'all, very jumpy. Head constantly swinging around, reacting to sounds coming from every direction. I promise I'm sober. I am. But this is a part of what I'm going to say, try to say, and what I can't tell my own crew. I can't share this at *my* meeting because I worry. Honestly worry, they'll question if I've been drinking. 'Cause it doesn't make sense. It doesn't. They're dead. My Addy and my Nathan are dead.

"So why do I keep seeing and hearing them?

"Why are they in the house? I'm sorry for all these tears, but this is tougher to talk about than the accident— they're…they're…*haunting* me.

"I know how that sounds. You're wondering has he slept? Is he on medication? I mean, I don't really sleep a lot, especially at night. But a couple months ago, I woke up one morning, and I heard Nathan in the kitchen; pans being knocked around, the tea kettle, a Stevie Nicks song from one of his Saturday Morning playlists. I smelled—the bacon cooking, heard it sizzling. And…I forgot. I jumped up like *oh yay, breakfast.*

"And then I got kicked in the chest when I went to the kitchen. It was empty. Nothing was cooking. Nothing there but the mess I'd left in the sink and the pizza boxes stacked on the counter. I could still smell the food. I could hear him humming along to his songs.

"I pushed the episode off as a half-asleep, half-awake kind of thing until a couple of days later when I heard Addy playing in her room. Her dolls were in the middle of acting out a telenovela when she passed. And I heard her voice from behind the bedroom door. I heard the dolls moving, their bodies being knocked against each other, and the playhouse. I couldn't go inside. I couldn't find the strength to open the door, but I held onto the handle, and I listened for twenty minutes, crying, like I am now, like I can't stop doing, and then the whole episode was over. Her room went quiet, and I remained in the hallway sobbing.

"I'd be fine, you know, finally in a moment when there were no thoughts, just blissful mindlessness where I wasn't being crushed by the weight of reality, and then something would happen: A door would close upstairs, the doorbell would ring, the air fryer would go off, my phone battery would up and die. Shadows moving around the house. Noises from other rooms. The feeling of being watched.

"These *events* keep happening. I was in bed a few nights ago and felt the covers move, and the pressure on the mattress shift, and a moment later—breath on the back of my neck. I didn't turn around right away; too scared of what I'd see. What if it was some*thing,* but what if it'd been him? His face looking at me from his pillow, his green eyes, his little nose, and that adorable smile. I think that would be worse. I finally did and, of course, nothing was there, but that side of the bed was warm.

"Sorry…but do you really not hear that? It's Addy's voice, calling out—Daaaaddyyy. I'll see her in the house, the back of her head as if she's there, sitting on the couch watching cartoons. I see those sassy curls, the ones I hate, 'cause she always knows how to flip them in the brattiest way, which would make me want to chop them off every time she flipped them at me.

"I tried to get closer to her that time. I stepped out of the kitchen quietly. I let the cartoons play. I wanted—*I needed*—to feel if she was real. I was scared, and the fear didn't want me to move. It locked my legs, but I forced myself. I inched closer and closer, with my hand reached out, fingers almost to her little shoulder. It felt like she knew I was there. She knew all I wanted was for her to turn around. How much I miss her face. I was close. I think my teeth were chattering, the room was so cold, but I didn't care…I was only inches away.

"And she was gone.

"I *swear* I hear her right now. It's like every day they get louder.

"I see some of your faces, those looks, see…who's gonna believe me? My own sister doesn't. I sound fuckin' nuts. She thinks this is my grief manifesting because I've not faced it, blah, blah—I zone out when she talks lately.

"I don't want to tell my friends. I've leaned on them so much already. And I can't take another dismissal when I know damn well what I'm saying is the truth.

"Are they going to believe I haven't showered in six days because right outside the curtain I see him waiting? I can tell it's him by the height, his stance. Why is he lingering there? Is he waiting for something? Is he going to get in? Am I going to turn around and see my dead husband in the shower with me? I can't close my eyes to wash my face. What *could* happen in the time they're closed?

"He just stands there!

"Silent. Watching me. Endlessly waiting. I'm too scared to ask what he wants. If it's Nathan, why does it make me so uncomfortable? There ha—

"DID you hear that?

"I saw…saw some of you react. You heard him; *baaabbbe.*

'Maybe it's a coincidence. I've written off a lot of stuff in the past couple of months as coincidences. I thought if I got out of the house, I'd be okay, right? Maybe cooping myself up there wasn't the smartest idea. But I love our home. I'm not ready to leave and I won't let grief run me off, either. There are *good* memories there and I want them.

"But *still,* I heard them. I think you all did too. Maybe it's this place? I come here so often, especially this past year. I lay bare my soul here. Why wouldn't they follow?

"I tried to go back to work. I'm a district manager for Lofty Barrel, the furniture store—sorry, the *lifestyle* store—whatever…but my office is in one of the stores. They followed me there. I saw Addy running around. I heard Nathan in the aisles, talking about styles and prices. It wasn't just me, the staff noticed things too; lights flickering, items moving around, and they heard her laughing.

"At the grocery store, I can hear Nathan in my ear; *hey Babe, I got the cookies you like.* I see Addy pointing at things she wants, but never full on, always the back of her. And in these micro-burst glimpses. As much as they scare me, they're hurting me.

"THERE. I know you heard that. What was that sound? Beer bottles. Is that what it sounded like? I see some of you are getting uncomfortable, that panicked *I want to leave, but I can't leave mid-share look.* I see it. That *was* the sound of beer bottles getting knocked down on the floor and rolling around.

"Beer bottles.

"Of course it is—I can't—I…I…I'm so tired. Don't know what to do. At least now, I know I'm not crazy. Yeah? You feel it too now. This is what it's been like. I don't kno—. Why is thi—It's like they're keeping me here. And I don't know wh—

"They're so loud. So many bottles.

"I wasn't responsible.

"No one questioned me. No one asked any questions. The other driver was coked out of his mind. He pleaded guilty. He had no license. He was trying to hide his car from being repoed. He's going to jail forever.

"No one questioned me.

"Those bottles…they're deafening.

"I'm tired…I'm so tired of running.

"I loved them so much. They were my whole life. I kept working at a job I hate because it afforded us a comfortable life. I gave them my time, my love. I would have never hurt them—but I *took* my chip.

"I'd been—um, it'd just been—what are you all looking at?

"Why are you all standing?

"I…feel them. They're right next to me, aren't they? You can see them. I only see shadows in the corner of my eye.

"I took *that* chip.

"I didn't want to go to that damn party.

"It'd been such a long week. Both at work and at home. I wanted a day to myself. I needed to decompress. I couldn't get any time alone. One Saturday, where I didn't have to move a muscle, is all I wanted.

"And I wasn't mad about going to the party; too tired to be mad. I was so stressed.

"When they were all singing Happy Birthday, I excused myself.

"I don't know WHY.

"Why…I snuck that one beer. One. Enough to give me a buzzy feeling to help me through. I wanted to enjoy the party. Enjoy life. It was stronger than I realized and I'm glad thirty minutes later, they both wanted to leave.

"I would have had another one.

"Nate was sloshed. He didn't notice I was buzzed. Addy fell asleep two minutes into the car ride. I—I—didn't feel…I didn't fully trust myself driving. I couldn't say anything. I was in the car and out the driveway before I realized.

"I took the longer route home. The one that felt safer; I'd have to go slower. There were more lights, more chances to stop if I needed a moment.

"*Safer.*

"Everything happened so fast after that.

"The accident, the recovery. I was swamped with sympathy; people bringing me food and reaching out to check on me, stepping up and doing things I didn't expect. And I couldn't bring myself in the middle of that whirlwind to admit the truth.

"I couldn't lose my sobriety too. I'd worked harder on that than anything in my entire life. I refused to lose that on top of everything else. Taking a day one chip? To bear and so deeply admit my failure in front of all of them. I refused. And I buried that beer down—that damn beer.

"*And* I took my ten-year chip.

"*And* I ate my cake and stood up there and spoke to all of them about how much they and my sobriety meant to me—when I should have admitted I'd relapsed. I'm such a hypocrite. And I was a coward in that moment, and many before it. You both trusted me to get you home safely. I'm sorry. I'm so sorry. I can't—

"Take *this*.

"Take this fucking chip away from *me*!

"I rebuke the damn thing! I'll admit it to everyone. I'll start over. From day one…right now.

"It was my fault, my loves. Forgive me, please…please, I beg you both…forgive me.

"—Listen.

"The bottles. Their voices.

"It's quiet.

"They've stopped."

Water Rites

ROOK RILEY

The screen door rested against my hip, halfway in and halfway out of my grandmother's house. Her 80th birthday had seemed as good a time as any to make my little announcement, but I knew it would be a mixed bag of reactions. It was supposed to go: love, marriage, then baby. But I'd never been one for tradition.

I looked over my shoulder to see Laban, or one of his progenies, standing near the pasture gate, watching me. He was a big old bull with giant bull dangly parts. He'd sired so many of the herd that his line, much like his mighty pizzle, went on forever.

"Who's letting flies in this house?" Mamaw called from the kitchen.

I let the door bang closed behind me about the time Aunt Sissy came around the corner to see who it was. It took her a couple of blinks before she recognized me.

"Good Lord, Jesse Wray, is that you?" she asked.

I laughed as she took in my thirty-two-week belly. "Surprise! It's a boy."

"Who is it, Sissy?" Mamaw came out on the screened-in porch, drying her hands on a dishtowel. "If that's one of the Risingers crabbing about the fence line again, tell them we ain't fixing it. It's their turn. You know they're just using it as an excuse to get their hands on old Laban. Best damn stud bull in the world."

My hard-as-nails grandmother's irate expression slipped, and she looked scared as she shook her head. "Oh no, Jesse. What have you done to yourself?"

It was the same words she used when I got my first tattoo, my first piercing, my first girlfriend, but the tone was different. She sounded defeated. It stole my hope and took my smile.

"Don't, Mama," Aunt Sissy started. "She doesn't know."

Didn't know what?

She put her hand on my shoulder and steered us into the living room. The rest of the Wray women were all drinking their afternoon iced tea, huddled around the window unit with the ceiling fan on full blast. It was still hot in here.

I wasn't ready for this. All six of them stared at my protruding stomach and shook their heads. It was a synchronized tsk-tsking.

"Y'all just look to see what Jesse's done to herself." Mamaw sat on the blank space left on the gold velvet couch that'd been in this room since before I was born.

Done to myself? Shit, I was pregnant, not Presbyterian.

"Go fix you a plate," my cousin Shelia said, "and I'll pour you some tea real quick."

But the East Texas humidity and heat, the forty extra pounds, and the weight of family disapproval took their toll pretty quickly. I didn't figure they'd throw me a parade, but this was hurtful. I pulled out my phone to see if I could change my departure date to tomorrow, but couldn't get a signal.

With a sigh, I put it back in my bag. "I'm not hungry. Just hot. And apparently, the worst thing that's ever happened to this family."

"There she goes, being all dramatic." Mamaw gave a dismissive, arthritic wave in my general direction. "Jesse Wray, you don't even know what you've got to be upset about. Headstrong and stubborn. Tell her to do one thing and she'd run off to do the other."

My mother had married into this insanity and left when she came to her senses. Of course, she died in a car accident not a month later, sending me back to live with Daddy in Dallas. Believe me, though, I spent every weekend and summer right here.

I dragged my bags into the back bedroom. It was the same one from when we were kids and the cousins would all pile into the wooden bunk beds, fighting over who would get to sleep on top. The only difference was the rearranged quilts. It even smelled the same.

I had just plopped down on the bed to re-evaluate my situation when Shelia came in with the tea.

"Where's all the menfolk?" I asked. "Did they run off because there's a queer in the house?"

She started to speak, and we wound up saying it at the same time, "Bow season."

I almost laughed. They'd have some moral argument about hunting—it always happened. After processing the deer, they'd donate most of it to Miss Opal for her foster kids, but somehow Mamaw would wind up with that venison chili she loved.

"What is wrong with them, Shelia? You'd think I came back as Lucifer for all the grief I just got."

"No one thinks you're the devil," she said. "Give them a minute, Jess. They're just startled, is all."

I took a sip and let the supersaturated sweet tea give me time to think of a response.

"When you joined the army," she continued, "none of us were surprised. You'd always been geared that way. But when you took the job in DC, I think that shocked them more than when you told your daddy you were a lesbian. They all figured you'd come home to work the cattle, girlfriend or no girlfriend."

I put the glass down on the nightstand and swept my hair up into a bun, securing it with a clip from my pocket. "It was never," I made sure to lay heavy on that never, "my intention to tend cows and deal with the auctions. I never considered it, to be honest." I folded up the pillow and put it behind my head to stretch out on the old twin bed.

The wooden frame creaked as she leaned against it. "You were good at it, though. There are things they didn't tell you because you're gay. Just remember that, okay? Things out here are a little more complicated than you might remember."

I closed my eyes for a moment. "What're you talking about?"

A sharp pain stole my breath. Great. This whole misadventure was giving me gas.

Aunt Sissy cracked the door to peek in at us. "Rita and Doreen just left and Mamaw's gone down for her afternoon nap. When she gets up, we're supposed to have this figured out, girl."

She and Shelia, looking like the before and after facelift advertisements, sat down next to one another on the bed across from me.

"Yes? What horrible dishonor have I brought down on our heads now?" Being here like this brought my emotional maturity down to my 15-year-old teen self, sarcasm and all.

To her credit, Aunt Sissy didn't sass me back, but she did lightly slap my leg.

"Jesse, I ain't ever hit a pregnant woman, so don't you be taking that from me." Her imitation of Mamaw was spot on.

I laughed, but neither of them joined in.

Shelia leaned towards me and in a conspiratorial whisper said, "You know we're cursed, right?"

All of us? I'd just thought it was me for being born into these back-pasture shenanigans. I picked at the quilt's yarn knots, wondering if they were all drinking well water or if the propane tank was leaking again. "Sure. Cursed."

Sissy's voice got quieter. "The first-born boys don't make it, Jesse."

Shelia put an arm around her momma's shoulders. "Your second cousin Jakob was four when that thing got him."

I vaguely remembered his name, but I'd always thought he'd had a heart defect.

"What thing?" This was getting weird—even for them.

Aunt Sissy didn't answer. When I looked up, she'd gone.

"Fine," I huffed, all out of breath from having my innards squashed as I tried to sit up. Oh hell. Been here twenty minutes and I'm already thinking like them again.

Sissy came back in with an armful of books—except that they weren't. Those were brass-edged and metal. And I'd never seen them off Mamaw's memory shelf in my life. I'd never even touched them.

"I cannot believe that you—"

"Joesph Wray, 1860 to 1867." She shoved the dusty tintype at me.

I caught it automatically and wished I hadn't. "People died all the time from lack of medicine back then."

"Henry Wray, 1887 to 1893." She let it go before I had a good grasp on it.

"That's sad, yes, but it's not proof," I said and caught it before it could fall.

Her voice grew sharper. "Frank Wray, 1922 to 1927." It clattered atop the last one.

"This is faulty reasoning," I said. "You're stuck in a loop."

"Thomas Wray, 1944 to 1948."

I turned his grimy glass smile face down as soon as it hit my lap.

I knew what was coming. She needed to stop. "Not enough data to support your claim."

"Jakob Wray, 1961 to 1964."

I got louder as the pile on my stomach grew. "Correlation does not imply causation."

After each name, she shoved another photo at me. With no lap, I struggled to hold them all. They slid against one another, their corners digging into my belly. If they fell and broke,

Mamaw would be devastated. Even so, I was waiting. Almost holding my breath for the last one.

She hugged it to her chest. And just like that, there he was, watching me with his red curls and bright blue eyes and his sweet little dimples.

I could feel it. Were we cursed? And it stilled my brain. It shut my mouth.

"Do you remember the last time you saw him? Think, Jesse. Do you remember that night?" Shelia asked.

I didn't want to. I had left this all behind me. I got out. I got away. I had another life, one that made sense outside of this place. I didn't need to be poor, lost David's sister. I was Rachel's partner. And soon I'd be James Wray-Collins' mother.

My throat was suddenly dry and the words quiet. "My brother drowned in the cattle tank. He was two and I was four."

"Your daddy never let us talk about it. And that's what run your momma off, Jess. Can't say that I blamed her, though."

"That's not true." I could barely speak. There hadn't been a splash. He never had a chance to scream.

But I did.

"Oh baby, don't you remember? I'm the one that found you. I brought you home and got you cleaned up before your parents came back from town. Y'all were supposed to be in the house. I don't know what possessed you to go outside."

"Kittens," I whispered. "The barn cat had kittens, and we snuck out the back door when you weren't looking. It was an accident." I don't know how she could believe me when I didn't believe myself anymore.

Shelia strode across the room and held up a glossy 8x10 under my nose. A chubby baby in a blue knit hat wearing the tiniest little diaper.

"His name was Michael, Jesse." Her voice quavered. "He was my son. Do you want to tell me I didn't see what I saw? We buried a pacifier because there was nothing left of him."

Aw, crap. How had I been gone so long? How had I forgotten that the flood of Facebook pictures had suddenly stopped just days after his first—his only birthday? How could I have forgotten another tiny coffin? Tears welled up, blurring Shelia's grief-lined face.

I didn't know anything about curses. Didn't want to know. But I had a lapful of morbid math staring up at me, and I couldn't help noticing the pattern.

Joesph had been seven when he died back in the 1860s. Henry had been five. David had only just turned two, and Shelia's son…

I glanced at that impossibly tiny diaper again, and then down at my belly. Dust and grime streaked my shirt where the frames had rubbed against me, like so many toddlers finger painting in ash. The only first-born son we had left was the one inside me— and at this rate, who knew if James would even live long enough to be born?

It couldn't happen. I wouldn't let it.

"OK." Tears rolled down the tip of my nose. "OK, I'm all in."

"IT WAS MY GREAT-grandfather who promised water rights to the Shochets before he died, the charitable man who he was. But it was his wife who never made good on it." The spoon clinked against her glass as she stirred her tea. She paused and took a sip.

"What happened?" I asked.

Mamaw spoke into her glass, never looking up. "Their herd died in the field. My granddaddy, who was just a boy then, used to say it was the most evil thing he'd ever seen. The only thing worse than those pitiful creatures lowing night and day was when it stopped." She met my eyes with rheumy tears in hers, spilling down along the deep crow's feet like rain trickling down a dry creek bed. "And then flies came."

Sin. There was no other word for it.

"They lost their land." My voice broke. "They lost everything."

I leaned against the countertop, scarred with generations of living. "What's been tried already?"

"Joseph was the first, and they just thought it was the filth and flies brought down by all the bloating. It took years for anyone to catch on. We've searched up the bones of those poor creatures, praying over and burying the ones we found. Men of God from multiple denominations came and blessed every room in this house when I was a girl. And after I married your Papaw, I had it done again—including the pasture and barns." She finished her tea and took it to the worn enamel sink. "I called every number the operator could give me for any name close to Shochet anywhere. Spent hundreds of dollars on long-distance calls, only to be told that there wasn't no one there by that name. After Jakob died, I put your daddy to work licking stamps and envelopes to mail out letters looking for them. They all come back: Not at this address."

I took my own plate and glass to the sink, my swollen feet complaining while Mamaw kept talking.

"Sissy looked for the Shochets on the internet, so maybe we could find a way to make amends for all that happened. Because it's them we owe." She rinsed out the glass and put it in the drying rack. "But you know, if they ain't got a Facebook account, they just don't exist."

"But what can we do, Mamaw?" I asked.

She sucked her teeth and cocked her head with that look I remember from the time I asked her about Bessie giving Laban a piggyback ride. "Well, hell Jesse. You're the government. I was hoping you'd tell me."

Unfortunately, if there was any agency that specialized in locating displaced deep-holler Hollows Grove folk, it was above my pay grade.

But that didn't mean I was helpless.

FOR THE NEXT FEW days, I pored over old scrapbooks and read from the family bible. Our Wray historians had taken their jobs seriously, and the books were full of So-and-so begat So-and-so, right down to J.T. Shochet's signature on the first Laban's bill of sale.

Sketches were made in the margins. Bulls, mostly, but even both families' brands were in one of the books. Different types of barbed wire, a couple of flowers, and a beloved cattle dog named Caleb were drawn in different hands, different styles through the years.

I read. I studied.

And on the third day I waddled forth to walk the fence line.

Sweat trickled down the back of my shirt and horse flies drew blood every time they landed. Occasionally, I'd find an old wooden post with the quartered circle brand of the Shochets or a rotting piece of burlap. But not much else.

It made a little more sense now. We were being Old-Testament punished for being stingy.

Another one of those sharp pains hit me. I was probably overdoing it again. Back home, Dr. Zimmerman and Rachel would have conspired to put me on bed rest or something equally awful.

Laban, the tenth of his name, stared at me. Four cows lay at his feet. It was a little regal to be sure. I tried to shoo him on his way, but he held his ground. I took the hint and went the long way around. The rest of the herd made a few complaining sounds as they ambled off.

I plodded along the barbed wire when I heard one of the Risinger boys holler at me. I waved and he waved, and we both went on about our business. And then it dawned on me that they were living on the old Shochet homestead.

I fought the barbed wire, stabbing myself in the hand with it, to get onto their property. He started my way. We met under a scrawny pecan tree and the shade was a blessing.

"Ma'am." He nodded a greeting. "You need something?"

"How long has your family owned this land?"

His good manners disappeared. "This land ain't for sale. You can tell your grandmother that again for me. If you don't mind."

Aw, crap. Leave it to Mamaw to piss off the neighbors. Was she trying to start up another feud? The damn Wrays and Shochets had been as bad as the Hatfields and McCoys.

"Wait, I don't want to buy it. I just want to look around. No one ever lived here when I was a kid."

It's hard for a southern boy to be rude to a pregnant woman. "Look at what, exactly?" But his tone did it well enough.

I told him the story. Every wild-eyed crazy word of it. I showed him the bones. And he showed me the ones that he'd found on his side of the fence. We found ourselves on his front porch drinking tea and speculating. It seemed that the Risingers built their house here and the original structures had gone to pot a long time ago.

After we'd exchanged names and pleasantries, Johnny asked, "Why do you think it didn't end when they died off?"

"I don't know," I shrugged. "But don't look to me for answers to this. My family's been picking up the bones around here for generations. One theory is that if we can find them all and crush them, the thing won't be able to manifest, I guess."

Thank God for running boards and free weights, or I'd never have hauled myself into that four-wheel-drive truck. He drove us out to the spot where the ruined buildings sat. The roof had collapsed. A wall had fallen over. It was probably full of skunks and wasps now, but at one time, this had been the home of the people that killed my brother. I walked out further to the ruined barn. I felt like I was missing something, but it was more of the same. No way in. Nothing to see but the rusted lightning rod reaching for the sky.

The next morning, I had something figured out. I already knew the death of the entire Shochet herd, and the ruination of their livelihood was the cause of our curse. And now, through the family history, I discovered that the original Laban had belonged to them. My great-great-grandfather gave his Shochet counterpart a whole dollar for that bull. If our families had just joined together, we could have all been rich. The Wrays might have had the land, but the Shochets had the stock.

If one were to look at it a certain way, the Shochets did have a living relative—and he was probably out in the back pasture chewing his cud right now. All he needed was the family name—or the 4H equivalent.

Over breakfast, Shelia asked me, "So you think if we give that old bull their brand, it'll break the curse? I don't see what difference that would make."

Aunt Sissy blew the steam off her coffee. "Can't hurt. We've tried everything else. The land and house have been blessed. The family's tried moving away. We've done everything but put sheep's blood over the door."

"Not everything," I said.

Change the brand. Change our luck.

The Shochet's brand was a circle cut into quarters. The Wray brand was a circle, with one line bisecting it. Both were simple—and simple to imitate.

While Mamaw found one of our old branding irons and Shelia rounded up the welding gear, fat storm clouds blew in, cooling off the morning. They wouldn't let me near the torch, so I settled for watching as they attached two metal lines. Now all I had to do was wait for Mamaw's little afternoon lie-down.

I took Mamaw's idea as my own and meant to just have an hour or so, but cramping, acid reflux, and the baby somersaulting around my uterus had kept me up all night. When I woke, it was pitch dark and the house was quiet. I reached for my phone on the nightstand to see that it was one o'clock in the morning. That gave me about four uninterrupted hours to take care of what needed doing.

And Mamaw wasn't going to like it.

Storm clouds had grown fatter, loosening huge drops of rain to pelt the roof and rattle the windows. Part of me wanted to get in that rental car and just drive, not stopping until I was back in the relative safety of DC.

But leaving hadn't saved David or Michael, and I couldn't trust that even a black sheep like me could avoid this plague. I was Jesse Eliana Wray, first-born child of Adam and Allison Wray, granddaughter of Miriam and Deacon, and heir to this evil.

I ignored the cramping that started low on my side as I tugged on my grandfather's old barn coat and boots outside on the screened-in porch. Nothing fit right. My feet were swollen and so was my belly. But my gut was full of resolve.

Wind whipped the treetops around, creaking and groaning. Rain blew through the screens. I took the shotgun down from the rack, just in case this didn't go as planned. I stepped over the squeaky boards and slowly opened the door to keep its complaining to a minimum. Mamaw would freak if she heard me out here. I thought I'd made it home free when I heard one of the boards I'd avoided.

"If you think you're doing this without me, Jesse Wray, you're wrong."

"Shelia," I hissed, "Shut up or Mamaw'll kill us both."

We snuck out, the rain immediately plastering my hair down and sending rivulets running into my eyes. She followed me to the shed and took the hand torch when I grabbed the branding iron she'd finished earlier. This wasn't the best idea I'd ever had, but if I bought into this curse mess, I had to be all in or we were lost, anyway.

We didn't speak as she opened the gate to let us both into the pasture. The mud sucked at my rubber boots, making it slow going. Sheet lightning flashed daylight, and I saw the cows pressed up against one another under the half-barn.

All of them except Laban.

He was standing on the low hill, broadside, as a warning. I'd never thought about how big he was. Or how much he weighed. Or how fast he could be in any terms other than breeding and money before. The closer we got, the more monstrous he became.

His horns were bone white and sharp. And the little light filtered through the clouds from the moon, lit up his eyes with an icy blue.

"He does not want us out here," Shelia said. "If he puts that head down, there's not a hidey-hole to jump in, Jesse. We'll have to shoot him."

Before I could argue, a contraction hit, doubling me over.

As I looked up, he charged. Hoofbeats thundered towards me, kicking up mud, and Shelia yelled as she ran towards him. He veered off course, but not before I got a good look at him.

Laban's eyes had widened and there was no hint of domesticated animal there. I could hear his ragged breathing even now, and smell the sulfur coming off of his hide. The Wray brand on his flank glowed. We had planned to come for each other the same night.

As the idea solidified, I yelled, "Get to the pen!"

She ran ahead to open the gate. I slipped and slid, moving at the speed of terror as he circled around for another attack. He would trample me, and if that didn't do the job, I'd suffocate in the muck. Either way, my son would never be born.

The gate was open. All I needed to do was lure him in without dying.

It was not a fair race.

Moving in a serpentine pattern slowed me down even more, but it might have saved my life. Burning pain ripped through my hip as his head sent me flying.

Sprawled on my back in the mud, I gave up on not being hurt.

I gave up on getting out alive.

I gave a bladder-busting pregnant lady grunt and shoved that shotgun stock into the mud, like Moses parting the Red Dirt Sea. By the time I pulled myself up, Shelia was already back at my side.

"Come on, you can do it," she said, half holding me up to walk. She handed me the torch. So, with the branding iron in one hand and the torch in the other, I surrendered the shotgun to the sucking mud.

I could barely stand. Another wave of contractions took my breath away.

Laban circled back, throwing his head and bellowing. It was more of a lion's roar. My cousin threw herself in his path again, and again he veered off to circle back.

Now he was cut off from the back pasture and the fence line. Shelia had shut the gate.

I teetered, unsteady on my feet. Another contraction started as I climbed the pipe fence. I'd gone numb and fumbled the torch. I dropped to my knees in the mud, scrambling to find it in the dark.

Laban balked mid-charge, shaking his head and stamping in the torch's flickering light.

Shelia climbed along the fence, getting down and running at him when the bull rushed my way. She kept him off me while I heated the brand until the head glowed cherry. He charged once more, and I already knew I couldn't get up or get out of his way.

This was it.

I flung myself down on my back, the hot brand in my hand. When he charged, ready to stomp me where I lay, I set the handle against my thigh. It would brand him no matter where it hit, and as he barreled toward me, I just had to hope that it would be enough to save the next generation.

And Laban slipped. His back end slid around, slamming the Wray brand straight into my iron, searing him into a Shochet in a red-hot instant.

The bull let out a bawl like a yearling calf. Stumbled. Staggered. And then all the might and bluster faded and Laban X, crowning jewel of the Wray brand, last of the Shochets, fell over dead.

And all I could do was sit there in the cold clay, mud in my underwear, slack in my jaw, staring dumbstruck as the last born Shochet crumbled to ash inches from the next to be born Wray.

Shelia panted, staring down the decaying carcass. "He should have died with his own."

"No," I said. "None of them should have died like that. But the debt is paid."

The tiny flutter of movement in my belly assured me that I was right. And I was also sure that I'd wet my pants.

I STOOD ON THE back porch of my grandmother's house, the screen resting on my good hip as I helped Rachel in with her bags.

"You're sure this is what you want?" she asked.

I snaked my free arm around her waist, and in my best Mamaw's bless-your-heart voice said, "Yeah, babe. I'm all in."

Smolder

CHRISTINA BERGLING

The shadows in the corner of my room smoldered, roasting in the smell of burnt plastic and flesh. A faint, red glow pulsed in the darkness, drawing a twisted, disjointed form. The shape twitched, moved unnaturally until it shuffled to the edge of the light.

She didn't look like herself without her skin. She didn't look human in so many jagged pieces. But I knew it was her. From the first time I saw her in that stone building in Baghdad, I would know her anywhere. Any piece of her. That first meeting haunted me more than the ghost that had followed me across the ocean, back to my safe, little apartment in the States.

"WOLFE," MASTER SERGEANT CARTER greeted me. He used his civilian tone, and his lip quirked on one side. "Got a new crop for you this morning."

"More from I-Corps?" I asked, matching his step as he marched down the marble hallway.

"Changeover is coming."

"What's your count at?"

His lip curled a bit higher, tempting a smile. "16."

"Not that you're counting, sir."

The sir cracked his grin, but he sloughed it from his cheeks before we walked into the training room.

The building housing the Army engineers contained an awful collision of cultures. Cheap, flat carpets covered the shiny marble tiles. Elegant curves of golden Arabic letters glinted embedded in the walls above canvas cubicles. Each workstation hosted black monitors and keyboards, their cords as twisted as the electrical infrastructure out in the city. The nest of wires known to electrocute gunners high in the basket of an MRAP.

Carter turned on his heel and escorted me to the front of the room. One soldier sat at a workstation, alone in the middle of the long table that held up five computers. Sleek dark hair cut along her sharp jaw. She perched on the dismal office chair, perfect posture in her bulky BDUs. Before I could think, my eyes traced the seams running down her back.

My breath caught in my throat at the sight of her. I tried not to react. I had not seen another female in a couple of weeks and none who looked like her since I set boots on this sand.

"Where's your team, Specialist?" Carter asked, fists planted on his hips.

"Out on an op, sir." She rolled back from the screen and found the backrest of the chair.

"Then why are you here?" The thick lines in Carter's forehead creased.

"I was nominated to become the expert and disseminate knowledge, sir."

Carter closed his eyes and lifted his face to the ceiling. I imagined he was running his countdown in his mind. "Guess you have a private lesson, Specialist."

"Yes, sir," she said, turning to me.

When they met me, her salient eyes were piercing. She would have been lethal in eyeliner. But only the middle-aged contractors who chased the combat sex culture had a use for makeup out here. I nearly flinched from her eye contact. A flush swept over me, and I looked to Carter to ignore it.

"Wolfe, expect follow on sessions." He nodded to me, clasping his hands behind him, and took his leave.

"Yes, sir."

I ignored the heat under my collar and gave her a smile. Glancing down at her chest for her name felt voyeuristic and warmed my skin even more. She observed me casually, one arm now slung over the back of the chair and her head tilted, all rigidity abandoned. I swore she saw the blush splashed on my cheeks.

"Ramirez," I read.

A grin grew across her face. She kicked out the chair beside her for me. I dropped onto the stiff foam and scooted the wheels toward the desk. Closer to her. I ignored my quickening pulse, covered it with words.

"How long have you been in theater?" I asked.

She looked up, digging in her memory. "Six days." Her smile was easy, crinkling the corners of those uncanny eyes. "But this is my third time on the merry-go-round." She looked me down, then up, quickly. "You?"

"91 days."

"But who is counting?" she chuckled.

Something in me roused while looking at her, something that had been dormant all these months in this place, something I had forgotten along the way. The sensation was thrilling, the way emotions are new in youth. Yet I chewed it back, hoping to present an indifferent surface. The arch in her eyebrow suggested my failing.

"Are you familiar with ATIN?" I asked, eyes fleeing to the monitor.

"Nah." She scooted closer, planting her elbows on the desk. "It was ODBP the last time I was in theater."

"Oh, same concept." My trainer voice spilled out in the rehearsed words. My tongue moved in muscle memory from daily recitation. "Except ATIN takes all of your reports and combines them with those from other communities like Intel, Psyop, Transition."

Smirking, she slouched in her chair, hand playing at her chin, legs spread like we were chatting at a bar. I could not resist the smirk as I turned to her.

"What?" I asked.

"You have, like, a whole spiel." She crossed her arms and nodded her head. "Don't let me stop you."

With a friendly glare, I delivered my speech, reaching across her chest for the mouse and navigating through the software. With each talking point, she drew a little closer.

"So, route clearance is what you care about, right?" I wound up for the interesting part.

She sat up in her chair, found her posture again as she shifted her eyes from me to the screen. "Yeah." Her face went serious, a stranger from whom I had seen the past hour.

"Let me show you route analysis."

I opened the map, zooming the street view on Baghdad and the roads just outside the wire. In practiced rhythm, I drew the arching shape along the route I used in every training example.

"So, you draw a shape on the map. You can use any of these or trace the route itself like this."

Her eyes widened, and she hunched toward the screen, cradling her chin in her hands. She watched every click and mouse stroke.

"Then when you search, it will show you everything that has happened in that area in the date range. SIGACTs, IEDs, even intel or interrogation reports that suggest a threat."

I retracted my hand, letting her absorb it.

"That's actually amazing." ATIN stole her attention, and I caught myself missing its warmth.

I marched her through the rest of the software, but her rapt attention on the screen waned once we left the map. Her focus wandered back to the side of my face. Catching her eye from the edge of mine had my pulse galloping again.

"Where you from, Wolfe?" she redirected.

"Colorado." I slid back from the monitor.

"Fort Carson?"

"Yeah, around there."

"Your husband stationed there?"

Husband. I should have said husband. I had been trained to say husband in this place. Always stand behind a man, even an imaginary one. I opened my mouth, but I hesitated. She clocked it, and her lips settled into a knowing line. She had clearly seen through to the solitary of me. And something else.

"Hey, do you want to go to chow?" she asked.

"YOU'LL BE MORE OF an expert than me after this," I said over her shoulder, watching her draw, then query the shape on the map over and over. Being our third follow-up session, she already knew what she was doing.

"It's important. I need to do it right. Every time. Show me again."

I lowered into the chair beside her workstation. Heat at proximity washed over my skin. "You got it," I said, quickly. "You don't need me."

She leaned in closer, lips near my collar. "Plus, I wanted to see you again," she whispered.

I stopped breathing, willing myself not to react. We were alone in her corner of the office, yet I still felt eyes all around, voices softly chattering down the hall.

Smirking, she pushed up, abandoning her chair and locking her screen. "Where are we going to chow?"

Air returned as I followed her. "Where do you want to go?"

"Liberty has the best desserts." She looped her rifle across her back and gathered her sunglasses.

"I like the grilled cheese on Victory." I gathered up my bag and kept step with her toward the parking lot.

"We should go out to BIAP, eat that fine Air Force cuisine."

The airport was a drive across Victory, at the edge of the complex. It would be a tempting amount of time alone in the dusty Pajero. I brushed the sand from the handle as I opened the car door, casting my eyes up. The sky felt lower. The clouds above loomed thick and orange. The taste of dirt was in the air.

"Air's looking pretty red," she mused as she took my passenger seat.

"Yeah, glad I'm not trying to fly today."

When we left the DFAC, full of grilled cheese and dessert, the sun had vanished behind the storm. Stray droplets turned into mud in their descent to my shoulder, painting my shirt brown. When I looked across the road, the wall of sand menaced in the closing distance.

"Where do you live?" she said from beside me.

"Dodge City North."

"Let's ride it out in your CHU."

I didn't have a chance to say anything. I was already following her back to the Pajero, already letting her ride down the dusty asphalt without her seatbelt, already watching her out of the corner of my eye rather than the road in front of us.

I rolled to a stop on the curb beside Dodge City North, a pad of rock and gravel lined with towering, gray cement walls that entombed each small, metal trailer. The bathroom trailers sat on each edge of the massive rectangle, a gender sign affixed to the T-wall outside the entrance. Arched cement bunkers peppered the walkways between rows.

My boot sank into the rocks, scratching and grinding with each step. Suddenly, the ground felt like quicksand, like we would sink and be trapped here for any passerby to see. My heart assaulted my ribs, sending tingles down my arms for the sensation to pool in my hands.

The wind whipped between the T-walls, blasting us with sand. The dirty cloud enveloped us as we hurried to my door. I fumbled with the key and got us in, shoving the door closed behind her. She stood in the little piles of sand, looking over the space. It must have been the same sad metal twin bed and particle board wardrobe in her accommodations. She looked at mine, then the vacant set on the other side.

"No roommate?" she asked, eyebrow arching.

"Not enough female contractors, I guess."

She nodded and stepped from her boots, propping her weapon against the wall. I was not even out of mine before she grabbed me. She seized me with tender aggression, sending me back into the door but cradling my head to spare me the impact. I groped at her, a flutter of forgotten sensations and repressed urges. I lost myself in a blur of touch and skin and mouths and hands until we flopped onto my squeaking bed.

As her fingers sank into me, I released a moan. The most honest sound I had made in theater. She clapped a hand over my mouth.

"Shhh," she breathed. "That is not what we want anyone else to hear."

But her warm breath at my neck had me bucking into her hand. She rolled me over so I could drown my pleasure in the pillow.

When we finished, our skin stuck together. I panted soft against her neck.

"Are you out back home?" she asked, fingers trailing over my bare back.

I lowered my eyes as I shook my head into her shoulder. "You?"

"At home, some places, with some people. Not in the Army at all."

"Why?" I asked. The closet did not seem like the place for her.

"Don't ask, don't tell and all that. If I were out, if I told them, it would be porn delusions of hot lesbians or a case of needing the right dicking down. I don't want to deal with either."

THE DAYS PASSED IN a homogenous blur. Significant activity report, improvised explosive device report, interrogation report, route clearance report. The abbreviated and summarized ugliness of this war filtered through my screen, and I felt it make a home in me.

My rendezvous with her were sporadic around her unit's operational tempo and my training schedule. She strategically scheduled training requests during my shift or sent subtle invitations to the DFAC to my secure email. Rushed lunches to sneak time in my shaky, metal bed. A late-night appearance drunk at my door after one of her unit had secured bottles from the Aussies. If the day was quiet, we would venture out to Camp Slayer for chow, farther away, where we would have a lower chance of seeing someone either of us knew. We still could not be us, but we could be two women pretending to be battle buddies where our appearance might not be drawn into a pattern.

As I clung to her sweaty skin, we were a bubble of beauty and truth in a war of lies.

"Are you doing Irish tomorrow?" I murmured into our shared pillow.

"You know I can't tell you that." But her face confirmed for me.

The shape of Route Irish was like a sunspot on my mind. I dreamed about it and the reports that exploded along it. I saw it now behind my eyelids, painted with hotspots of enemy activity. My pulse hurried, and my breathing struggled. She kept tracing an indistinguishable message on my skin.

I wanted to melt into her. I wanted to fuse with the scratchy sheets and never leave. Yet the clock ticked for her, down to when she would be counted, expected. I wanted to cling to her, fight the lean muscles I loved to admire, to keep her just overnight. Yet she gently slipped from my grasp and gathered her uniform from my floor. She dressed efficiently as she cast mischievous glances at me.

"Hey, Erica." She hesitated at my door, holding the thin wood. Her fingers teased at the doorknob. When she turned back to me, I flushed at the look in her eyes.

Pulling the abrasive blanket up on my chest, I rolled to face her. "Yeah, Dani?"

She smiled with a softness I had never seen, a softness that looked out of place here. "Nevermind. I'll tell you tomorrow."

And she closed the door behind her.

I SHOULD NOT HAVE looked at the report. But Route Irish was the first thing I checked when I got into the ATIN trailer. Every type of report in the past twelve hours, well covering her shift and any time she would have been out on the patrol I wasn't supposed to know about. When I clicked Search, the shaded line on the map peppered with icons. Yellow circles, red diamonds, orange triangles, nothing good.

Compulsive, desperate, I clicked through the symbols, exposing the report previews. All details painfully familiar. Reports I had scrolled through day after day that had never reached out to touch me. Then it was there: the IED report. My eyes leaped to the unit callsign, the casualty count.

Hand quivering, I opened the full report. Something heavy and hot sank in the pit of me. I couldn't breathe under its weight. My eyes and sinuses were already tingling.

I opened the scene pictures, my need to know a masochist. Those sharp eyes stared back at me from a cratered mess of exploded flesh. Clouded now with black granules clinging to the surface. Even in the unrecognizable pieces, I knew it was her. Her arm near the camera, fingers curled toward the blackened palm. Her face missing a jaw amidst the rubble. Her mouth that had kissed me, her fingers that had been inside me.

My vision blurred and flickered. The terrible world closed in around me.

A SHUTTERING VIBRATION ROCKED my bed. The way a distant IED explosion rippled through the floor of the ATIN trailer. Something I had never felt in my CHU. I jerked up in my bed, squinting around the dim morning light.

Somehow, I had left the ATIN trailer and gotten to my CHU. Maybe Moore had escorted me. Maybe I had driven the Pajero into the curb outside. I did not know, and I did not care. I didn't even care if a rocket had made it over the wall.

Flopping back down to the flat pillow, I curled into a ball. I could not hold myself tight enough. My eyes wandered to the door, searching for her there. I wanted to call her back to bed. I wanted to beg her to stay. But the blistering pain in my chest and my raw sinuses reminded me it was too late.

I glared at her vacancy, at the increasing light sneaking in under the door. Then I noticed a small pile right inside the threshold. Where she had first stepped out of her boots on a sandy day, where I had seen her yesterday.

I poured myself from my bed, landing hard on the tile, and crept across the floor. My muscles felt atrophied and resistant as I dragged. I squinted through puffy eyes. Not sand. The sand was everywhere. Not dirt. As I drew closer, I saw it was not granules but feathery flakes. When I pinched them between my fingertips, the ashes smeared across my skin.

In horror, I threw myself together and rushed to work. Nothing stopped when KIAs appeared on my monitor every day. There was no bereavement for a secret relationship.

Moore had taken the Pajero for his early shift, like every morning. Shouldering my backpack, I traced the sidewalk with my head hanging. My feet knew the way, so I only trudged along.

The desert sun baked down through a painfully clear sky. Sweat sprouted under my clothes and in my boots. I glowered at the gleaming T-walls lined up beside me, then froze in my tracks.

Wisps of smoke spiraled up from the closest bunker. I gaped, bewildered, but unwilling to approach. Inside the shadow of the bunker, something moved. Something about the shape twisted my stomach.

The air was silent. No sirens, no C-RAMs. Even the range was quiet from morning exercises. I glanced back and forth to find any reaction. When two soldiers marched past the bunker unfazed, I squeezed my eyes shut and shook my head. When I looked back, nothing.

I wasted the day detached at my desk, pinning the tears deep behind my eyes where no one would notice. Some crisis called most of the trainers and services guys out, so I counted the minutes until I dove back into my bed. I slept restless, dreamless, and miserable.

When I opened my eyes and peeled my cheek from the pillow, she was waiting for me.

It was not the woman from the training room. Not fierce eyes and flawless skin. It was the pieces from the IED report scene photos stacked back together.

She crunched and crackled as she emerged from the shadows on the empty side of the room, exposed bones grinding together, skin fluttering off like ash. She left a trail of embers as she shambled toward me. The ragged edges of her cheeks quivered over her missing jaw.

I choked on my horror, a ball of nausea and fear filling my throat. My instincts sent garbled and confused messages through the static of my grief. My muscles contracted to flee, yet my mind was mesmerized by her. I wanted to hold her. I wanted to touch her face again. I wanted whatever was left of her.

Ignoring the putrid smell packing my trailer, looking through the disfigured specter, I slipped from the bed we had shared so many times. The tile was sickly warm against my bare feet as I crept towards her. My fear faded with each inch I gained, with how she looked more like her living self in my eyes. I told myself the crinkle in her burnt cheeks was a welcoming smile.

She tilted her bald and blistered head as I reached her. Tears streamed down my cheeks like the Tigris. I reached for her with trembling hands.

With a peeling shriek, she snatched me. Her broken, disjointed arms fumbled around me, smearing me with charred flesh and blood as they held me vice-tight. I writhed against her, hands sinking into her destroyed flesh. Then her touch seared me. She left welted handprints on me as she groped at my neck and face, clutched at my arms. The burns spread, filling me with heat until I felt like I might combust.

Screaming, I bucked against her. I slapped against the tile in an empty, quiet room. Without the ashes of her around me and with nothing but a scalding handprint on my chest.

I FINISHED MY ROTATION numb and detached. The months passed mechanically. Sometimes, I slept. Sometimes, I ate. I worked. Then I repeated. I let the routine beat me into compliance.

And every night, I waited for her. The sweet smell of her charred flesh caused my stomach to flinch. I never got used to it.

Her blistered, melted specter lingered in my bedroom door, as always. The skin on the swollen fingers cracked to reveal tender meat, oozing with puss and fluid. As her grip twitched around the knob, the splits branched to expose more raw wounds. Her hair had not survived, yet her eyes glinted clear and undeniable above her unrecognizable, scorched cheeks.

The muscles and tendons in her exposed throat flexed and worked. Her top lip quivered above the gaping space that used to be her mouth. Her lower jaw was missing, blown completely from her face with her left ear. The chasm left behind choked on words she could not speak.

Even without the crisp lines of her features, I knew that look. She had given it to me before and now was trapped, repeating that hesitation at my threshold.

Yet, my countdown finally reached 16, then wandered down through single digits. I allowed muscle memory to carry me to the end of my commitment and onto my flight home.

I watched Iraq recede into sand, then under clouds from my window. It felt like I was leaving her, abandoning her to haunt my shitty little trailer. Even though I knew the pieces of her had gone home months before. I would never know where she was buried, could never visit where she rest. I didn't even know if her parents were some of those people who truly knew her.

As my grief flattened across time, she felt more like the ghost screaming from my nightmares and casting burning figments onto my nerves than the sweet touches we had hidden or the honest words spoken. I had no pictures of her living, no evidence of the moments we stole in theater. I hadn't even conjured the courage to tell anyone about her, in Iraq or back home. It was as if we had never happened. I went back to saying the word husband and dying inside with each syllable.

I didn't know how to exist back home. My world had contracted down to a simple routine, the same day on repeat for months. Besides her. I didn't remember how to have free time or options. The comfort and abundance abraded me, but I could not tell where the rage was coming from. I just knew that when I walked into a Wal-Mart, I wanted it to burst into flames.

So I didn't go out. I didn't socialize. I didn't eat. I didn't sleep. I crafted a new routine of working, watching Netflix, and mourning, waiting in the dark each night, both terrified and excited for her to haunt me.

"I guess I just don't understand why you're struggling so much. It's not like you saw combat," my mother said as she unloaded groceries into my cabinets. She worked around the neglected stacks of dishes.

"It was a war, Mom," I said, curled up on the couch. "I saw horrible things."

"But you didn't." She paused. "*See* them. Right?"

"People I knew died."

"But no one you were really close to. Right?"

This was my moment. This was my opportunity to make it real. To honor her. To say how much I loved her in those fleeting months. To be myself.

Instead, I pulled the plush blanket tighter into my chest and watered it with my tears.

SLEEP DEPRIVATION MADE THE world surreal. Like when I switched from days to mids. One foot floating away in dreams, one snagging down in reality. I lay in my bed with a sandstorm in my mind, wanting it to bury me.

Just as I started to wander off consciousness, the smell announced her, snapping me fully awake. My throat flexed, wanting to retch the odor from my sinuses, yet my heart also fluttered. I wanted her to hurt me, to punish me for denying her. Anything to not be alone in this wake of war and her.

Fear and longing entwined to string my nerves taunt. When her smolder lit the shadow, I drew up in my bed. My stomach begged my legs to run, yet I was done listening. She had followed me so far across the world. I had to see what was left of her.

The shadow peeled back to reveal her skinless form. The burned skin and blisters had fallen away to reveal her bare, callow flesh. Bloody veins mapped her disfigured terrain. Clear eyes burned out from her destroyed face, as piercing as the day I met her, unmarred by death. Her dismembered joints ground against each other as she planted wet footprints across my floor. She staggered toward me a few steps before turning toward my door.

She took the knob in her hand, toying at it with slick, raw fingers, drawing her fingerprints in blood. Lingering in the threshold, she turned those blazing eyes back on me.

In that instant, looking past the grotesque to her shape, I saw that final moment in my CHU. The epiphany buried me like that sand cloud. I glimpsed the moment in which she was trapped. I read past her missing lips to the words her shredded throat was trying to form. I knew what she was saying. Then. And right now.

Clarity erased my fear and disgust. Throwing my blankets aside, I rushed to her. I stood where I should have when she walked out of my trailer. I nearly choked on the taste of charred death and regret. Yet I stared into her eyes unflinching.

"I love you too," I said.

At my words, her burned throat stopped undulating in unsaid words. Her exposed muscles relaxed and her bloody shoulders lowered. Her eyes softened on the edges like they did when we were all alone in my bed.

I held out my arms to her. When she staggered into me, I folded her into my embrace. I didn't feel the slip of her blood against me or the crunch of her burned muscles. I only felt the weight of her against me. And how much I had missed it.

The heat blossomed between us. It radiated from her, roasting into me. Some part of me wanted to flinch away, wanted to flee the incandescent pain. I clung to her tighter. I leaned into the hot edge of her touch, and we burst into flames together.

My Lover, The Muck

BENJAMIN LARNED

July 27th

Charles wins again. Rather than luxuriating in a tropical paradise, I am stuck in a manor on the Irish moors. Never let an intellectual plan your holiday.

Odd duck that he is, Charles has fallen in love with it. He leaves me alone most of the day, tromping through bogland, looking for god knows what. It isn't that I mind, as long as he enjoys himself. But as the guidebooks warned, bogs are dangerous. There's always a chance he won't make his way back.

We spent the prior weekend in Dublin, half in museums and half in pubs, the warmest places in the city. At least there I could watch the pretty Irish boys get drunk. The museums, as one might expect, were dreadful—and none more than the history museum. They had a mummy exhibit on, complete with some-thousand-year-old corpses dug out of the local bogs. These dead boys kept their hair, nails, and skin, even as the muck dissolved their bones and organs. What remains is a suit of flesh, tanned to a ruddy brown and horrid to look at. But my Charles was enamored with these poor souls. He spent all day taking notes, snapping photos of their awful, twisted skin.

Gloomy prospects all around. This is a sad place, and a sad country. Unavoidable, perhaps, due to the weather; all we have seen thus far is rain. Not an ideal climate for a romantic getaway. Did I marry a toad? I fear that, with each passing anniversary, he becomes more ranine. Let us hope he does not start to croak.

July 30th

I thought I was so clever, forbidding Charles to pack more than one book. Lo and behold, the manor comes with a fully-stocked library. I believe Charles did not want a vacation, just more time for reading. He might have said so earlier and saved us several thousand dollars. All day he disappears into "research" while I putter about, drinking and staring through the window. At least, once the light drains and his eyes get tired, he joins me in the drinking.

When he isn't reading, he wanders the bog, oblivious to the chance that he might take a wrong step, sink below, and turn himself into one of his obsessions. I try not to think about this as I wait for him to return. He hasn't invited me to join him—not that I would accept if he did. I have no desire to cover myself in mud.

The house itself is an utter tomb, almost without charm. Its sparseness mimics that of the land, most of it razed by the English for timber. The Catholic memorabilia is plentiful—everywhere you go, there's a reminder of your mortal sin. It would be magnificent to host an orgy here; though Charles, being shy in the nude, would never agree.

CHARLES GROWS STRANGER BY the hour. He speaks of this house as if it belongs to him. He has met the previous residents, it seems, through their records and journals. They were wealthy landowners from the early Celtic days, and managed to survive the invading British heel, though the potato famine seems to have finished them off. Their bodies are interred in the bog nearby. Perhaps this is what occupies Charles, looking for their graves.

I am pleased for my husband, though. He has regained color, animation, and focus. We've been having a good time in bed, I'm surprised to say; the rain has done wonders for his libido. I think of those Irish pub boys as we make love. Charles seems to think of someone else, too. He asks me to lie still and pretend I am asleep, so he can explore me unhindered.

I love the man dearly. I would not have stayed with him for twenty-five years if I did not. And in these moments of youthful excitement, I remember why. He is pure as a child in his needs and wants, and his means of getting them; but he is damnably silent about them as well. Sometimes I wonder if I displease him. If that's the case, shouldn't he tell me? Is it my responsibility to coax him out, indeed, like one would a child?

But we agreed long ago that our companionship was not built on those expectations. And isn't his evasiveness—dare I say it—a little sexy?

August 1st

Rain worse than ever, and I haven't seen Charles all day. The manservant said he left for a walk at dawn. It sounds like Charles, but in this weather? Toad or not, he doesn't have the constitution.

Of course, it is too soon to worry. I have just begun to dread this empty house, the way its floorboards creak and shift in the wind. I never know who I might find in these endless rooms. There is no one to find, of course, besides my awkward reflection in the mirrors. This is not an exciting enough place for a ghost.

PAST TWO AND NO sign of Charles. The manservant said he left without lunch—so like him, to forgo mortal concerns in the face of ambition. He's eaten nothing since dawn, and the rain has not let up. We are in the marsh, with deep wells all around us, any of which might swallow a man and leave no trace. Such a lonely way to die.

NIGHT AND HE IS still gone. The manservant has called the police. They won't be able to help us until morning, they say. Whatever happens, it is out of our hands.

Is it wrong that I cannot react with any great emotion until I know for certain that he is gone? God dammit, I sound like a tragic bride, my husband already a ghost, forever lost to the earth… or perhaps I'm just drunk. I will wait for him. I must believe he will come back.

I AWOKE TO NOISE, shuffling in a distant room. I ran toward the sound, down one hall and out another, into the library. A dripping shadow leaned against the window. I stopped in the doorway, and it lurched towards me. I shrieked—the apparition said, "What's the matter, sweetheart?"

There was Charles, my dear toad, getting bog-muck all over the antique rugs.

That idiot did get lost, he said. He was frozen through, covered in mud. I bathed him and fed him dinner, after giving him a piece of my mind. He's warm now, tucked in bed, safely dreaming. I feel more relieved than I ever thought possible. The thought of returning to America alone, a widower—well, best not to entertain the notion.

CHARLES LEFT AGAIN IN the night, fumbling down the hall. When he came back to bed, his hands were wet. I didn't ask why. It is enough that he's here. As long as he stays put.

August 2nd

My husband has become drearier, if that is possible, since his adventure. He spends all of his time with those books and records. I'll relate what little he deigned to tell me over our lunch:

The manor's first owners practiced old Celtic rites, forbidden at that time by sword and pulpit. The women were heads of households, sorceresses, and lawmakers. The men, hunters and providers. They held ceremonies for the earth, which provided little respite when the famine came. With their ancestral wealth dried up, they lingered in degenerate strands, occupying the house like squatters—until the last descendent was chased into the bog, and the property went up for public sale. According to legend, townsfolk discovered the tragic heir seducing a young peasant boy. The mob chased him into the marsh and never found him. His body is still in the bog, they say.

I haven't seen Charles this excited in years. And isn't it funny how excitement can make a man lose all his charm? How his passions turn him so far inward that he might as well be talking to himself? Silly to say, of course; Charles is having a grand time, while all I do is mope. He would say it's what I do best.

Another thing I've only just noticed. One of the upstairs rooms is locked, and neither of us has a key.

NOISES AGAIN TONIGHT, SPLASHING and frantic. Is someone running through the halls with wet feet? It couldn't be—Charles is asleep, snoring beside me. Nothing to fear, only the rain. But when I close my eyes, I see people dancing, naked, covered in mud.

August 3rd

This occurred late at night, so I cannot trust the memory. I awoke to a pesky bladder. Without disturbing Charles, I went to relieve myself. When the old pipes finished clanking, I thought I heard something outside—movement, shifty and damp. Assuming a drenched vagrant had snuck in, I balled my fists and thrust open the door, but I found no one.

I let out a sigh, bemoaning my anxieties. Then my eye caught something past the window. Just outside of the moon's glow lurked a figure, horribly bent and reeking like garbage. It took a step closer—or so I thought, hearing a wet slosh—then a second figure appeared, pulled the first into a nearby room, and shut the door.

I stumbled for the knob, but it didn't budge. I listened through the door for some time, pondering that awful smell. I must have fallen asleep on my feet—the next thing I knew, Charles was shaking me awake, demanding to know what happened. When I said I'd seen a ghost, he shook his head, led me back to our room and tucked me in. That dreadful smell followed us. But I suppose it was, as Charles insisted, a dream. It makes me feel safer to think so.

THE LONELIER I BECOME, the more strongly I feel the house's presence. I suppose it's more of an absence, really. Charles hasn't left the grounds, not even for a short walk, but I still don't see him between breakfast and dinner. I can't find him in the library or the parlor, the halls, or the study. Wherever he sequesters himself, he's utterly quiet. Let him choke on the dust, then. I can have my own fun.

I feel like a veritable governess, unstable and overwrought, though less from nerves and more the good Irish whiskey. I spend most of my day stewing and waiting for a "manifestation," whether it be my husband or the theoretical ghost. It may happen anytime—a sigh, a moan, a muttered word drifting to me from nowhere. The house's pipes carry sound, but from whom? The voice I imagine is too hollow to be my husband's.

I *do* tend toward melodrama, as Charles loves to remind me, but I never entertain fancies as truth. I prefer not to be known as a "colorful character." The atmosphere has simply gotten to me.

And I hate to admit it, but I miss my silly, amphibious man. What could occupy him so long in this house? What gives him the excitement that I cannot?

August 4th

Charles is more evasive than usual this morning. He set to work without breakfast, as he tends to do around midterms and finals. I have been left once more to wander the house alone.

For good measure, I checked the door by the stairs. I found it locked, just as before.

I'VE CONFRONTED THE GHOUL in the flesh. And what flesh it has.

The noise woke me again, crashing in the dark, this time downstairs in the parlor. I felt for Charles in the bed—he was not there. In a white flash of panic, I imagined him on the floor somewhere, limp, not breathing. Had he been frightened, had he called for help, and I didn't hear?

The idea smothered all logic. I rushed to his side. I am not graceful when I run; by the time I reached the parlor, I was panting, gasping his name.

I found the ghoul sitting upright on the couch, bathed in moonlight: a corpse, leathern and preserved. Its grin seemed to widen at my appearance. Staring it down, I found that I could not scream. Terror is a funny thing, I tell you, it overwhelms all your faculties and renders you moronic. I wouldn't even have been able to run had the thing attacked.

But it didn't—it has long been incapable of movement. Its bones and organs were all dissolved, leaving only the husk of a boy.

Between its legs, however, alive and quite preoccupied, was Charles.

I'D RATHER NOT DESCRIBE the scene in greater detail.

As you can imagine, I had little to say to my husband. He begged me to listen, but I couldn't look at him, with mud smeared on his lips like that. When he tried to grab my hand, I flung him away, went back upstairs, locked the bedroom door, and drew the covers over my head.

He pleaded for entry until dawn, but I ignored him. I was and am not interested in discussing the matter. There are limits to a person's understanding. I have found mine.

August 6th

Since my discovery, I have not left my chamber. From my bed, I swear that I can hear him—them—in the infernal locked room. He must have been hiding it for days, sleeping in my bed, cradling me with the same hands he used to touch *it*.

Nobody will ever hear about this. I believe Charles has enough sense to ensure discretion. I will not ask how he found it, or where. I assume that he was looking for it the moment we arrived. No wonder he was so insistent on this godforsaken place.

I can't help but imagine what he thought about each time we made love. When fucking me, did he wish me dead? Did he fantasize about mortified skin, rigored muscle, and expelling fluids? Was he ever in love with me, or was I just a convenient shield? By kissing him, have I also kissed a corpse? But I won't ask these questions. I won't dignify him that way.

I will wait until our time is up, and then I will go to the airport, fly home, pack my things, and call the lawyer. Charles will not be able to afford a trip like this again, not without my support. He will have to find other ways to exercise his desire.

How quickly a person can fall out of love. My disgust is more powerful than my fondness ever was. But even after all this, I cannot help but wonder: is it the body of the pervert, the house's last owner, chased to his death over a century ago? Why did I think that its face-folds betrayed a touch of glee, as my husband serviced its hollowed-out cock? What does the dead boy give him that I cannot?

I WILL NOT BLAME myself. I was simply on my way to the kitchen for more whiskey. When I entered the hall, I heard bed springs creaking in a familiar rhythm. I put my head down and stalked past the locked room. But Charles, in his haste, forgot to close the door. There, in plain view, were his flabby buttocks, writhing atop his new lover.

A man with more resolve than I might have kept silent, but I was already in the room, hands on my husband's neck, pulling him off the corpse. His erect member, thighs, and mouth were covered in matter—exposed to living fluids. The corpse had begun to decay again. Even in his abjection, my husband was smiling.

"How long have you wanted this?" I asked.

Charles blinked at me like an imbecile. The corpse did not move; it did not mind that I was making a scene. I screamed like a jealous lover, "Twenty-five years and all I've done for you—*this* is how you spoil it?" It did not matter that the boy was dead. I never made Charles smile like that.

He couldn't answer. The toad was never good at self-expression. I left him slack-jawed and dazed with his lover. The cursed stench lingers in my nostrils; how does he bear it? I suppose one can bear much for a good lay.

I will not leave the room again, not until I must. The whiskey will sleep next to me. When it's gone, I will gather my things and fly home alone. There is no use staying with a man so enamored with death.

OH, NO.

I did not last long in my resolve. I tried my best, but no one, not even the most disciplined masochist, could stay put with that *smell* in the air, the weighty miasma of something I can't describe. It leaked through the vents and the floorboards, permeating the entire mansion. I could not stand for it. This indignity would be the last.

I went to the forbidden room and found it unlocked and empty. Shouting for my husband, I stomped downstairs, likely appearing as haggard as I felt. In the library I found his lover propped against the window. Framed by the howling rain, it looked triumphant.

Glaring into its sockets, I bellowed my husband's name.

There was no answer. I bellowed again and again, until he staggered from upstairs, bleary with sleep, robe open around his mung-stained stomach. "What, what?" he said.

"Put this filth outside," I answered, impressed at my calmness. "I can smell it from my room. The manservant will smell it too. You won't embarrass me like this."

He addressed *it*, not me. "What are you doing out of bed?"

I looked between them. "Don't play games, Charles."

"I'm not. I was asleep. Did *you* put it here?"

I took the corpse by the neck and dragged it from the library. Charles lurched, took my arm, and babbled, "Please. You don't understand."

"If you love it so much," I said, wrenching myself away, "then sleep with it outside." I brought it to the foyer, opened the front door, and through the threshold it sailed.

The body collapsed in the mud, a heap of leather and keratin, no longer so lifelike. Charles's expression became pitiable, so helpless and twisted, I wanted to smother him for his own sake. "Go on," I screamed, "you deserve each other." I gripped him by the collar and pushed him out. He tripped onto the porch, arms wrapped for warmth, looking at me with that face, that pleading toddler's whimper.

I couldn't bring myself to shut the door. I went outside with him, heedless of the rain, and used my slippered foot to stomp the corpse into oblivion.

It took great effort. My legs were drenched by the time I finished, my face splattered, frozen in a snarl. I turned to Charles, who had been fixed to the spot, powerless to stop me or save his lover.

"We are leaving," I declared.

"Not we," Charles replied.

His expression changed in a way that I will never describe, except to say that in his dumb triumph, he resembled the corpse.

He fell to his knees, pulled up the half-ruined body, and with it in his arms, raced off into the night.

I did not follow. I went back inside and crawled into bed. When I woke the next afternoon, I called the police. They conducted a search, which I monitored from a hotel in Dublin. Five days later, Charles was declared lost, a victim of his bog.

LIFE IN AMERICA FEELS more predictable now. I have adjusted well. I go to work and socialize, even date now and then; there are still men in the world who like them older. It's easy enough to make friends. I am jovial and pleasant, and I don't bring up my lost husband; not that anyone ever asks.

I've always been a good performer, perhaps something I learned from Charles. Behind my facade, I am far from recovered. I still smell that miasma, as if it has bonded to my nostrils. I see his last expression, too, printed against my eyelids, that empty corpse-like grin. I did love him, but I did not know him. And I'll never find a love as complete as his. That is what bothers me most.

Sometimes I imagine his condition, after all this time in the muck. How like his lover he has become. I think, how happy that would make him. And I think, how beautiful he must look.

Gänger

G.B. LINDSEY

On the thirteenth day, Gerte, looking over her shoulder, saw that she had picked up a gänger.

It wallowed on the path among the weeds twenty meters behind, the size of a small dog. Its limbs were knobbly, lumping from its sides without fingers or toes. It looked like a child, if a child were wet-skinned and gray.

Gerte rose from where she sat on a fallen log and picked up her pack. She was thirsty and her chest hurt. She had thought to fish in this lake today, but the pool had dwindled from blue to yellow sludge. Now, the gänger—the *thing*—rocked back and forth in the road, and the clouds scudding from the south looked darker than before, swollen on the horizon.

As she stepped closer, the thing mewled from the cracked earth. The cry was hoarse, a throat as dry as the soil on which it lay. Blue veins ran beneath its skin like roots. The gänger's head was distended, its surface undulating like hills. Two mounds where eyes would be, and nothing but a cave for a mouth.

Gerte hurried away from the thing in the road, its cries following in little flayed gasps, and headed south, chasing the storm. Rain tonight, maybe. Dear God, please. But there would be no running water until then; the riverbeds had all dried, the water skulking deep in the earth. She found the stream bed she had passed that morning and stepped across it as it wound a thin snake through the trees. Along its edges, flowers reached sallow heads toward the sky. It was nothing but a trickle, the water thick and sluggish with dirt, but it was moving. With luck, the thing would not be able to cross.

She walked fast, her boots *sshhh*ing through brittle leaves. The land was as thirsty as a bleached skull and the weight of that thirst leaned heavy and orange over everything. The sun slid toward the hazy line of mountains. Gerte walked and walked, and in an hour, she came over a rise and saw the city again, and knew for certain that even now, five years after the ruin of the world, they could not stay there.

Something old and foul had moved in.

The buildings tilted against the sky, their tops ragged shards. Black virga dripped, pooled in the streets, a great sooty gloom that swallowed the city's legs. Here and there, though they faced away from the sinking sun, their windows glittered with milky gold light.

Warmth, they promised. Shelter.

Gerte knew better. There were other beings than gängers in there. She went left along the tree line, did not look directly at those lighted windows, and presently she came away from the city's broken shell. The windows followed her like eyes. Even beyond the city limits, she felt the tug of the place and what lived there, catching at her wrists where her blood flowed closest to the skin. Ravenous, seeking to draw it out.

Warmth. Shelter.

And then there was a prickle close on her nape, and she knew what she was nearing as the road bent around the trees.

The woods to the left petered out as the road widened, spilled from its channel until asphalt merged with dirt. Even the weeds had not made headway except in the fissures where the tarmac had split, and there they drew sickly brown rivers through the black, like the veins under the gänger's skin. Gerte stopped in the road, rocking her weight from foot to foot. The sun dipped lower still.

If the places where people had lived once were no good, it was worse where they'd died.

In the pines' shadow lay great furrows of earth, thrown and turned and so gorged on rot that thousands of flowers grew atop the mound: hungry pink bells with yellow insides, flat-faced blooms of bright blue and dark red, green stalks topped with feathery purple. A wild bouquet marching down the spine of a mass grave.

There was no other way to pass by and keep out of both the city and the woods. Neither was safe after dark. The last pit she had seen, on the other side of the city, had not even been covered over. The silence was as thick as the fetid clots pulsing from the pit's mouth. And under that silence, she was sure she had heard movement within. The patter of falling earth.

She had not looked in at what was making the smell. She just hastened by, holding her breath. But she could pass this one now. A gänger had already crawled up from the loam and found her; another would not come.

She reached the old farm shed with the sun just touching the earth. It had been three nights since she had left Birgit there. Gerte did not stay long, lest the place gather her scent back into its walls and draw the gänger on. The shed listed, gray against the hill behind, the door forced shut in its frame. Her sister was not there; Birgit's bedroll lay neatly in a corner and her narrow boot prints ghosted the dust on the floor. Gerte took the pouch from the hole they had carved into the wall and ate a handful of what was in it. Then she scratched a note with charcoal on brittle paper, and rocked from foot to foot again, the paper held in one hand.

Birgit—
Came for almonds. I have a shadow.
(She dared not write the real word.)
I am at the dam. Don't stay. Don't follow.
—G

In the end, she left it on the table for Birgit to find. The gänger would not be able to read yet.

IN THE DAM WAS a room whose walls were gristly with dead moss. Broken tile sagged across every surface, and the side opposite the windows housed cubicles with pipes jutting from the wall where showerheads had been torn off. The reservoir outside was nothing but a striated crater reaching into the earth.

There was a table with a crack running up the center and one tilting wooden chair. Gerte laid out the bag of almonds and her empty water bottle, then sat down and ate at that table. She would be human still, if the rest of the world would not.

There was a bathroom: more cracked tile, dark green water stains. Gerte peered into the mirror, around patches of rust and splinters in the glass. Two faces, three, four, stared back. Her eyes looked old, faded blue, offset in her face, and her mouth was waxy, the skin sun-stretched. Her features were barely hers anymore. She pressed her cheek up and watched it fall back into place.

She wondered what she looked like to the gänger, if the gänger could look before it had eyes, what it was about her that it wanted to become.

At nightfall, Gerte returned to the room with the listing table and Birgit was there, sitting with her back against the wall, knees up.

Panic prickled at Gerte's teeth. *Why are you here?*

Birgit shrugged, looking down at her boots as she chewed on a root. Her hair was lank and dull, a paler brown than Gerte's own hair, and dirt clung to her neck where sweat had dried. Her eyes were the same sharp green as before the ruin of the world.

You must be more careful.

Birgit nodded. She chewed her root and watched the steadily darkening window.

The room was too quiet, both of them in it, not speaking. Gerte licked her lips and opened her mouth.

O'er land I walked, cross quickening stream—
And a mem'ry of me in the sun's cruel beam—

She could not sing. She was thirsty. Her tongue tasted of the spindrifts outside. In five years, too much had changed, and her throat was not right anymore.

BIRGIT USED TO TALK in her sleep, nonsense words. The wisdom of the world, their parents had joked. Gerte would creep into her sister's room at night and listen, and then touch Birgit's forehead until she rolled over and went quiet.

It's a clear memory: the rug between her toes, the nightlight in the shape of a star burning in the corner. The rest, the between—

(the chaos in the streets)

(the dwindling water)

(the first morning of true silence)

(the soft squeal of the front door in the night)

(the parents that were no longer their parents, white hair still, and wide feet with long toes but not the same, not the same)

(the look on Birgit's face, staring down the hall as their mother closed in on dragging steps)

Five years since the ruin of the world. One year while the land grew dark, and the birds all died, and their parents…went. And then four years of sun-charred earth and turning from the reaching shadows of the cities and walking, always walking—it all blurred.

The two of them used to sing together. Birgit didn't sing anymore. Birgit didn't speak anymore. For four years now, Gerte had heard no voice but her own.

IN THE PALE MORNING, a man crossed in front of Gerte and Birgit through the field.

When things began to feed off the dead—growing upon the bodies like fungi—the living put the dead away from themselves. They piled corpses at the lips of great trenches, rolled them into the hole. And then they ran.

And then the things growing upon the dead got up and followed them.

The man in the field wore a torn shirt and filthy pants. His hair was patchy and grown out, veiling his face. He walked a few steps, then stopped and swayed. He reached out. His fingers stretched. Curled. He walked a few steps in the other direction.

He opened his mouth and closed it, and stared toward the horizon for something he clearly thought should be there.

He turned. He came back the way he had gone before. Turned. Came back the way he had gone before. The grass was bent down in a flattened track.

Do you think he's human anymore? Gerte whispered.

He was in full sun, which discounted a number of things he could be, but not everything. Birgit watched him pass slowly from right to left, left to right. She shook her head no.

No humans left. Gerte had not said it aloud yet, even to herself. But it crept farther down her tongue today. She was tired, and the sun beat down atop her head. She was tired, and she wanted to sleep.

We should keep moving, she said.

Birgit nodded.

They walked and they walked. No birds sang. The roads lay barren and black under the baking sun. The world was so very silent.

You used to talk, Gerte said when they sat down to rest. She was so tired. But it was nothing to worry about. She had checked the road behind them again and again. It was only the heat.

Birgit shrugged and pushed the end of a weed through the dirt. It was thin and sharp at the edges. Birgit looked small against the ground, limbs tucked nearly inside her body. Some days, Gerte barely recognized her. Birgit was like a copy of a copy of the sister she'd known and held and bathed as a baby, whose hair she had braided, whose laugh had been wild, whose smile at graduation had been bright. Birgit now sat faded and slouched, like Gerte felt. The whole world was a photo negative, turned around and made to face into a sputtering sun.

It's because of what happened, isn't it? Four years ago. And then what happened after.

Birgit shrugged. Pushed her sharp little weed. A wind moved through the grass at the far edge of the field.

There was no wind. Gerte looked up.

The gänger leaned like a bending sapling, a bulbous head now rolling on its too-thin neck. Its skin had gone from gray and slimy to raw pink, and strange pebble-teeth hung in its mouth. Earth-brown hair grew out of its scalp in clumps like dead grass. It walked toward them, the field parting around its malformed legs.

Gerte seized Birgit's hand and yanked her up. She ran, and Birgit ran behind her, the sun a swollen flame against Gerte's back, her breaths harsh in her ears, the grass sharp and *ssshhhh*ing on their shins.

THAT NIGHT, GERTE WAS so tired. Her muscles ached and her head swam as though pushed by a sea. Around her were dim walls of warped wood. Birgit lay against her side in silence, one hand clasped around Gerte's.

Gerte thought about the day Birgit had stopped talking: the light fading quickly even though it was morning, their not-mother lurching down the hall, closer and closer, until Gerte grabbed Birgit's hand and pulled her out the door.

She squeezed Birgit's hand now. She was very tired.

THEY WALKED FOR A day, and another day. The city slouched behind them against the light, a canker rising from the face of the earth. In the morning, Gerte found an elder branch and broke it into a stave, just in case. But her limbs hurt, and her lungs burned just crossing the flats, so she had to use it as a walking stick. She felt her strength draining, far faster than it should. She recognized it, a half-formed memory. Birgit held Gerte's pack when Gerte had to sit down, and all day they saw dirt and weeds and dead trees, but… nothing following behind.

Maybe they had outrun the thing in time.

Maybe it *was* just the heat.

There were places they avoided, places they had tried before. Rooms with withered husks lying silent in corners. Mouths stretching open around dirty teeth. Fingers curled. She and Birgit remembered those places, the look of those doors, the heavy stain of certain houses, and walked past them. Gerte could not look at them anymore, and turned her eyes away. Their hair on those husks strung across the floor like her own hair hung down her back. Their wrists were thin and tight, like her wrists might be in another week. They looked too familiar.

Gerte and Birgit came to a house with a smashed door and shattered windows, and no husks inside. They had not been here before. They went into one of the rooms and hung tattered blankets over the windows. There were books with broken spines on a shelf, so Gerte took one down and read a story to Birgit like she used to. Mostly it was to keep herself awake, but Birgit listened with an unbroken gaze. Sometimes her mouth would open, and she would make the shapes of the words. No sound, though. No sound.

Eventually the dark pressed in from outside, even with the windows covered. Gerte lit a stubby candle that had been sitting on the desk. Birgit lay down along the east wall and did not move from her position on her back, one hand resting on her stomach. It was hard to tell when she fell asleep. Gerte shielded the candlelight with a piece of wood, curling herself around the flame. She read for a bit, chewing a fibrous tuber, then put the light out. She was tired now because it was night. That was all. She rolled over and slept.

When she woke, the gänger lay twisted in the corner, half in the sunlight where it had pulled the blanket down. It was more arms than legs, too many elbows for each limb. Its eyes were blue and glassy, like wet daubs of paint, fixed upon her.

Gerte shot backward and hit her head against the wall. She lay with her ears ringing, neck strained where wall met floor, and the thing in the corner bloated like bread rising, its flesh the color of uncooked salmon. It sank back, then bloated again, and Gerte realized it was breathing. Trying to breathe. It breathed in the knobbish appendages that would be legs, in the span connecting bulging head to pasty torso, as though bladders swelled just under the skin.

Birgit lifted her head from the floor, then turned half onto her side and stared at the thing as it grew and shrank, as it rolled once away from the corner, into the room.

Gerte scrambled to her feet, snatched up the elder stick, and stuck it through the gänger's engorging body, pinning it to the floorboards. The thing made a sound as sore and bitter as burnt flesh. Gerte grabbed her bag in one hand and Birgit's arm in the other, hauled her off the floor, and crashed through the doors into the silver morning.

IT GOT UP AND followed them.

Each day it was there, trailing behind. They ran faster than it could walk, but it always caught up in the night. It scraped itself against the doors, and when it grew hands, it scraped those against the doors instead. There were no more elder branches, and no running water to bar its path. It came into the rooms where they lay, and it stood over Gerte, and it bent down and—

And they ran.

No, Gerte sniffled as twilight bore down and the gänger drew closer up the road. *No.*

Now it had long brown hair and blue eyes. It wore fleshy rags that looked like a shirt and pants and gathered color like blood in water. Its mouth had lips, and they opened and closed, and it limped from foot to foot as Gerte limped.

Ohhhh, it said, gusting through a newly formed throat. It lapped her strength with every step. *Nnnn…ohhhh.*

Help me, Gerte said, and Birgit took her arm and led her down the road as the gänger crept nearer.

I just want to go back to the way it was, Gerte sobbed as they floundered into the woods. *I want to go back to the way I was.*

Birgit's mouth was a tight line.

Say something. Come on, you can do it.

Birgit's mouth opened, but nothing came out.

WHY WON'T YOU SAY *something?* she screamed at Birgit. But she knew why. Because of what had happened, and then what had happened after.

Do you even remember Mom and Dad?

Birgit looked at her. Her sharp green eyes blinked once.

Maybe Birgit remembered some parts of Mom and Dad. Like Gerte remembered parts of Mom and Dad, fewer and fewer as the months dragged on, as they walked and limped and ran. Curly white hair. Smiles. Wide feet with long toes.

You aren't even her anymore, Gerte cried. *You aren't even her.*

She had said it aloud before.

Birgit said nothing.

It had been four years since Birgit had been Birgit.

THE LAST DAY AT their home, four years ago—a year after the ruin of the world—Birgit had stared at their mother, the face that was trying to be their mother's face. She had stared at their father down the hall, one hand with too many joints curled around the door jamb, trying to pull itself through. Gerte had grabbed her, and they had run.

They ran away from the city and all the unpeople in it. They took to the woods, ate animals until the animals disappeared, and one day, they stumbled across a great, open pit in the earth that smelled of death, and after that, something had come along behind, walking in Birgit's shadow. But Birgit walked and walked, and grew more tired day after day, and never once had she found it in herself to speak.

And so, the thing had learned not to speak either.

IN THE MORNING, THE gänger stood in the corner with cool blue eyes and earth-brown hair. Its lips were pink, and its skin flushed with the flow of blood. It had ten fingers, ten toes, and it said to Gerte where she lay winded and wasted on the floor, *You aren't even her anymore.*

Gerte's limbs would not move. She tried to sit up, but she had no strength. Her muscles were dead things, cut from all bone, and even as she watched, the extra flesh drained from her wrists and feet, leaving them withered. Sucked dry.

Not again. Not again. This part was always the worst.

She tried to speak, but her breath whistled from her throat, stirring the dust before her. Instead, she reached. Stretched her fingers toward the indistinct shade that was her sister.

Birgit did not look at her. Birgit had turned to the thing in the corner, the thing that stood upright, that opened its mouth and whistled from its throat, and stretched its fingers toward Birgit.

BY THE TIME THE sun rose, the old Gerte was a parched husk on the floor, and the dust sat disturbed around the tips of her fingers and her bare heels where she had struggled. The new Gerte had clothes now, and the shoes from the old Gerte's feet, and she came over and lifted the pack and put it over her shoulder. She turned her eyes away from the husk. The places with husks were bad places.

We should keep moving.

Birgit nodded.

The sisters walked and walked. They passed the lowering city and its two mass graves, the filled one and the open. They went to the dam, and the field where the not-man trod back and forth under the sun. Eventually they remembered the shed, and they went back to it and carved a new hole in the wall and put a bag of almonds in it.

On the thirteenth day, the younger of the two, looking over her shoulder, saw that they had picked up a gänger.

Imposter

TOSHIYA KAMEI

As autumn light slants through scarlet kaede leaves, you emerge over the tree-covered hill like a specter, armor caked in dust and blood. The song I'm humming dies on my lips, and I stop picking berries. Despite the sun warming my skin, I shiver and gather my kimono around me. The memory of your hands on my throat makes me flinch.

"I'm back, Tsumugi," you say as you stop before me.

"Kikuchiyo." Your name is all I can manage. With the rest of what I want to say stuck in my throat, I force myself to stare at your inscrutable face. Dismay crushes my chest as I realize it was premature to revel in my widowhood.

"Let's go home," you say. I pick up my basket of berries and follow you down a narrow path out of the forest. To my surprise, you slow to my pace and stay abreast of me as if you care about me. There's something different about you, but I can't quite pinpoint what that is.

We cross the threshold of our thatch-roofed house together. Once inside, I help you off with your armor, and with your back to me, you slip into a new kimono. I notice you're thinner. Your body seems to have shrunk, and the contours of your ribs are visible beneath your torso. Your cheeks hollow out, making your eyes appear too large for your face.

"Have you lost weight?" I ask with feigned concern.

"That's what war does to a man," you say, your expression still unreadable. When I try to scrutinize your face, you turn away.

Hearing you, Rikichi looks up from his toys, and you scoop him into your arms. You smile, revealing pearly teeth and dimples. The boy's knotted face loosens into a grin. Still holding our son, you approach me. I brace myself for castigation, but nothing comes. Instead, you pull me closer and plant a gentle kiss on my lips. When I glance at you, a warm light flickers in your ember eyes.

I blink in disbelief. Before you left for Sekigahara to make a name for yourself, you showed no affection for anyone, not even for Rikichi. Even on your good days, you treated me like a servant rather than a wife.

"Are you hungry, Kikuchiyo?" I ask. "I bought some unagi from a traveling fishmonger." Salt-grilled eel is your favorite meal, but then again, we can hardly afford other kinds of fish.

"I'm starving," you say, smiling, and set Rikichi down on the dirt floor. I feel like humming again as I head for the kitchen.

I scoop three live eels from a bucket. As I cut off their heads, the smell of raw fish permeates the air. I sprinkle salt over the unagi before placing their limp bodies on the grate. Your laughter reaches my ears, and Rikichi's follows. One thing is certain: something happened to you in battle to alter your demeanor. I have no idea what accounts for these changes or how long they will last.

I light the charcoal, and the flames soon burn yellow-white. Smoke rises, and the aroma of grilled unagi tickles my nose. When the eels begin to curl up, I flatten them with a spatula.

When the eels are ready, I serve them with bowls of rice and miso soup. You pick up a piece with chopsticks and place it on top of your rice.

I steal a glance at you while you shovel rice into your mouth. Rikichi follows suit. I can't tell whether he's consciously imitating your mannerisms, or they come to him naturally. You don't ask for another bowl.

"Do you want me to heat sake?" I ask.

To my surprise, you shake your head.

"Are you sure?"

You nod.

You used to drink sake after dinner, become irritable, and strike me for no reason. The memory of being beaten by you makes me tremble. Instead, you remain affable, and I can't quite bring myself to believe it. You get down on all fours and pretend to be our son's horse. The boy's laughter reverberates around the room, lifting my spirits. Despite myself, tears of joy almost rise to the surface. Rikichi falls asleep while riding on your back.

I loosen my hair and let it fall over my shoulders. I lay out two futons, side by side, and place our sleeping son between us. Staring at the ceiling, I recall the pain and humiliation I endured at your hands. I flinch as you slip into my futon. When you kiss me, tender and sweet, my fear thaws.

"You smell different," I whisper.

"What do you mean?"

"You don't smell of tobacco anymore. Did you stop smoking?"

"Yes," you say, and joy once again surges through me. When I asked you not to smoke in front of our asthmatic son, you yelled and hit me. My left eye was swollen shut for days, and when he saw me, Rikichi burst into tears, saying I was as ugly as Oiwa, who had been poisoned by her husband and met a horrible death.

"You smell like citrus," I say, and we kiss again.

Kissing gives way to caressing, and neither of us can control our passions. I worry about waking Rikichi until I hear his soft breathing. You position your head between my legs, and I feel your lips suck me into your mouth. Voracious. Incessant. I climax, and the world darkens.

"What's gotten into you?" I say when I catch my breath.

"I missed you." You hold my hand and give it a gentle squeeze. "It turned out I wasn't cut out to be a samurai. I must be content with the quiet life of a farmer from now on."

"War is a terrible thing, darling," you continue with a sigh. "I have no stomach for fighting, let alone killing."

"Don't worry, Kikuchiyo," I say. "There's no need for you to be a samurai anymore. Not one bit." I squeeze your hand. "I'm glad you're home."

"So am I," you say.

My eyelids feel heavy, and I yawn. Before long, I drift off to sleep, content.

At dawn, I wake with your arms around me. A warmth fills me, and I feel loved for the first time in my life.

"I can't believe this," I mumble. "It's like I'm dreaming."

"Dreaming?" You kiss me. "What do you mean?"

"How can I put this?" I ask, pausing. "You've been acting different since you came back."

"Is that a bad thing?"

"No." I shake my head. "I rather like it." Suddenly, I don't know how to continue. I fist the sheets until my knuckles go white. I watch you—your interest turning to confusion, to concern—and my heart races. I want to be right. I need to be right. The hooting of a nearby owl allows the dark night to intrude again, and I force myself to breathe.

"I don't know if you're my husband," I say.

"Excuse me?"

"Maybe you're not Kikuchiyo; maybe you're someone else."

"Don't be silly. Of course I'm Kikuchiyo."

I say nothing, and an awkward silence weighs between us. Punishment for adultery is death in this region. If the authorities find out about us, my life will be in danger. Even if you're an imposter, I have no choice but to go along with your ruse.

"There's something you need to know," you say, turning serious. You take my hands between yours and close your eyes. Your throat moves in a heavy swallow.

"What is it?" I don't want to scare you, so I try to keep my voice soft, fragile, and I feel that way as well. With one awful word, one terrible explanation, my newfound peace will shatter.

"I was wounded in battle."

"Wounded?" Fear coils in my stomach, and I try to recall if you seemed stiff or pained while playing with Rikichi. Every moment before this one, though, seems far away. You finally open your eyes.

"Here." You take my hand and place it on your crotch where your penis used to hang. I gasp as my fingers brush something soft and wet. The same thing I have between my legs.

"I can still make love to you, but I can't give you any more children."

"Don't worry," I say. "We already have Rikichi."

Truth be told, I'm relieved. You used to leave me sobbing after rough sex, and dread choked me every night your hands sought me. I seethed with horror as you satisfied your needs. Afterwards, my bruised thighs would always throb.

Days pass without incident. I imagine you met my husband in Sekigahara and decided to take his place. But why? Is the real Kikuchiyo still alive? Did you have anything to do with his disappearance? These questions circle like flies.

One thing occurs to me: If my husband comes back and finds me with you, he'll make trouble for us. I stash a knife in the breast of my kimono for protection.

"I'm going to town to get supplies," you say after breakfast. "Do you want me to get you anything?"

"Why don't you take Rikichi with you?" I suggest.

"What do you say, son?"

"Yes, Father!" Rikichi cries, bouncing about in his excitement.

You take our son's hand, and we kiss goodbye. I follow your image down the path into town until you disappear from sight.

I love being with my family, but alone time will do me good. I kneel in the garden and tend to my flowers. The day is bright and warm, perfumed with the scents of dirt, clean wind, and leaf rot. I watch a butterfly flutter among my flowers, and I can't help smiling. I never thought life could be like this. I never thought I could be happy.

I stay out for hours, my skin turning red, and only when I hear footsteps approach do I set down my spade. I sigh and wipe sweat off my brows. A shadow covers me with its cold touch.

"All done?" I ask. "What took you two so—"

And my question dies swift and silent as I look up. As the real Kikuchiyo stares down at me.

"Can I help you?" I ask. My heartbeat rings in my ears.

Silent, he comes near me, and it takes everything in me not to tremble. "I'm your husband." He moves with a slight limp and grabs my wrist. I struggle to free myself, but he tightens his grip and pulls me toward him.

"You adulterer!" he shouts in my face. "You're living with an imposter! She's a fellow soldier I met in Sekigahara. While recuperating in an infirmary, we told each other about ourselves, and we decided to trade places."

"Why would anyone do that?"

"I don't know." He pauses to gather his thoughts. "I failed to make my mark as a samurai, and I was sick of my old life."

I want to tell him that I too was sick of my life until the imposter appeared to replace him.

"However," he continues, "when I went to her home, it didn't take her family a second to expose me as a fraud. It was only then that I realized she was a woman. She duped me!"

"Leave me alone." I raise my voice, still trying to pull away. "My husband will be home soon."

Kikuchiyo hurls me to the dirt. He sits astride my shoulders, and he wraps his rough hands around my throat. I gag, saliva drools from the corners of my mouth, and tears roll down my cheeks. I almost pass out, but Rikichi's smile floods into my mind, and I manage to stay conscious. I grab a handful of dirt and throw it in his eyes. He cries out and loosens his grip.

My shoulders heaving, I pull out my knife, and Kikuchiyo looks at me with a mixture of hate and fear. I stab him again and again. The blade flashes in the sunlight, and his blood splashes all over my face and kimono. He groans as he collapses with a thud. I hold my breath and regard him with disdain. I kick him hard in the ribs to see if he's alive.

When there's no response, relief overwhelms me, and I can't help remembering the feel of your caress; I know you'll approve of my deed.

I wipe the blade clean on the dead man's chest before disrobing him and setting his clothes on fire. As orange flames flicker and crackle, the desire for revenge stirs inside me with a renewed intensity. I trim the fat from his flesh and cut the meat into strips for drying in the sun. As luck would have it, the sky shows no signs of rain.

By the time you come home, I've marinated Kikuchiyo's meat in soy sauce. Nothing goes to waste. That was his motto.

"What happened?" you ask, staring at the blood stains on my kimono. "Are you hurt?"

"I'm alright," I say. "Your imposter showed up. He claimed to be you, my husband. He said you two had switched places. He attacked me, and I had to defend myself."

"He must've gone mad," you say, frowning. "Sadly, that's what war does to so many men." You kiss me on the top of my head.

"Don't worry." I shake my head. "He won't be bothering us anymore. You can be sure of that."

"Are they ready to eat?" Rikichi asks, peering at the meat.

"No, darling," I say. "We have to dry them." I place the strips on a rack.

You and I exchange knowing glances, and as Rikichi goes off to play—his laughter sweet and ripe—I swear I will never again speak of the imposter.

The Carers

SEAN EADS

There has to be a way out of this, Greg thinks, pulling at his hair as he sits on the couch listening to voices from the bedroom detailing how a Mayan god is, in fact, an extraterrestrial. Or a time traveler—there seems to be a diversity of expert opinion. Greg doesn't know this one despite all his nights enduring Robbie's need to fall asleep listening to the show. How many episodes of *Ancient Aliens* are there, anyway?

He's just gotten home from an evening work shift filled with more signs and omens. There was even a syringe embedded in the tread of the driver's side front tire. Brady's way of telling him to confess or else Robbie gets harmed. That's the best way—the only tangible way—to hurt Greg, after all.

There has to be an escape. Someplace even Brady can't reach us, Greg tells himself. He can't conceive where or what it would be.

He stands up slow and cold at the sudden screeching noise of leg chairs moving across the kitchen floor. In the next instant, a table chair comes into view, its sound softened by the transition from tile to carpet. Greg puts both hands over his mouth. The chair comes to rest, facing him, from the other side of the coffee table.

"Brady?" Greg whispers into his palm.

The chair rocks a little.

"Make me confess and Robbie will hate me. That's what you want, isn't it? Your best revenge?"

The chair rattles.

"Greg?"

Ancient Aliens has ceased. The bedroom door has opened.

"Robbie, don't come out! It's not safe."

"Not safe?"

Robbie enters the room. He's just 23, a little short, very slight of build. He's the only guy Greg knows who wears pajamas to bed. Throw in his tousled hair, and he looks about 12-years-old.

The chair wobbles a little. A trick of light? Greg raises his hand to point at it. Robbie looks but shows no reaction. Does he *not* question why the chair is even there?

"Are you going to be mean to me again?" Robbie says, moving toward the chair.

"Mean? When was *I* ever mean? When did *I*—"

Seeing Robbie sit in the chair sucks the air from his lungs. Greg shakes his head. All he sees in his mind's eye is Robbie sitting submissive and humiliated in Brady's lap.

He's giving in and he doesn't even know it, Greg thinks. Brady will never stop dominating Robbie's life. I was trying to protect him, but I've just made it worse.

"Robbie," Greg says, trying to be calm. "I want you to get up."

"Why?"

So innocent, so ignorant of the danger.

Hold me. Protect me.

Greg grits his teeth, lunges, seizes Robbie by the arm and pulls him up. Then he pivots to put himself between Robbie and the chair. God, even in the blackness of his fear, protecting Robbie feels so good, so right. The erection's back. It'll always be a miracle. He stares down at himself, 50-years-old and fat, wearing only boxers. Then he looks Robbie in the eyes and says, "There's something I have to tell you."

AS AN ER NURSE for over 20 years, Greg had seen his share of suffering and pain, but no victim had anything on the young man in Examination Room Three. He knew it was a hell of a thing to think, considering the patient wasn't bleeding. Wasn't even bruised. There'd been a woman huddled in that room last week, beaten all to hell by an alcoholic husband, her purple, swollen eyes a horror out of Greek mythology. Somehow, even she seemed better off than this helpless guy hunched forward and sobbing like a little boy.

"He won't stop doing it, and no one cares. Why doesn't anyone ever help me?"

No one had figured out Robbie's exact story, even an hour after his admission. Greg was alone with him and felt a kind of privilege that this shy, sensitive person was opening up to him. The quality of despair in his voice drew Greg closer, and before he knew it, he had planted his hand between Robbie's shoulder blades.

"There are people who care. I promise you that."

Robbie nodded, his body shivering beneath Greg's touch. His body was warm and solid, and he had a pleasant scent that wasn't chemical in any way. No waft of lotion or cologne. The aroma of goodness and naivete, perhaps. *Poor, sweet guy, I wish I could make things better for him,* Greg thought. And in the next instant, he was rock hard. The sudden erection proved a genuine shock. He'd been experiencing erectile dysfunction for a few years now, and at 50, he considered his sex drive dead without an unhealthy amount of Viagra. But he had steel right now, sudden and glorious, commiserate with the desire to make Robbie feel safe.

"Do *you* care?" Robbie said.

He pulled Robbie into a full embrace and held him. Greg could only thank his stars that no colleague entered the room just then. In all of his many years as a nurse, he'd never done something so unprofessional. Robbie wasn't even his type. Yet there Greg was, holding him close like a boyfriend. Vulnerability *shouldn't* be erotic, and it felt perverse to even consider it, like some sort of mirror sadism where he was getting off by inflicting compassion.

Robbie looked up at him with a shy smile. His eyes were wet, pale blue, and a little protuberant.

"Who's hurting you? Who in the *world* would want to do that? Is it…a boyfriend?"

"Hell no. I don't go for assholes. I like nice guys. Nice *men*. Like you."

Greg leaned forward. "So who's the jerk who is not being nice to you? And where is he, so I can kick his ass?"

Robbie blushed in the most beautiful way.

"His name's Brady. I've known him since kindergarten, and he's always made my life hell."

"The classic school bully, huh?"

"A lot worse than that. He lived next door. Our moms were best friends, only mine worked and Brady's stayed home. So they had an agreement that she would watch me after school and on snow days and during the summer. Brady was always good at making it seem like we were best friends. Like, he'd hit me on the shoulder like it was playful, but he'd make sure to keep tagging me on the same spot until my arm was so bruised I couldn't move it. I still remember the first time he told me to get in his closet. We were six. He shoved me in and I just sat there in the dark, trying not to cry while I listened to him playing with his toys. When his mom found us, Brady said we were playing a game. And I—I nodded."

"Hey, it's okay if you don't want to—"

"I hate myself for nodding. My whole life might have changed if I'd let her know Brady was bullying me. But I was stupid and afraid, and Brady saw it. I was in his pocket and the bullying became a pattern. I just accepted it."

"I think that happens to a lot of people. It's psychology. Don't be hard on yourself."

"It just kept going and going. Eight years old, twelve years old, fifteen. Puberty was the worst. He developed fast. I—didn't. My voice didn't really change at all. This is as deep as it ever got."

Greg could only wonder how many times Robbie had answered a phone, and the caller called him *ma'am*.

"By our senior year, we had an inmate relationship. One's always in charge and the other is the bitch. He always knew how to pick his spots. I swear to God, some of my teachers even thought Brady and I were best friends. Pull back the curtain, and it was pure hell. I did what he wanted. No shame, no self-esteem. I just don't get it."

Greg put his hand on Robbie's right wrist. "What's not to get? You've been an abuse victim since you were little."

"But I had chances to escape! I thought college would do it, but we both end up staying in the state. Then Brady asks me to move in with him. Be his roommate. And goddamn, I did it. Like we're friends. Friends, hell. The bullying was worse than ever before. I became his butler. He'd sit on the couch and watch me clean the apartment. He'd have me in the corner ironing his shirts. I had to drop out of school to keep up with his demands. I know, it sounds insane."

"Was it ever…sexual?"

Robbie's miserable expression turned into pure hate. The transition was so immediate that Greg felt like a terrible pervert for asking it, as if that had been the sole reason for the interview. As if he was *hoping* to hear that it had been for his own sick fantasizing.

"Brady's straight. But he knows I'm gay. He has to know. But no, it's never been like that. Yet. Guess I've still got to wait to see how low he'll make me go."

"You're still living with him?"

Robbie nodded. "In his house."

"A house, at his age?"

"He makes a good income working for his family's construction company."

Greg stepped back, aware of the sound of approaching footsteps. The shift doctor was coming, and Greg snapped back into his job duties. Doing so felt strange, as if he were just pretending to be a nurse. As if he'd infiltrated the ER to reach Robbie.

The doctor had a brief conversation with Robbie, focused on psychological angles. Trying to discern if Robbie was suicidal. Greg listened with growing annoyance. The doctor was pressing too hard. His tone was too sharp. Badgering and bullying. Bringing poor Robbie back to the edge of tears.

"Sorry about that," Greg said in a low, gentle voice once they were alone again. He rubbed Robbie's shoulder. "That asshole has no bedside manner. He needs his butt kicked. Like *Brady*."

Robbie put a hand over his mouth and giggled. He flashed a smile like everything was right with the world. This made Greg feel giddy. He was so hard.

"Can I ask exactly what happened tonight that made you call 911?"

"We were at a work party."

"He took you to his work party?"

Robbie's head drooped. "He got me hired in his office. Without a college degree, I didn't have much choice."

"What do you do?"

"Whatever's needed." Greg could guess the title Robbie didn't want to say.

Secretary.

"The party was at Brady's house. There were about 20 guys there. People from the construction crews. None of them know me because they're never in the office. So they're all drinking, and I'm fetching them beers, and it's obvious they're wondering who I am. Brady points at me and says, 'That's the company fag.' I just froze. Everyone did. Then he said, 'Sit down' and pointed to his right knee. I started trembling. They're all watching my reaction. Brady says it again, and this time he snaps his finger and points at his knee. People started to snicker as I trudged over to him."

"You sat down on his knee."

Robbie's bottom lip trembled. He was dissolving into tears again, and Greg grabbed a handful of paper towels and pressed them into Robbie's hand. His fingers slid down to hold Robbie's wrist.

"What I remember most are the faces of the other guys. The smirks. They broke me. Even in high school, he hadn't bullied me too much in front of a lot of people. This was so public. I ran out of the house. For a while, I thought I was going to kill myself. I called 911. You're right, I was trying to prove to myself that there are people in the world who care. And I found one."

That's right, Greg thought. You did.

THEIR NEXT MEETING WOULD be two days later. In the ER. Same examination room. Greg heard the intake receptionist say, "That sad kid from the other day is back," and he rushed to see Robbie.

"What happened? Brady again?"

Robbie raised his tear-stained face and nodded. He wasn't bruised, but he was stricken. Greg understood the power of psychological abuse, and it was clear Brady had full control of Robbie's life.

"I want you to stay with me," he said. "At least for tonight. You need a safe space."

"But I still work in the office with him."

"Then you need to quit the job. I'm serious. Look, I've got plenty of money. I can take care of you."

The sentiment, the certainty, came out of Greg with a maternal ease. He was rock hard again as he placed one hand on Robbie's shoulder. It wasn't until Robbie flinched that he had some sense of the inappropriateness of his actions. Touching a trauma victim without asking? Inviting an ER patient to come live with him?

"You do make me feel safe. I think that's why I called 911 again. Hoping to see you."

Greg grinned. "Hey, I do even better away from work. We're going to start making things right for you."

His shift ended about an hour after Robbie's discharge, and per their arrangement, Greg found him waiting in the parking lot. As soon as they got into Greg's car, Robbie took his right arm and snuggled against it. The act was the most erotic thing Greg had ever experienced, though he had no thought of fucking Robbie, even if his erection was stronger than ever. Instead, he saw many hours—a lifetime, even—of Robbie snuggled against him, needing him, wanting to be comforted. Like any fantasy object, Robbie had no existence beyond their time spent together. Work, transportation, meals—what need of these against the backdrop of Greg's nurturing?

"I guess there's something I should tell you," he said as they entered his apartment. "I only have one bedroom."

Greg already knew it wouldn't be a problem, so he was a little surprised when Robbie looked to the couch. Greg pulled him down the hallway, unbuttoning his shirt along the way. He pushed Robbie into the room and shut the door.

"It's a big bed."

Robbie looked at the floor. Greg patted his shoulder, threw his shirt on the floor, and went to the other side of the mattress. He dropped his pants and pulled back the sheets.

"Turn off the light and undress. Let me hold you. You'll feel better."

"Maybe I shouldn't—"

"You've got to be tired," Greg said. "It'll be okay."

He looked so lithe and cute standing there, his shyness and uncertainty an alluring quality. When he didn't move, Greg tried again.

"Come on, I'm tired too. It'll be good. Nothing sexual."

That was the truth as far as he was concerned, despite the ongoing presence of his very obvious hard-on. It was a different erection than he'd ever had before. It wasn't just stronger than what he'd experienced before his dysfunction. Its *character* was different. Moral. *Upstanding.* Eschewing vulgar carnality. It was as natural and firm and constant and uncomplicated as his affection.

Why wasn't Robbie moving? Why was he just standing there?

"Right now!" Greg shouted, and Robbie flinched and turned off the light. He got into bed without undressing, and Greg reached over to hook his arm around Robbie's waist. It was all just fine and perfect until he saw a light and realized Robbie was on his phone.

"You're not texting Brady, are you?"

"I just have a habit of falling asleep to YouTube videos. Is that cool?"

Greg gave him a squeeze. "Anything you need, anytime you want."

An hour later, he had his first episode of *Ancient Aliens* under his belt.

CARING FOR ROBBIE BECAME the cause of his soul. Greg knew it after that first night together, and every subsequent night over the next month affirmed it. He'd come home to find Robbie despondent from another day of bullying, and he'd clutch this wonderful guy against his body and hold him in a rocking fashion, telling him how strong he was, pouring out his compassion. He could not get enough of caring for this wonderful, sweet young man.

"It's time to take the next step," he said on the night of their five-week anniversary.

"What do you mean?"

"You've managed to separate yourself from Brady a bit, but you won't be able to escape him until you have a new job."

"But where? My whole resume is that job."

"Marie is a good friend of mine in HR. I was telling her about you, and she said there's an opening for an administrative assistant. She thinks based on your description that you'd fit right in. I think so too. We'd almost be working together. Wouldn't that be great?"

He saw Robbie getting the job, and sure enough, it happened. After all his years of loneliness and hopelessness, Greg now experienced a queer sensation that he could bend reality to his will. Robbie was safe and protected by him during the day and night. Robbie was his. This beautiful, wounded young man was his to cherish and nurture.

Greg could see Robbie benefiting from his protection. He lost his anxiousness, he became relaxed and unguarded, he showed off that boyish smile more and more. It was all so perfect.

Then around the sixth month of their relationship, Greg noticed a certain backsliding in Robbie. One day, a touch of skittishness. Another day, he kept his head bowed. Greg didn't want to acknowledge it at first, but it was as if Robbie had rocketed into the air, reached an apogee, and now he was falling back. Being reclaimed by gravity.

By Brady.

At last, driving them both to work one morning, Greg could stand it no longer. "Are you in contact with him?"

"With who?"

"Don't treat me like I'm a fucking idiot, Robbie!"

He only just stopped himself from slugging Robbie's shoulder. He couldn't believe the impulse and it made him grip the steering wheel until his knuckles went white.

Robbie didn't say a word. His head was bowed, and he sat on his hands as if he were trying to make himself as small as possible. A complete regression.

Goddamn you, Brady, Greg thought.

When they parked and got out, Robbie said, "Some of the people in HR want to have drinks after work."

"I don't know if I can."

"You're not in HR."

"But I'm your boyfriend."

This had never been discussed, though, and Greg winced to let his aspirations slip out like that. Boyfriends with a 25-year age difference? Well, why not? It wasn't so uncommon among gay men. But he just knew it wasn't what Robbie wanted. What the hell did Robbie want, anyway? Why was Greg letting himself be used like this?

"Yeah, fine," Greg said, red in the face, unsettled by his changing mood. Before he opened the staff door, he gave Robbie a fierce hug. "I care about you more than anything, you know that? You and your happiness."

They had no other communication that day. At the end of his shift, Greg drove home without texting Robbie about his travel arrangements or an expected return time. Robbie came home around 2AM and Greg, sleepless, stared at him in the dark. Robbie then did something he'd never done in all their time together. He shed every bit of clothing and got into bed, inching his naked, burning flesh against Greg.

"Hold me," he whispered. "Protect me."

Greg's erection was instant, almost eternal as he draped his left arm across Robbie and cinched their bodies together.

"*Always.*"

The morning revealed the huge, shocking bruise on Robbie's right shoulder. Robbie wouldn't say anything about it, but Greg's memory went straight to the childhood story of Brady punching him in the arm. He started to press Robbie about the injury, and then stopped himself. What could either of them say? There was a massive lie between them. Robbie hadn't been out with the HR crew last night.

Brady had gotten Robbie under his thumb again.

Something had to be done.

IT ALL CAME DOWN to Marie. He got a copy of Robbie's resume from her and found the name of his former employer. J&K Construction Associates. Under References, he found two names. How it galled Greg to see the name *Brady Rassmussen* listed above his own.

Robbie's addicted to him, Greg thought. He's addicted to being bullied.

Addicted. The word was like an electric charge, like an answer from God. A couple of days earlier, the ER had treated a man who overdosed on fentanyl. He swore up and down he thought he was taking a muscle relaxer a friend gave him to help with post-gym soreness. That could be true. The main point was the guy was fit, white, and young. No doubt a demographic Brady clone and the new face of opioid addiction.

The hospital had fentanyl on hand, of course. The staff joked all the time about raiding the supplies to make a few hundred thousand dollars on the street. Monitored access wasn't a barrier to a nurse whose reputation was beyond reproach and who only needed to steal a little. It was as simple as filling the barrel of one syringe and replacing the stolen amount with a little saline solution.

Casing Brady's house was the harder task, as he had no idea what he was doing. He knew enough to park up the street, which made him feel a little devious. Brady lived in a modest suburban place, nothing like the gated community mansion he'd been imagining. But how was he going to get inside—break a window? A sign near the front door boasted of a security system, which was enough to fill him with tremendous despair.

Robbie, meanwhile, was having *drinks* with his co-workers almost every night. Such a pointless pretense at this point, the sort of flimsy excuse only the true addict would find convincing. *Hold me. Protect me.* Greg would never forget those words whispered in the dark, a soul's plea for help.

There was only one way to answer it.

He waited until one of the evenings Robbie was having *drinks*. He took off work early and parked near Brady's house. Robbie arrived in an Uber about an hour later, near sunset, and knocked on the front door. It opened at once and Greg got his first limited glimpse of Brady, a somewhat husky man who took Robbie into a bear hug and hoisted him off the ground and shook him. The overwhelming physicality was obvious. Robbie was a rag doll to this man.

He checked his emotions enough to wait half an hour before leaving the car. He got to the porch and felt the outline of the syringe in his right pocket. Then he tried the knob.

The door opened. He stared at the revealed space and thought, If I go through, I'm trespassing. No, I'm *already* trespassing. If I go in, I'm breaking and entering.

He stood fixated on the sudden mathematics of criminality and how it seemed to take a hundred smaller crimes to add up to a big one.

An angry shout came from inside the house.

"No, you listen to me! You're not leaving again. Got that? The way you act, maybe you fucking deserved everything. What is it about you, man? Everyone wants to hurt you except me, and you run away? After all I've done? Now *come here!*"

"No, Brady, please…"

"Saved you in gym class. Saved you in the hallways. Got you a job where I could keep you safe. You'd be nothing—"

"Brady—"

"*Nothing*, goddamnit! You'd be dead!"

Greg stepped through, almost forgetting to shut the door behind him. He ducked inside the first space he found—the coat closet in the foyer—and huddled there, hands over his mouth in the dark.

This is what Robbie felt like in Brady's closet, he thought. This is the crap you're going to save him from forever.

"I expect you to be a little goddamn appreciative at least!"

The fight was terrible. Brady went on screaming about Robbie's ingratitude. Hearing the bully demand thanks from his victim was almost more than Greg could stand. At last, they seemed to be arguing in the foyer itself.

"You'll never find someone who looked out for you like me, you piece of shit!"

The door slammed. Quiet descended.

Greg waited.

He checked the time on his phone. More than two hours passed before he risked leaving his hiding space. He took out the syringe. The sound of the television drew him further into the house. Son of a bitch, Greg thought, realizing he knew what was playing. No wonder Robbie couldn't stop watching *Ancient Aliens.*

Brady was half sprawled on the couch, his head lolling. There was a half-empty bottle of Wild Turkey on the coffee table in front of him.

Greg uncapped the syringe and tried to catch his breath. In Brady's stupor, he could almost stand in front of him and give him the shot. He opted to go in from the side. The approach *felt* stealthier.

Brady noticed him. His bleary eyes blinked.

"Come…came back…"

Brady's left arm was out, the crook of his elbow exposed. Greg's hands were shaking.

"Mine. Stay. Me."

Mine.

His fingers found their resolve. "You'll never bully him again," Greg whispered, and completed the injection.

In his imagination, he'd seen himself leaving right away. Reality told him he needed to wait. Needed to make sure the deed was done.

It was almost midnight when the effect hit, and not in the way Greg expected. Brady spasmed and got off the couch. He looked at Greg, eyes widening. Greg experienced a moment of horror at this sudden strength and lucidity. "You…"

Greg retreated, thinking the game was up. As the weight of his failure sank in, though, Brady turned and pointed at the wall. "Who are you? Why are you here? What do you want from me?" He looked back at Greg. "You see them, don't you?"

He fell face down on the floor. Greg stood in place for a few minutes, shaken by what he'd witnessed. Then he went to check Brady's pulse.

Nothing.

"HOLD ME, YOU SAID. Protect me. Well—I did. I'd do anything to keep you safe," Greg says, approaching Robbie as he gets out of the kitchen chair. "It was the only way to stop Brady from harming you. I wasn't worried about ghosts. Not until—"

He still can't make himself say it, even after all he's experienced the last week. The sudden occurrences of the letter B around the apartment and at work. The syringes appearing in his pants pockets. And then, this morning, as he tried to type out a message to Robbie, all that wound up on the screen were individual letters from various words that spelled *watch out*.

Greg turns to the chair and points at it. "What else do you want me to do? Go to prison? But I won't let you hurt him ever again. Never."

He picks the chair up and shakes it.

"We've got to leave, Robbie. I know this must all seem crazy, but I have to protect you. You're all that matters."

He slams the chair down hard, splintering its back. Robbie jumps back and cowers near the hallway door, shaking and sobbing. Just as Greg moves to seize him, the door opens, and a man steps out. Brady! Greg thinks, falling back. But no. That can't be.

This man is taller. And far larger. Like some sort of gym trainer, muscles on top of muscles, with a broad round face made fiercer by a shaved head and flaring nostrils.

The man's big hands somehow make even larger fists, like two medieval flails dangling from the heavy chain rope of his arms. This guy could crush Robbie in a second.

"I couldn't listen anymore," he says. "You were right about this guy. But you're safe now. I'll make sure of that."

Quicker than his size suggests, he grabs Greg by the neck and jerks him so hard that Greg releases Robbie, who runs into the far corner and squats down, both hands over his mouth. Greg shouts for him to run from this madman, but Greg doesn't get out more than a couple of words before getting sucker punched in the gut. The pain blinds him and puts him on the floor, breathless, reduced to a helpless wheezing.

"You're trash, dude. Robbie's a great guy and a pathetic fuck like you comes along and abuses the hell out of him."

"I never—"

"You're done. There's only one way to keep him safe."

Greg's eyes widen as the beast gets down on his knees and straddles Greg's chest. The first punch socks him right in the mouth, sending his front teeth into the back of his throat. Immediate shock numbs the pain and gives Greg the feeling of an out-of-body experience. He doesn't feel the second blow or the third.

Then Greg realizes he *is* standing outside of his body, which is a bloody mess. To his right, standing by the broken chair, is Brady, shaking his head. Greg starts to speak but notices there are many others in the room as well, a silent chorus line of men of different sizes and ages, their dress style spanning centuries. Greg looks from them to his body, from his body to Robbie, who remains in the corner, hands over his mouth, but not quite concealing the little smile of pleasure one gives when all is right with their world.

When We Laid Down Our Arms

SUMIKO SAULSON

He followed Alex home
Scent of cinnamon tea
Like a puppy at his heel
As they ran through the fields

They first met in the trenches
His breath on his cheek
In the blazing sun
Knees buckling
Until his hand
Lifted him

Alex saw him in the mirror
When he leaned in to shave
Lovers smiled at one another
Finally able to share a home
After so many years of
Hiding their love

Alex touched the dog tags
And the vial of ashes
Around his neck
And knowing
Their love
Transcended death
He smiled
At the spirit
Beside him

The Elixir

MAY WALKER

Neatly labeled bottles arrayed the wooden shelves, glittering faintly in the half-light.

"How do you even give someone temporary beauty?" Nola asked the clerk.

"It's a glamour to enhance your features. Most people use it on their wedding day. Shall I wrap one up?"

Nola shook her head. "What I need is courage."

"Excellent choice." The clerk scanned the bottle-lined shelves. "I'm sorry. It appears we're out of Courage. Perhaps Valor would be an acceptable substitute?"

Nola bit her lip. "Well, I am planning to ask for a raise, which feels like preparing to go into battle. And dangerous when your boss is a lech."

"I'll wrap it up." He plucked a bottle of bronze colored liquid from the shelf and settled it in a velvet-lined box.

"How long do the effects last?"

"No more than twenty-four hours. You'll need to time it carefully. The effects can be…unsettling. You'll need at least twenty minutes of privacy."

"Is it painful?"

"It's an—individualized experience. The more foreign the trait you introduce, the greater the side effects."

He tied the box with a tasteful green bow before placing it in an unmarked bag. This was a product people didn't want to advertise.

HER BOSS HAD SET their meeting for the end of the day, his typical ploy to get women alone after hours. With mornings already chaotic, Nola decided to take the elixir the night before.

She sat in her bathroom, watching the contents swirl like liquefied pennies. At last, she uncorked it, held it to her nose. The fragrant scent of lilies wafted out. Roses. A hint of earth like a garden after a storm. She tipped her head back and swallowed. Felt the elixir slide down her throat. It had a bitter aftertaste.

Immediately, her fingers contorted. The beat of her heart grew so strong Nola imagined that, had she been able to stand, she'd see it pounding through her skin like a cartoon character in love. Sweat slicked her palms, her underarms, easily overpowering her natural deodorant with the sour scent of fear. Her jaw clenched, teeth grinding to dust. A whole-body Charley horse overtook her, had her writhing on the cold tile. Had she been able to open her mouth, she'd have screamed. Tears mingled with her sweat as iron butterflies erupted in her stomach, frantic for release. Five minutes. Ten.

As she was nearing her capacity for pain, her muscles relaxed. Her jaw released. And then something unexpected—euphoria. It rushed through her veins, shimmering beneath her skin. Her body was a wondrous place to inhabit, all pain eradicated. She was ready for anything. Was this how the average person without anxiety felt?

Suddenly, fatigue hit. The glowing in her veins faded. It appeared even the invincible needed sleep.

A TWIST OF SHEETS. Summer sun on golden hair trailed kisses down the length of Nola's stomach, a sure and steady path. Nola's moans filled the room, pressed against the ceiling, floated out the window on the warm breeze.

She tried to hang on, to stay in the moment, but someone's infernal alarm was going off, steadily increasing in volume.

Nola opened her eyes, disappointed.

Getting ready was a revelation. She didn't question her outfit, or second guess her lipstick choice, opting for the bold red with the unbroken seal. Found a parking spot and didn't triple check the sign. Didn't break a sweat in the elevator. In fact, she didn't sweat at all; her dress was still pristine by day's end when she strode into her boss's office. Nola sat across from him and leaned back, entirely at ease. She didn't even consider what to do with her hands.

"Nola, what brings you in?" He looked at her appraisingly. Her skin crawled, but she didn't back down. He knew what she wanted, but thought if she had to say it, she'd give up. That was yesterday's Nola.

"A raise. Twenty percent."

He scoffed, forgetting himself for a moment. "That's impossible. As you know, costs have been increasing—"

"Exactly. That's why we all deserve more money. That so-called cost-of-living bump was a pay cut in this economy. Furthermore, I was promised a five-year raise that never materialized. Ditto, my ten-year. I've earned twenty percent."

"The best I can do is three. Anything more needs board approval."

Nola leaned in, smile predatory. "I have a better idea. How about I tell the board about all the women you've coerced? The spiked drinks?"

His face turned an ugly shade of red. "Now, let's not be hasty. No need to throw around baseless accusations."

She sat back. Crossed her legs. "Sharon recorded you spiking my drink at the Christmas party."

His mouth fell open.

"I think we're done here." Nola left, ignoring the threats he hurled at her back. Took the elevator up to his boss's office, a man who in fact worked when he worked late.

Forget a raise. It was time for a promotion.

NOLA LOCKED THE DOOR to her apartment and slid to the floor. She'd gone to the bar frequented by the staff after work. Regaled them with her good news. And, still in the throes of Valor, promised to make her first official act as manager an appeal to the board for universal raises. Already it felt impossible as the effects of the elixir drained away. Anxiety, settling back into the familiar grooves on her shoulders, had never felt so heavy.

The next day, she moved into her new glass office. Looked out at her staff. She'd never be able to honor her promise. Not without another bottle of Valor.

Thankfully, she now had the money to procure it.

ON PAYDAY, SHE YET again opened that nondescript door.

The clerk smiled. "The pain proved worth it; I see."

"I'll take another bottle of Valor. You can skip the bow." All the velvet in the world wouldn't lessen the pain she had coming. Was it somehow worse to know what she was in for?

This time, she cracked a tooth, but otherwise came out unscathed. Valor spread like melted gold through her veins, assuring her that keeping her promise had been worth the pain. Normally, worry over her tooth would've consumed her. Instead, she smiled, with teeth, at her reflection, blood highlighting the split.

She fell asleep easily that night.

Nola was on a beach, her hand intertwined with the blonde woman's. She pressed it to her lips, sun-warmed and smelling of coconut. Took a slim finger in her mouth.

"Nola, there are children here," the woman laughed. The teasing lilt of her voice was everything. They drifted off to the sound of waves.

Yet again she woke disappointed. And alone. Who was this woman? Wren wiggled her cracked tooth, copper flooding her mouth. Maybe she could see a dentist while her fear was nonexistent.

SHE STRODE INTO HER meeting with the board and strode out, raises procured. Nola had thought it had been her, and a handful of women who'd left the company, but it turned out a lot of the women shared similar stories but had feared speaking up. Women who'd had one drink, yet woke in bed with their boss, and no memory of how they'd gotten there. There wasn't yet enough to take to the police, but there was enough to cause a scandal the board would rather avoid. Especially when she'd reminded them of how, while all that had been going on, they'd been giving themselves raises and doing stock buybacks.

ALL TOO SOON, NOLA was on her way to purchase another bottle, this time to battle the eviction notice the landlord's lackey had unceremoniously shoved beneath her door.

"Back again so soon? Perhaps you'd be interested in our loyalty card?"

Nola shook her head. "This is the last time. One bottle of Valor, please."

"I've recently unpacked a shipment of Courage if you're interested."

Nola picked at her cuticle, not stopping until she drew blood. She'd heard grumbling in the lobby of her building, others whose leases were up and had received eviction notices. She had enough problems without taking on everyone else's. If she took Valor, she might make more promises she'd be obligated to keep.

"Sure, let's try the Courage."

THIS TIME SHE PUT in the mouth guard she'd picked up when she'd gotten her tooth repaired and walked away with nothing more than a burst blood vessel in one eye and claw marks the length of her thigh.

Again, Nola fell asleep easily, but this time she didn't dream. Yet again, post-elixir-Nola woke disappointed. She wasn't, however, disappointed by the rest of her day.

Because anxiety-riddled Nola had kept receipts she'd been too timid to use, courageous Nola had ammunition, and her increased paycheck, with which to bargain. The building was going condo, and she'd negotiated a good price on the apartment across the hall. That way, she could remain in her clean, comfortable home while she chose all the finishes in the new condo.

As the Courage wore off, and her anxiety flooded back, guilt hitched a ride. She liked her neighbor across the hall, yet Courage had made her unafraid to screw him over.

NOLA KEPT THAT IN mind when her best friend announced her husband was cheating. Another Valor it was.

The process was brutal, as always, but with her mouth guard and freshly trimmed nails, bearable. Or perhaps she was getting used to it? Either way, the post euphoria made up for it, as did her dream. Music pulsed, sweat dripped, and women writhed, uninhibited, in the absence of men. The blonde woman was back, Nola gyrating against her.

"Tell me your name," Nola whispered in her ear.

"You know my name," she shouted over the music.

"I like the way you say it."

The woman leaned close, soft lips grazing Nola's ear. "El," she said, voice breathy.

"Kiss me, El," Nola whispered back.

Nola missed El when she woke. And then she missed her opportunity to use her Valor. Paula's husband's flight was delayed, and with it her chance to confront him before the elixir wore off. Nola escorted Paula to her apartment, and made some arrangements on her behalf, but with him getting in that evening, she needed a plan.

She needed another bottle.

Nola smiled as she climbed into her Uber. She was going to see El again.

"BACK SO SOON?"

"The timing didn't work out. Another, Valor, please." He plucked the bottle from the shelf and began the tedious wrapping process.

"You know it's weird. Every time I take Valor, I dream of the same woman. But when I took Courage I didn't dream at all."

He dropped the ribbon and looked at her, eyes wide. "Every time? The same woman?"

At her nod, he disappeared into the back office, returning with a thick ledger. Took out the bottle and compared the numbers. "This is most unusual. Please wait here. I need to make a call."

"Is something wrong with that batch?" Nola asked when he returned.

"The owner is on her way. She'd like you to wait. She'll be here in five minutes." He took her package and squirreled it away behind the counter, effectively holding her hostage.

She drummed her fingers on the counter, Nervous-Nola back in full force. It was an interminable five minutes, pinned under the glare of the clerk, who watched her from his desk in the back office.

At last, a woman entered, amber eyes glittering like one of her bottles. She held out a slim hand, nails long and ruby-slipper-red. "Violette."

Mesmerized, she took Violette's cool hand in her sweaty one. "Nola."

"Pleasure. Now, I hear you're having dreams. Can you describe them to me?"

Nola glanced at the open office door, face flaming.

"I see. One moment." Violette disappeared, returning with a stack of papers. "I'll need you to sign a confidentiality agreement."

Nola signed without reading. Paula was waiting for her.

"I wonder if you'd indulge me for a moment." Violette pulled out a paintbrush from beneath the counter, centered on a velvet tray as though it were a diamond necklace. "If you could touch this. Tell me what comes to mind."

"I don't have time—"

"Please."

Nola picked up the brush, surprised to sense it buzzing slightly in her hand. The urge to create overwhelmed her. "It's making me want to drive to the nearest artist supply store and buy one of everything."

Violette inhaled, air whistling through the gap in her front teeth. "I'm going to reveal to you something of our process. Keep in mind that you signed a nondisclosure, and we have a team of lawyers at our disposal." Violette held up a hand. "No need for anger. Just listen, and you'll understand the need for discretion.

The main ingredient in our elixir is derived from a—questionable source."

"Questionable how?"

"They're derived from the qualities of real people. Deceased people."

"Are you saying you used bodies in the elixirs?" Nola gagged, her black coffee and ill-advised breakfast sandwich threatening to come up, the only thing she'd managed to eat that day.

"No, not at all. We purchase objects from the estates of the recently deceased. They're coated with a residue. A residue only I've been able to sense. Until now."

Nola's eyes widened. "The paint brush."

"Precisely. It will be used in crafting our Creative elixir."

If Nola hadn't experienced the elixir, dreamed of El, who'd turned out to have been a real person, or felt the vibration of the paintbrush, she'd have had a much harder time believing Violette. But since she had, instead of doubt, all she felt was curiosity. "What object did you use for this batch of Valor?"

"It wouldn't be unethical to disclose that, I'm afraid."

"I think we surpassed ethics one questionable ingredient ago. Please, I need to know." Nola didn't like the desperate pitch to her voice.

Violette opened the ledger to the page the clerk had marked. "We created this batch from a bronze star with a 'V', awarded posthumously to one Eleanor Jones of Connecticut."

El. Nola pulled out her phone and searched. "It's her! The woman from my dreams." She ran a finger over El's face. "How many bottles do you have left from her batch of Valor?"

Violette ran a bejeweled finger down the page. "Of the twenty created, we sold three to you, plus four additional bottles."

Nola couldn't stand the thought of others having had those final pieces of El. But it also meant she could visit El thirteen more times. "I'm assuming you make batches because you can only create a finite number of bottles from each object? What if I find something else of El's? Something bigger?"

"The number of vials we can create from each object is the same, regardless of size. And, unfortunately, the residue concentrates on only one object. One person, one batch."

"Then I'd like to purchase all the remaining vials."

Violette sighed. "Eleanor's residue seems to have been extra potent, which explains why, even with your sensitivity, you only had dreams under the influence of Valor. That potency then transferred to your emotions. So, I know it feels dire, but you have to understand, these dreams have real consequences for Eleanor."

"What consequences could there possibly be? She's already passed."

"And failed to pass from this plane of existence. That's what the residue is—a sign a ghost is lingering. That connection is usually severed through the creation of our elixir. It helps them cross over. Occasionally, after we sever the bond with their object, a spirit will transfer to another object. Or a sensitive person. Which is why I never use my own products."

"So, she's haunting me?"

"More like your dreams are activating the inert pieces of her suspended in the elixir. And the dreams are reminding her of what it is to be human. They're like a train she keeps missing because you're blocking her departure. If you care for her, you'll allow us to set her free. Before it's too late."

"And how do you do that?"

"Look, I've never come across another person as sensitive as me, so I've never run into this issue. But, usually, a batch of elixir will stop glowing. We'll then look for a nearby object that has taken on a glow and destroy it with the batch of bad elixir. In this case, the elixir is still glowing, which indicates that destroying the remaining vials should be sufficient."

"No! You can't do that. I need to see her again." Nola tried to rein in the desperation in her voice. It wouldn't do to sound like an addict in need of a fix, though that's what it felt like.

"Can't I have one more bottle? So I can say goodbye?"

Violette tapped the counter with one long nail. "One more time won't hurt. As long as you take it tonight. But then she needs to find her way onto that train. Any longer, and passing will become extremely difficult, if not impossible. You don't want to see what happens to the ghosts who become stuck."

Nola shuddered.

"But I have one further condition. I'd like you to consider working for me. Helping me search for objects. I'm sure we can come to a financial agreement that would be to your satisfaction."

"I just got a promotion at work. I can't quit." That's what had started all this.

"Wouldn't you rather be your own boss? See the world? Take a few days. Think about it. Either way, you need to let her move on. And then do the same yourself."

Nola checked her phone as she waited for her Uber. Twelve missed calls and a barrage of texts. Paula's husband was on his way to the apartment, which meant there wasn't time for privacy. She pulled out the bottle, the bronze swirl glinting in the dying sun, as captivatingly beautiful as Eleanor. Swallowing it down, she imagined she could taste El on her tongue.

She was in the back seat of the Uber when the effects took over. Should she warn the driver? Her jaw locked. Too late. This time was worse than the first, the pent-up anxiety of the week vying for release. Her body arched with spasms, the pain of her broken heart pressing against her skin, oozing through her pores. The despair was so great it was lucky she didn't have a weapon. In that dark moment, had she been armed and capable of pulling the trigger, she would've. She felt like she was in the bottom of a well, slowly perishing from want.

"What's going on back there?"

The sounds of gridlock fought through the darkness. The fear in the driver's voice.

"Are you having a seizure? Don't die in my car, lady. We're ten minutes from the hospital."

All she knew was pain and the ceaseless blaring of the driver's horn. Slowly, but forcefully, the elixir expelled her anxiety, euphoria rushing to take its place. Her fingers released. Her arms. Her jaw. "Would you quit laying on the horn?"

"Jesus." The driver looked at her in the rearview, taking in her sweat-slicked but peaceful face.

"No need for the hospital. I have medicine at home. Get me there as fast as you can."

"If you say so. You nearly gave me a heart attack, lady."

It sounded better than her broken one. The one waiting for her on the other side of euphoria.

She reached her apartment in time to see Paula's husband pulling her out the door by her hair. Nola looked around for a weapon, a break-in-case-of-fire ax. Then she realized she had the greatest weapon of all in the palm of her hand. It was painful to watch and not intervene, to step into the shadows and hit record.

Nervous-Nola could never. She recorded the first hank of hair coming loose. The pop of a collarbone. The snap of a wrist.

Enough.

"I'm calling an ambulance."

He froze, arm pulled for another blow.

"If you stop and agree to our terms, the next call won't be to the police. And this video." She held up her phone. "Won't go to the press. You're a public figure. Think of what this would do to your career. And before you do something stupid, I'm still recording, and it's all backed up to the cloud."

Nola ignored the threats and slurs he spit in her face. That was the problem with alpha men—they couldn't withstand a bruised ego. Her standing there, unflinching, was withering his already shrunken manhood. At last, he brushed past her.

Nola called after him. "You'll leave her alone. You'll give her the house, her car, any belongings she desires, and half your assets. And don't bother trying to hide any money. I've already hired the best financial investigator in town."

He hesitated, perhaps debating if he could throw her down the stairway or if she was truly bluffing about the cloud.

Nola continued. "If you harass her, or get someone to do it on your behalf, this video goes public. Should anything happen to me, this video will automatically post." Nola collected Paula and shuffled her inside. Her heart raced, but she didn't quicken her step. Valor made her brave, not inhuman. She didn't breathe easy until he'd left, dragging his shattered ego like a torn security blanket.

Paula looked at her, wide eyed. "How could you only watch? Who are you, and what have you done with my Nola?"

"You really want her? Cause this Nola has already had your exterior locks changed. Now we're going to get you fixed at the hospital, change your alarm code, and then I'll pack his shit."

As though she hadn't suffered for Paula. Who was looking at her like she'd shape-shifted into another creature. In a way, she had.

EVEN VALOR WASN'T ENOUGH to make saying goodbye to El easy; their kisses salt-tinged. At work, she sat in her office, looking out at her staff. Had she even wanted this job, or had it been the Valor? Without Valor, did she have the courage to change her life?

Perhaps, like El, it was time to move on.

Nola accepted the position. Her first official duty was destroying the remaining vials of Valor. What she hadn't expected was that in releasing El, Nola would also free herself. That the intensity would dissipate, and her heart would mend.

She relished traveling across the country, seeking objects to help set spirits free. As she was. It turned out the objects had a somewhat indirect role in the elixir's creation. The proprietary ingredient was grave dirt, which Nola was tasked with collecting on the first full moon following a death. Only the top half-inch was viable, which is why Violette was only averaging twenty bottles per grave.

Nola had to time things just right. She'd scour for estate sales and the corresponding obituary. If a full moon hadn't yet occurred, she'd hit the road, looking for an object with a gleam. If she found one, she knew the dirt would be elixir worthy. Once there, she'd bury the object and allow the moon to work its magic.

She thought she'd hate digging in cemeteries, but it turned out she enjoyed getting her hands dirty. Gathering dirt and any flowers left on the grave under the patchwork cover of darkness, the petals adding a certain potency to the formula. The scent of flowers and earth always brought the elixir, and thus El, to mind.

On those haunted nights she'd search out a club, like the one she'd gone to with El. Nola might never be a courageous person, but she'd learned a few things from her brush with valor. How to live for herself. And that there were plenty of beautiful women in this world.

Living women.

Devil's Tree

AMANDA DIER

Black and white photos flashed on the television screen in the dark room one by one, faster and faster until they blurred. The next image showed a set of women's headshots fanned across the screen like a yearbook page, but the somber music in the background made it clear this was no mere keepsake. They ranged from class photos to drivers' license headshots, but the grayscale overlay did a lot to make them homogenous. It also drove home the fact that the women weren't counted among the living.

"All sixteen women were chosen for their vulnerability," a female voice said as the pictures shrank. "All were picked up while hitchhiking through New England, and only six partial sets of human remains were ever recovered."

Stacey's mind immediately presented a memory. *Partial sets of human remains,* a few bones laid out on a white sheet along with a skull. She'd seen pictures in other case studies in her class, but this documentary was tailored for a broader audience, not an academic one. She brushed the memory aside and turned her attention to the documentary.

The screen zoomed out to display the face of a man superimposed over the women's photos, then changed again to show a display of what had to be the murder weapons—an assortment of knives. Beside her on the couch, Stacey's girlfriend squirmed.

"You sure we have to watch this?" Annette groused.

"It's for my class, babe," Stacey said. "I need at least one non-written source for this paper."

Six sets of remains and confessions for twelve more victims. She wrote on her notepad as the narrator continued.

The room lit up as Annette unlocked her phone and started browsing the web, and despite Stacey's interest in the murder documentary, she couldn't help but be annoyed.

"Why don't we watch something a little closer to home?" She asked. Annette liked horror movies, just not the real-life horror of serial murder. Maybe this would be enough to get her adrenaline pumping, so Stacey wouldn't have to finish her research alone.

"Like what?" Her girlfriend asked with skepticism as she stared at her phone. It lit up her face, but not much else.

"You know Shell Oak Park down the street?" Stacey asked.

"Mmmhmm." Annette sounded disinterested.

"What if I told you someone once buried bodies there?"

Annette actually looked up. "Who?"

"Timothy Wayne Geisel," Stacey said. "He used to be a cop down in Minnows and they say that before, during, and after he was a police officer, he'd drive around looking for girls." She leaned in close, breathing on Annette's neck. "Pretty girls," she said, lowering her voice. Her fingers crept up Annette's bare shoulders, barely touching, making her squirm.

"Girls like you!" she shouted and goosed her girlfriend. Annette shrieked, quickly reduced to begging.

"Okay, okay, okay," she cried, laughing. "We'll watch your stupid thing on the cop guy!"

Stacey flopped back into her spot on the couch and changed documentaries before Annette could change her mind.

From the moment the old oak tree with twisted branches crossed the screen, Stacey was pleased to see that her girlfriend had put her phone down.

"From the moment that men scavenging for aluminum cans found bones emerging from the ground on Highfin Island in Florida, authorities knew there was someone very dangerous in their community."

Grayed-out pictures showed a smiling, round-faced man with glasses, eleven photos of women and girls around him in a circle, interspersed with white question marks against a black background. *"Timothy Wayne Geisel himself estimated his number to be at least eighty, but he can only be directly linked with eleven victims..."*

Stacey happily noticed that Annette seemed fixated. Stacey's legal pad bounced on her knee as she continued jotting notes about Geisel's methods of hanging, disemboweling, and sexual assaults. Normally, Annette would be hunched with all of her attention bent on her phone, but tonight, Stacey could see the device was dark in her girlfriend's fingers as Annette leaned forward. Her other arm groped for Stacey's knee as the documentary alluded to a little of the fantastical.

Oh, *that* had caught her attention. Of course. Annette was a paranormal junkie. If the two weren't watching criminal justice documentaries, they were watching ghost hunter shows.

"*I don't know about the man himself,*" a woman's voice said. The accent made her sound like a local. The tree was back on the screen, flashing between normal colors and a negative print. "*But I have been there late at night, and if you look close, you can see the bodies hanging from the tree.*"

They were both quiet until the documentary ended, then Annette immediately bounced up. "Let's go see it!"

"The tree?" Stacey asked, still mentally organizing her notes into an argument for her paper.

"Shell Oak Park isn't far," her girlfriend cajoled. "You're always saying we need to get more exercise. Let's walk over."

Maybe I can work it into something like the community impact section, Stacey thought. "Alright," she sighed, putting the notebook down. "Let's go."

Their walk was short, only fifteen minutes. "Half-a-mile there, half-a-mile back," Annette said. "That's a lot of steps. Ten thousand a day, right?"

Stacey nodded, observing the rapidly darkening sky overhead. The sun was getting low, turning the sky into an array of pinks and corals that seemed appropriate for Florida, but she worried about finding a particular tree in a park full, especially in the dark.

Annette already had the park map pulled up on her phone, along with website directions to find the tree.

"I guess we aren't the only ones looking for it," she giggled, leading them into the park and down a path. Stacey couldn't tell one tree from another, but Annette quickly had them standing under the reaching branches of a thick oak. The bark on the trunk was blackened, though Stacey couldn't distinguish whether it was from fungus or fire. Other than that, it looked like every other tree.

Spanish moss dripped from the branches, and weeds and dead leaves littered the surrounding ground.

"It's so old-looking," Annette said, laying her hands on the trunk. Her fingertips traced the grooves. "The website said it's *really* old, like a hundred and fifty years!"

"That's up there," Stacey agreed, looking at the other trees around them with trunks of similar width. "Did they say how old the rest of the trees in the park are?"

"Who cares?" Annette said. "If you come here on certain nights, you can hear the snap of a rope. The lady in the documentary said you can see bodies hanging. I wanna come see them."

Stacey rubbed her arms as a chill crept through her veins. "I'm good without," she said uneasily. "Let me get a picture for my class and we can go."

It took more prodding than she wanted to coax her girlfriend away from the tree to take the shot, then out of the park entirely.

"Want to finish the other video on Lyman?" she asked as they walked home.

"Sure," Annette said, looking down at her phone. "Maybe I can find more stuff to watch on the Devil's Tree."

During the next two weeks, as Stacey finished her essay, packages containing used books arrived almost daily, and Annette's normally studious nature kicked off into overdrive, with one subject as her focus.

The video-sharing app on the TV became inundated with crime shows and "weird Florida" type videos that Stacey had never heard of, and when she watched a few out of curiosity, she realized they all had the Devil's Tree or Geisel in common, and usually both were at least mentioned in every show.

A binder with photos of the victims grew fatter and fatter, containing faces that hadn't been featured in the original documentary.

"Wow, you're really getting obsessed with this," Stacey commented as she read over Annette's shoulder. Her girlfriend was punching holes into the edges of a drawing of a woman who had been bound with her arms behind her back and a piece of wood wedged under her elbows. "Did you print that out?"

Annette shook her head and slid the drawing into the binder rings before clipping it closed. "I drew it," she said dreamily. Stacy noticed her fingertips were stained gray with pencil lead.

She decided not to pursue it, but that night she deleted everything crime-related from their 'To watch' queue, even the stuff for her classes. Stacey could always re-add it later or at the library, but that drawing had spooked her more than she wanted to admit. With long, dark hair, and pale skin, it was hard not to think about the fact that the drawing resembled Stacey herself.

Annette never commented on it, but she carried her binder around like a teddy bear, never letting it out of her sight. Stacey drew a line at throwing out the drawings, but she wished her girlfriend would drop the obsession.

"Let's go for a walk," she said one night when Annette had paused in her frantic scribbling to add a fresh sheet into her binder.

"At a park or around the neighborhood?" Annette asked. The bags under her eyes were deep, and Stacey knew she hadn't been getting much sleep. Maybe tiring her out would work.

Stacey shrugged. "Around the neighborhood, I guess."

She had assumed they would wander around the neighborhood until they found a street they recognized to make it home. But Annette steered them left onto Via Cuervo instead of the right

Stacey was expecting, though the houses they were walking past looked familiar, especially the molded fiberglass manatee mailboxes. Stacey shrugged and glanced around, looking for interesting landscape ideas the neighbors had completed in their front yards, and wondering if she could copy the designs on the cheap.

The empty lots between houses grew more numerous, and ahead of them, the street curved to the left. Stacey turned to follow it, but Annette caught her by the arm.

"There's the park!" she pointed out.

Stacey felt a weight drop into the pit of her stomach. Her girlfriend had led them back to Shell Oak Park, the one place she hadn't anticipated.

She had wanted to get them away from Annette's newest fixation, not go directly to the place outside of the house that had started it. Stacey bit her tongue as Annette led them to the tree, committing the path to memory. The idea of coming back in the middle of the night with a chainsaw and a gas can was tempting, and she imagined being alone on the path with gas-filled jugs in her hands, stalking down the path like a murderer herself with one goal at the end.

Annette dragged them straight to the tree, stroking the trunk like a dog she had missed. Her eyes searched the branches. She never looked at her girlfriend.

I'm getting really sick of this tree, Stacey thought, imagining fire licking up the trunk and leaping from branch to branch as it used the dry moss as tinder.

She looked down at Annette, who now had her forehead pressed to the tree like she was communing with it. Her knees were pressed into the sandy soil surrounding the trunk, and Annette's fingers dug into the dirt like she was searching for a bone.

"Let's go," Stacey said, hoping to ward off the chill creeping up her spine.

Annette didn't move.

"I'm going to leave without you," Stacey said loudly.

"Mmm," Annette said. Her eyes never opened.

"I'm sick of this," Stacey announced. She turned and walked back toward the entrance, hoping she'd hear the crashing clamor of her girlfriend racing to meet her. Annette always chased her whenever Stacey walked away after a fight.

What trailed Stacey now was silence.

She walked home alone and spent the rest of the night fuming and looking at psychological studies of murder groupies on the campus's digital library. Annette wasn't home when she went to bed, though Stacey woke up with a warm, familiar presence in the bed next to her. She ignored her sleeping girlfriend and went to her first class, anger still burning in her gut.

Though Professor Crume had worked in several prisons while studying serial homicide along with violent criminals in general, Stacey hesitated to approach him about her concerns. She knew she herself was a murder nerd, one of the teenagers who'd grown up watching nothing but the Forensix channel and true crime shows that aired 24/7, but being a fan of something was different from admitting that *something is terribly wrong with my girlfriend.*

So, she kept her hand down, wrote notes instead of the list of questions she wanted to ask about where to get help, how to make Annette's obsession stop, and the more personal one, '*Is my girlfriend obsessed with a serial killer?*'

It was her long day at school, with classes that stretched from nine in the morning to ten at night, with hour-long breaks in between. When her last class ended, she still hadn't gotten a text message from Annette. Not a 'Hey, I miss you,' or the long-desired 'Sorry.' Only silence since the last excited message 'I got three more books!' the day before.

Annette was in bed and asleep by the time she got home. *Had she ever gotten out of bed?* Somehow, the stack of books on her nightstand had grown.

Stacey frowned when she saw the small glass jar next to the books. Was it weed?

She leaned in with the light from her phone for illumination, hoping she wouldn't wake Annette, then recoiled when she saw what was in the container. Pale gray, sandy soil with dry, broken brown leaves mixed in. The exact soil the trees in the park somehow drew sustenance from.

Stacey Ritter was *not* jealous of a dead man, she told herself furiously. She was *not*. But this had gone too far. She would throw out the jar tomorrow in front of Annette, and they were going to the school's counseling center. Enough was enough.

She did her best to ignore the feeling of someone observing her. Annette could play her stupid game of pretending to worship Geisel beyond the grave, but Stacey would not get sucked into it. She bundled herself into bed, keeping a pillow between the two of them to avoid touching her girlfriend.

Their life outside of this little snag was great. They needed to get back to where they had been, instead of this weird game of obsession and derailment.

Stacey's plans stalled when she woke alone. The bed was cold, and Annette wasn't a morning person, so Stacey was trying not to panic when she saw it was seven in the morning and Annette's car was gone.

She checked the phone tracker app and noted that Annette was on the interstate past Orlando and heading north. Was she going home to Georgia?

Stacey's calls to Annette calls went to voicemail, but the tracking app stayed on. Her text messages went unanswered. Midway through the morning, she debated following the phone signal to wherever Annette was when she realized the dot's movement had stopped in Starke, Florida. Barely south of the state border, she acknowledged, zooming in.

Raiford? What's in Raiford?

Other than the state prison, Stacey couldn't think of a single thing. What if Annette had a new obsession? What if she was pen pals with another serial killer? A living one this time?

The car moved down roads that weren't marked on the map, appearing to drive through forest and over an unlabeled river before stopping again. It stayed there for a long time, at least an hour. Stacey checked anxiously every five minutes while reading more studies on hybristophilia, and when she checked again to see that the dot was slowly meandering back south on state and county roads, her shoulders slowly lowered. Tension she hadn't known she'd been holding eased out of her spine as Annette's car crawled down the state toward Stacey's marker, faithfully still, as it had all day.

She was so relieved when the car lights swung across the front window that she couldn't gather the strength to be angry when Annette walked in, all smiles and giddy happiness.

"Look what I got!" she announced, holding up another plastic jar.

"Where were you?" Stacey interrupted.

"Raiford," Annette said carelessly, shaking the container. Dirt bounced around inside, darker than what was in the other bottle Stacey planned to throw out.

"I saw that," Stacey said, emphasizing every word. The anger was bubbling back up, and she was getting an ugly feeling about where Annette had been.

"I went to his grave!" Annette exclaimed.

"Geisel's?" Stacey said. "He's buried in a damn prison cemetery. How did you get in there?"

"I walked," Annette said, glowing like it had been a great triumph. "There are back roads, you know," she burbled. "I drove a few and got within walking distance and strolled right in. I guess they weren't burying anyone today! No one tried to stop me or anything!"

"You broke into a prison!" Stacey exclaimed. "Do you have any idea what could have happened to you?"

"Clearly nothing did," Annette said, brandishing her prize like a macabre maraca. "I got back here, didn't I?"

"You could have been arrested!" Stacey said. "If you got arrested, that would have looked horrible for me!"

"Horrible for *you*," Annette echoed derisively. "Everything is bad for you. Can't ever get in trouble with the police, can't smoke, can't drink too much, or have any fun because of a *career* you don't even have yet."

Stacey cringed. It was an argument that was brought up whenever Annette wanted to do something that wasn't wholly law-abiding. Going into old, abandoned buildings to look for ghosts? Setting up shop outside someone's *house* with a camera because she'd read online that it was haunted? Staying in a movie theatre to watch a horror movie for a second run-through after they'd only paid for one showing? Stacey wasn't willing to throw away a career she was taking on student loans in order to get, which meant not doing a lot of things Annette wanted.

"I'm going to bed," she muttered, turning away.

"Run away, that's what you always do," Annette mocked her. "Go on, go to sleep. I'll be here watching the shows you always tried to get me into."

Unwilling to let the tears fall, Stacey shut herself into the bedroom and buried her face in her pillow. She'd go to the campus counseling office tomorrow, though if it was for Annette or herself, she didn't know.

The TV in the living room never turned on. Stacey fell into an uneasy sleep, hoping Annette was rueing her own words as much as Stacey was. She drifted in and out, wondering when and if Annette would come to apologize for being so savage with her words.

Half awake, Stacey turned in bed to get comfortable. Her hands brushed across the covers to smooth them out, and grit rolled beneath her fingertips. She jerked awake, sweeping off the duvet in disgust.

She flicked on the nightstand light and froze. It wasn't stuff tracked into the bed from the floor that had woken her. It was *dirt*. Annette's containers lay empty atop the dresser, and Annette herself was nowhere to be seen.

"Baby?" she called cautiously. "You in the bathroom?"

The door was closed, but no light shone under the door and she couldn't hear a sound.

Stacey checked the other side of the bed, but it was still cold.

Her phone displayed the awful truth that it was three in the morning, and she swiped past the screen to get to the phone locator app. Annette's phone was in the house according to the app, but when Stacey called it, the vibration coming from the living room made her jump.

Their house was dark, and the TV screen was black when she cautiously wandered out, hoping Annette was asleep on the couch and not looking to pick another fight.

The screen read, *Missed call from Stacey,* when Stacey fished it out from where it had fallen half under the table.

She looked back into their bedroom at the dirty bed and the stack of books about Geisel on the nightstand. *The park.* That stupid, stupid park, and that stupid tree. Once she got Annette home, she was going back with the gas can.

She pulled on jeans and shoes, ignoring the car keys by the door in favor of her own feet. Walking over there might cool her down, and god knew she needed it.

The night sky was bright overhead, lit by the full moon illuminating everything as she walked the familiar road to the park.

Resentment curdled in her gut as she looked for the two manatee mailboxes so close to each other, remembering how Annette's pace sped up a little after they made that last turn onto Via Cuervo to get to the park.

It loomed ahead, a darker space at the end of the already murky street. This area of the neighborhood had few streetlights and even the one in the parking lot seemed dimmer than usual.

She ducked under the swing gates at the entrance, glad she hadn't driven. The walk hadn't actually calmed her down, but leaving her Camry at the entrance could have meant talking with the police if they'd spotted it, and she didn't want to deal with that right now.

The parking lot was empty, because of course it was. Annette didn't want to hang out on sun-cracked asphalt, she wanted to sit under the stupid tree and bask in the tree's aura. Stacey followed the usual path, walking along the edge of the canal and looking at the houses on the other side. Everyone in them was undoubtedly asleep, like she desperately wanted to be.

Her shoulders hunched at the thought of the spiders living in the Spanish moss hanging from the old oak trees, and she wished she'd worn something with long sleeves. She pushed down the path toward the tree and stopped.

Annette was nowhere to be found. The base of the tree was empty. Stacey listened for movement, thinking maybe she'd beat her girlfriend there, but there was no sound of leaves crunching underfoot, no one breathing. Nothing stirred the night, except for a faint creak she couldn't quite place.

Maybe Annette had climbed the tree? She peered up into the branches, hoping her girlfriend hadn't been stupid enough to climb it.

She shuffled sideways a little, peering around the bulk of the trunk, and froze. Above her, Annette's still form twisted slowly, spinning at the end of a noose under her own weight.

Swollen face, will most likely exhibit petechiae when examined up close, tongue sticking out, body limp, her mind gibbered even as it cataloged.

"Ann?" she whispered. If Annette moved, twitched, did *anything*, she could get up there and cut her down, and maybe—

She hadn't heard any movement, but something scraped at her ear, and she shuddered. It was a sensation she hadn't felt since high school. Men's stubble. She jerked away, and the weight of a rope settled around her neck.

Behind her, a male voice whispered, "Gotcha," and the rope tightened.

Bloom House

JOHN GROVER

Every town had that home. The one the kids wouldn't walk past on their way to school. The one everyone in town said was haunted, but no one could prove it. The anemic house, with its dilapidated roof and ravaged walls that shouldn't still be standing, but did, despite monster storms and natural selection.

That was Bloom House in my hometown. More than an eyesore, a monument to the salacious and insidious. A product of gossip by the kids in my neighborhood. It had always terrified me, even though I had never actually seen it. Until now.

Not too long ago, I was a combat medic in the Iraq War. It was where I met Liam, my commanding officer. He was everything I wasn't. Brave. Strong. Handsome as Hell. We had a brief physical affair. This was still a huge deal at the time, and we kept it a secret. No one knew. Not a soul. It was even more scandalous that I was having an affair with my CO, but my heart didn't care. I'd been looking ahead, the two of us getting out of the war, moving in together, starting a new life.

That dream was shattered the day the roadside IED took him from me. I can still see his blood on my hands as I held him in my arms and watched him die. There almost isn't a night that goes by that I don't wake up in cold sweats, witnessing the shrapnel tear through him again and again.

When the war ended, I moved to San Francisco. I wanted to lose myself there, let the big city show me its wonders. I went from guy to guy but never quite found someone like Liam. Then I got the call…

Home again. This big city boy came back to this Godforsaken New England town after vowing I never would. Dad was dying, and I decided I needed to be there—for mom. Dad and I never saw eye to eye. Especially after I came out to him and Mom. He even tried putting a lock on my door to keep me from seeing other guys. The fits I threw when I found myself trapped in my room were so surreal that I swore I remembered climbing out of my bedroom window and falling two stories, breaking my arm. Mom claims that didn't happen.

Eventually we made our peace, but it was a long, hard road. His illness had taken its toll on Mom—long nights at the hospital, downsizing into an apartment, the loneliness, the money, everything. When he passed, it was like relief. Mom could begin her life again and I could sort mine out.

What was I still doing here? It was simple—there was no place else to go. The house I scooped up to be near my parents was now worth next to nothing, and I couldn't sell it even if I wanted to. The market had sunk.

My dating life was much like the Housing Marketing—missing in action. That didn't stop me from seeking out unconditional love. I got a dog. A cute little lapdog. She was black and white and had such a bubbly personality. Not a yippy little thing like some small dogs. No, she was a little ball of snuggly fur who I named Bandit because of the markings around her eyes.

I liked routines. After dealing with the family issues, I tried to put order back into my daily life, like the military had taught me. Up at 6 a.m., walk the dog by 6:30, eat at 7 a.m., shower by 7:30, life was grand. The dog led me on the same path every morning, straight down the street to the baseball field and the state forest behind it. On the way there, we would stop at the edge of a yard belonging to the abandoned house in the neighborhood, on the corner of Blackstone Street, *Bloom House*.

Damn house gave me the creeps. Of course, the dog insisted on stopping at its yard each morning to sniff the ground. I tried to pull her away every time, but she fought against me. Stubborn little pooch.

The old bungalow sent a shiver through me. I referred to it as the derelict house. It had no owners, no life, no heart. Built around 1909, the house had been ravaged by a fire decades earlier, and never recovered.

The outside of the house had dark black scorch marks down its clapboard walls like bloodstains on a murder scene that no one could scrub away. Some of the windows were boarded, charcoal shutters missing slats and hanging precariously.

The windows that still owned their glass reflected nothing but shadow—doorways into a different time and place. There was one window on the second floor, smaller than all the rest and oddly shaped, so that I could see the sunset within, illuminating the slanted ceiling of what could have been a bedroom. The remains of front and back porches, without stairs, sagging and rotted, left no way to the doors. All doors were boarded. No way in. No way out.

Grass grew thick and wild, choking the home's foundation and overtaking the gravel driveway. The chimney was broken at the top, the roof pocked with holes and gutters twisted with ruin, like the broken bones of a dying behemoth.

The stories about Bloom House began coming back to me, pieces of them flitting through my thoughts. My memories had been jogged by finally seeing it in person. It was said that George Bloom burned alive inside the house. Unable to escape such a small and unimpressive house seemed illogical, but that was the story. Some say he set the fire himself, trying to end his own misery and take his wife Margaret and son James with him. They survived; he did not. Afterward, his wife and son moved away and were never heard from again.

These events happened before Mom and Dad lived in town. They never mentioned the house, never talked about the stories. I asked mom once, but she dismissed me, saying she'd never heard such stories. It was simply a burnt-out house no one wanted anymore. Neglected. Abandoned.

A sigh of relief escaped me when Bandit opted to move on and head for the ballfield. I couldn't help but look back at the dilapidated house. I sensed its eyes on me.

In the fall, the sun shrank away earlier, and a chill laced the air. Darkness appeared everywhere. Long shadows stretched in every direction. I walked Bandit along my road, dead leaves crunching under each step, and saw the house waiting for me as I reached the top of the hill.

I turned the corner onto Blackstone Street and came face to face with it. The leash pulled in my hand. This time, my girl did not want to linger; she wanted to go, and now. I didn't blame her. The house looked more desolate by night. Soulless, a shell, but not without presence.

A light came on in the house. *A light!* It glowed on the left side, that oddly-shaped window. I didn't know what to think. It was impossible. There were no electrical wires running to the house. No phone lines. There shouldn't have been any light.

A stone sat beneath the window, big enough for me to stand on. I could probably see in if I climbed onto the stone. The light remained. I sucked in some air. My dog waited patiently. I made my move.

It was stupid. I had no business being here, but I stepped into the yard anyway. Mud squished beneath my shoes. The smell of rotting vegetation wafted past my nostrils.

Closer.

My feet trembled a bit. A surge of excitement swelled in my chest, and my heart fluttered. The moonlight caught the stone under the window, illuminating it like a beacon. I tugged at Bandit's leash, and she followed me reluctantly. My gaze locked onto the window as I drew closer. My foot tapped the stone. I stepped up and—

A snarl escaped my girl. I froze. Her growl rose. She was definitely afraid. Her hair bristled; her snout crinkled. I stepped back and looked at her. She stared at a tree across the yard, part of a thin patch of woods that surrounded the backyard. Suddenly, I felt self-conscious. What was I doing? What would the neighbors on Blackstone think? What if someone called the police?

I rushed out of the yard, pulling Bandit with me, and scampered toward home. The wind started up, and a chill caressed my face. I looked back and the light in the house was out. Was it ever on? Had I let my imagination get away from me? No, it was there; the light was there.

The rest of the night passed without incident. No police. No neighbors. No house. I carried on, dinner, TV, and bed, but I couldn't get the house out of my head. I wanted to tell my old friends. I knew they would get a kick out of it. Some of them were amateur ghost hunters. Especially my friend Katie. She would be all over this.

Sleep eventually did settle over me. Dreams—choppy, confusing, chaotic—messed with me, but I was used to that. The remnants of the last one had faded away, except this time, it wasn't about Liam. It was about me—pounding on my bedroom door, my father bellowing at me from the other side. *You'll stay in the closet until you straighten the hell out!*

I woke. My eyes popped open and for a moment, I felt lost. The room was pitch black, and I realized it was still the dead of night. A bit of sweat drooled down my face. I wiped it, sensing I wasn't alone in the room. I caught movement out of the corner of my eye and looked up.

The silhouette of a man stood in the doorway. He was darker than anything else in the room, like a living shadow, blacker than any night. My heart jumpstarted, pounding against my chest. My throat went dry as I tried to form words. A nervous feeling swelled in the pit of my stomach. My feet went numb.

The man lifted an arm and pointed at me. He took one step closer, and I nearly screamed. Where was my phone? An intruder had—

"Liam?" I whispered.

I didn't sincerely think it was him. That's when I started to panic.

"Stay away from my house," the man rasped, holding his ground.

I wanted to speak, wanted to answer the cryptic warning, but was struck mute. My limbs felt as if they weighed five hundred pounds.

"Stay away from my house. It will be your undoing."

With his last words, the man faded, and as the last of his visage vanished, I caught a glimpse of a face full of charred flesh.

I had been visited by George Bloom.

THE NEXT NIGHT, MY close friend David came for a visit. He and I had crushes on each other in high school, but we never did anything about it. George Bloom's words still replayed in the back of my mind. I wanted to mention it to David, but it sounded insane. A dead man paid me a visit? Right. I cooked David dinner, and he devoured it. We settled onto my couch in the living room and an awkward silence fell between us.

David put his hand on my leg and leaned in for a kiss.

I recoiled. It was an instinctive reaction.

"Oh God," he said. "You're not ready. Of course you're not. I...God..."

"It's okay." I forced a smile. "Forget it."

A moment later, I changed the subject and told him the story of the house. He was more of a believer than I, and, of course, my tale both fascinated and captivated him. I knew I was in for trouble.

"Let's go check it out," he said.

"Are you crazy? I think the place might be haunted."

"That's the point. It's obvious something's going on there."

"I think I should stay away from it."

"You chickenshit. You would never pass up a chance like this. Remember all those houses Katie took us to?"

"I didn't live a few feet away from them. I get a bad feeling about that place."

"It's settled; we're going."

"David."

"C'mon, it's the perfect season. Halloween is coming. Look, I'm getting goosebumps. C'mon, let's go. Please…we might be able to capture an image on our phones." His grinning face got to me, the glee in his eyes like a six-year-old going to a carnival haunted house. "You know you want to! It'll be scary fun."

"Okay. Let me grab a flashlight."

This time Bandit stayed home.

We walked slowly down the sidewalk, desiccated leaves rolling in the deserted street, the moon a sliver in the purple-black veil of the night sky. I tightened my hand around the flashlight. My spine stiffened. I saw the house taking shape over the hill.

David was full of anticipation and wonder; he loved every tense moment. I couldn't believe I let him talk me into searching the dilapidated ruins. My breath started puffing into the air. The temperature was dropping. Finally, the house was upon us. The bungalow looked even more sinister to me tonight. Thankfully, I had some backup.

"Oh my God," David said breathlessly. "This place is creepy. You were right."

"I told you."

"Look at the scorch marks. The old foundation. There's a basement, too. I wonder what horrors happened down there?"

"Stop it. No horrors there. Only a fire. Let's go."

David followed me into the yard. Everything was still and dark. The window where I saw the light come on was pitch black. I stared at the stone beneath it and then turned to David.

"Okay, go ahead," I said.

"What?"

"Go to the window, take some pictures."

"It's dark."

"So?"

"I won't get a photo with my phone. Why don't you go first and see if you can see anything?"

"You're scared."

"No, I'm not." David shook his head and smirked. That nervous smile of his. I'd know it anywhere. Of course he was scared.

"Yes, you are. Now who's the chickenshit?"

The light in the window suddenly came on and we both stopped cold. Our voices dying in the frigid air. Amber light rippled from the old window and crested over the weed-filled yard.

"And there it is…" I whispered.

"Go." David nudged me. "Here's my phone."

I shook my head. "So help me, I'm gonna kill you." I snatched the phone from him and turned the camera function on. "Never should have listened to you."

"We're here now. Quick, get a picture of the inside of the house, then we'll run all the way back."

"You're such a bastard."

I walked to the window and stepped onto the stone, juggling the flashlight and the phone. I leaned against the house and peered in. A lamp with a stained-glass shade glowed inside. It looked like an antique or something…then…my legs buckled. I almost tumbled to the ground, by God. There was something there…holy God, a body. I saw a body. I didn't imagine it. A man lying prone on the wooden floor. The camera went off. My heart leaped into my throat.

"David…" I turned to get his attention and saw him standing frozen on the edge of the yard. He was shivering, his face pale. Behind him, a figure appeared, tall, cloaked in shadow. It was a man. An arm reached for him.

"Behind you! David…there's someone…!"

The world spun. I looked at the sky and the stars winked. Darkness swallowed me. Nothing but black. Nothing but…

IN THE DISTANCE, I heard the faint sound of IEDs exploding as if I was right back in Iraq. Terror surged through me. My head felt like it might split open. I opened my eyes slowly and noticed I was not outside anymore. I was inside. Inside the house! Inside *Bloom House*.

"How did I…Jesus Christ! David!" My scream echoed through the house.

David's body lay beside me, covered in blood, glassy eyes staring right at me. Screaming, I tore myself from the floor, but fell again. There was blood everywhere, covering the walls, the old wooden floor. The stained-glass lamp illuminated the ghastly sight. I crawled to his body and checked his pulse, then started CPR, but it was too late. He was gone.

"David!" I screamed again, as if it would change the situation. I climbed back to my feet and looked for a way out. Everything was boarded up—the windows, the front door. I stood in what appeared to be the living room and dining area in one. A dust-covered dining table stood feet away from me. Four empty chairs. There were oil paintings on the walls, some throw rugs, hardwood floors blanketed in dust…dust that was recently disturbed.

Footprints trailed through the dust to the blood. A bloody footprint was near David's body. Was someone else in the house with me? Panic swelled inside of me. I felt close to passing out again. My head swam. My eyes welled as I stared at my best friend's body.

"David…" I whispered before hearing footsteps creak above. There was someone in the house. *I have to get out of here.*

I ran through the room, checking the doors and windows. None of them would open. A few of the windows were exposed, but wouldn't budge no matter how hard I pushed, and there was nothing to break them with. My flashlight was gone. The phone, too.

I raced down the hall and into the kitchen. A dripping faucet called from the shallow light. I crashed into a table and fell again. Footsteps shuffled above, rattling the floorboards. I glared at the ceiling. "No…no…no..." Tears streamed down my face. I pulled myself onto weak knees—felt sick to my stomach—then I spotted a door in the kitchen, half open. It was the basement.

I ran to the door and threw myself down the basement stairs, almost killing myself in the process. Darkness swallowed me once again. The room was cold, with rough floors, dank and musty. An earthy, damp smell hung thick in the air.

What do I do? How do I get out? My hands trembled, my chest ached from my heart pounding inside of it. I felt weak again, dizzy, my legs weakened.

No. I can't die here.

I reached out for the nearest wall and felt my way around. Footfalls thudded across the kitchen floor. Finally, I saw light glinting outside the only unblocked window in the basement, a streetlight! The basement door creaked. Footsteps clanked on the stairs.

No! I pushed myself against the window with all my weight. The glass popped, and I forced myself through it, falling to the ground. The next thing I knew, I was running at full speed, screaming until I reached home. Warm lights and the comfort of familiar surroundings calmed me down. I scrubbed my hands in the bathroom sink and into the mirror. I didn't recognize myself…I had aged. After catching my breath, I stood there and cried. David…

I found my way to the house phone and called the police.

"WHAT WERE YOU DOING in that house, anyway? That house is condemned…don't you know that?"

The officer's words stung. He was so angry at me. "I'm sorry, but you have to believe me. My friend David is dead. We were attacked. Someone or something pulled us into the house. There was blood everywhere. David's body was beside me on the floor. I was trapped in the house. The windows and doors were boarded up. I was stuck in there."

"Then how did you get out?"

"I crawled through the basement window. Someone was there, officer." I strained to remember his name, then glanced at the name on his shirt. "Officer Edwards. I heard him running around upstairs, then he came after me."

"There's no one there. The house is empty."

"There *is* someone there. He's killing people. David's wasn't the only body I saw. Open it. Open up the house."

"Calm down, sir."

"I'm not making this up. Please."

"We had calls come in of you screaming, running through the street. You're the one scaring the neighborhood. What are you trying to do?"

"Open the house, Officer. Do it, please. Open it!"

Hours later, in the dawn of the morning, we stood outside the house with a pissed-off looking man from the state. Apparently, the state-owned Bloom House, and they had never decided what to do with it.

The state's rep, Thornton, took us around the back of the house to a small basement door. He fished around for a bunch of keys and tried one or two in the lock. Finally, the door unlocked, and we eased it open. We went inside.

There were assorted colors of graffiti all over the rough stone walls. A layer of dirt covered the floor. It looked undisturbed. *Where were my footprints?* In the corner of the room, I saw the old furnace with its copper pipes sitting on a cement block.

We climbed the basement stairs to the main floor. More graffiti. Dust everywhere. Faded wallpaper rotted on the walls. Burnt wood, charred beams, and timber littered the room.

"Watch your step," Thornton said. "Last thing I need is some damned lawsuit."

We moved from the kitchen into the dining and living room. The ceiling leaked. The floor was cluttered with debris. Walls were black and scorched. I turned to my left and saw the one uncovered window, sunlight streaming through it. The antique lamp stood pristine on a table, but no blood. No bodies. No David. The room looked as it had for the last twenty years. My heart sank. *I'm losing my mind.*

"Satisfied?" Officer Edwards said with sarcasm.

"He was here." I pointed at the floor. "I didn't imagine it. I was in this house."

"Well, there's nothing here now. No murder. No crime scene." Officer Edwards turned to Thornton. "Sorry to bother you. We just had to be sure."

"Whatever. Let's get out of here. Place is dangerous."

"Exactly."

It was a silent walk all the way back to my house with Officer Edwards. I felt the contempt in him. We stopped in my driveway.

"I don't want to come back again," he said. "Stay away from that house. Walk your dog on another route. Don't go near that place again. Forget it even exists."

"Okay. What about David? I didn't imagine his visit."

"He probably went home in a panic after you passed out. Give him a call. Maybe this whole incident is a big joke he was playing on you."

"Maybe." I nodded. "That does sound like David."

"Get a good night's sleep." He climbed back into his patrol car and skidded off.

THAT NIGHT, AFTER ANOTHER dinner alone, I called David's apartment, but there was no answer. The only other thing I could think of was to call his sister Amy.

"Hey, Amy."

"Oh my God, hi! I heard you were back."

"Yeah, for a little while now. How have you been?"

"Oh, you know, the same."

"Sure, sure. I'm calling because I've been trying to reach Dave, but he's not answering. Is everything ok?"

"Yeah, he's great. He's in the Florida Keys on vacation with his boyfriend."

"He is?" *That's not possible. He was here. I know he was.*

"Yep, for almost a week now."

"Wow… that's…ah great. So good to hear he has a boyfriend."

"He's so happy. The two of them are inseparable. You have to meet Greg."

"Yes, I do. Well, I should go I…"

"Is everything ok?"

"I'm fine. Thanks Amy. Bye now." My voice grew softer. My thoughts drifted. Did I imagine the entire thing? No! David was here. He was here!

Maybe I did need to get a good night's sleep. I hadn't been sleeping well at all since…Dad…no further back than that. Ever since… Liam.

Bandit watched me with some concern as I crawled under my covers. I wanted the entire world to go away. I was done with this. No more house. No more ghost hunting. No more.

A loud rhythmic booming noise woke me in the middle of the night. Bass pounding from a car radio. The walls of the house vibrated. I listened to the car roll slowly up the road, up the hill. Rude.

I threw my covers aside and headed for a drink of water, eyes half open, stumbling into the hallway only to be greeted by someone standing there. A translucent figure draped in shadow.

My mind went instantly to George Bloom, but it wasn't exactly him. I wasn't sure who it was.

"David?"

The man turned away, his face still in shadow, and walked down the hall. I followed until he slipped right through my kitchen door. I raced to the door and yanked it open. Icy air bit into my face. A chill slithered through my soul. I reached the deck and saw Bloom House. A light on in its window. Damn that house!

The next thing I knew, I was running in the street barefoot, gravel and cold tar assaulting the soles of my feet. I didn't care, it was time to find the underlying cause of that blasted house. I was tired of looking at it, fearing it, needing it.

I stormed through the yard, eyes fixed on the window and its golden light, jumped onto the rock, grabbed the window ledge—

"What the hell are you doing?" a voice called behind me.

I turned to see a police officer standing in the yard with me. "Officer Edwards? I—"

"Didn't I tell you to stay away from here?"

"You don't understand. Something is going on…see the light?" I turned back to point it out. It was gone. No light. My hands trembled. "It was right there. I saw it!" I turned around to see someone rise behind Officer Edwards.

"Behind you!" Darkness swept me into unconsciousness.

I WOKE IN THE kitchen, staring at its blackened ceiling, listening to the deafening drip of the sink's faucet, and coughed before catching my breath. My eyes were heavy, blurry. I looked around the room and saw Officer Edwards' body. A knife protruding from his chest. I screamed. Rage surged through my body. Screams turning to wails. I crawled across the floor, hurling chairs out of the way, pushing the table across the ceramic tiles. I couldn't find my balance, my strength. I was too weak to get up.

"No! Goddammit no!" I looked around the room. "Where are you? Who are you?"

Like an answer to unholy prayers, footsteps scuttled across the floor above. I trembled as someone stepped onto the stairs, descending them step by step.

"Show yourself!" I pulled the knife from the police officer's chest. "You son of a bitch, show yourself!"

Shadows shifted across the walls. A man turned the corner, emerging from the dining room. I tightened my grip on the knife and looked into my father's eyes.

"Dad…"

He stared down at me, dressed in the jeans and white t-shirt I had always remembered him wearing, his face pale, his hair a mess. His mouth dropped open, and a baleful moan wailed out of him. He pointed an accusing finger at me and howled again. His face morphed, flesh shifting…

"Dad, no!"

He was Liam now… his eyes pain stricken, his body tearing apart in front of me, reaching out to me for help.

"Liam, why…? Why!"

The walls settled in around me, tighter, closer. Gunfire rattled outside. Bombs exploded all around the house. The room looked like my bedroom except there were no doors or windows. I pounded on the walls over and over. "Let me out! Please, let me out! Dad! Liam! Let me out…!"

I covered my eyes and screamed.

"You're okay now," a soft voice said.

I reopened my eyes to find myself in a hospital bed with a woman sitting beside me. "What happened?"

"I'm Dr. Levitz. Your neighbors heard you screaming and called the police. When they arrived, they found you unconscious. Paramedics brought you here. We couldn't find anything wrong with you, but we kept you hydrated, and here you are."

"They found me at home? In my house?"

"Yes."

"I wasn't in Bloom House?"

"Bloom House? No, you couldn't have been in that house. There hasn't been a Bloom House in over twenty-five years."

"What are you talking about? I live down the street from it."

"That's not possible. It was destroyed in a fire."

"What? God…what is happening?"

"It's okay. Your next-door neighbor explained. It's been hard for you, losing your father, your best friend, your dog, all within months of each other. It would be hard for anyone. You'll be okay. You just need to rest. You can go home in a few days, and we'll give you the name of some excellent professionals."

"But I…"

"Why don't you get some rest."

She got out of her chair and left the room. I stared into the hospital hall, nurses and visitors walking back and forth. Lunch carts, IVs, machines, stretchers, wheelchairs, all familiar trappings. I let everything drift past me and cried.

Bloom House.

I couldn't have imagined it. It was there…

I'm still there.

The Elevator in FKD Mall is a Hungry Sukebe

R.J.K. LEE

Definitely something in that shitty elevator. A presence in the one beside the FKD mall entrance near the first-floor food court that closes too early in our post-Covid era. Its hungry *sukebe* maw opens on the third floor between the coffee shop and game arcade, facing the costume shop, Halloween Hallows.

When you bicycle in and park at the fast-food court side, you can see the outside wall, beyond which the elevator rises and falls and waits, stained in pigeon shit and mold. You'd think the powers that be would clean that. Stereotype though it may be, Japan usually keeps things clean. Until they don't. Apparently. But it's not their fault. Don't blame others, my counselor told me, and like a good teenager I take my meds for POTS and everything that goes with it, autism or depression or imagining things or simple exhaustion and relentless pain. Japan doesn't provide great care for people like me, but I make do. I survive.

I do agree with my counselor, though. Don't blame other people. Blame the elevator itself.

I loved going to the FKD mall instead of taking the train one stop to another mall, because it gave me an excuse to bicycle with Sachi. Wind blew through our hair and our chatter sparked such joy. Nature unfolded before us, open spaces where we could escape the crowds and the pressure to be somebody else. At the bridge, we rolled our bicycles to the riverbank and stood them beside us like shields. While fish jumped in the river, our hands slipped together, hers sweaty and mine tingling with her warmth. We pumped our bicycles onto an empty farm road. I let her get ahead and admired the strength in her calves. We parked our bicycles before the rice fields and sat, watching grey herons wade through the mud to snatch up smaller amphibians to munch on. Then she kissed me and, shivering, I brushed her hair back from her forehead. Under the cover of our bicycles, we found freedom. The steel frames of those bicycles imbued with a guardian spirit that protected us and brought us that chance to find heaven in each other.

In contrast, some evil shitty *baka na mono* lurks in the generic steel gray frame of the FKD elevator. A darkness that doesn't protect. I knew it was watching me like a *sukebe* when perverse fingers brushed down my spine, likely mulling over abducting me when I entered its walls. To devour body and soul, I assume. Just the sort of crime peaceful malls in Tochigi need.

I've begged the unexplained presence to get it over with ever since the incident. Pathetic, I know, but maybe I'll see Sachi again that way. *Mata aitai na.* She's the best.

Her bicycle is still parked in front of the McDonald's side entrance. No one ever asked me where we parked our bicycles or looked for them, so I left hers there as a touchstone to remember our freedom and our joy, to encourage me to keep looking.

IT WAS ON THE first of October that Sachi entered the elevator on the third floor without me. She said she'd fetch us strawberry ice cream from Thirty-One while I finished choosing my costume. If only I hadn't waffled so long between vengeful ghost and horny alien.

Sachi was already slaying it with hers, a voluptuous devil with a pattern of curling flames. Stylish slices in the leather revealed plenty of her pale shoulder, boobs, and black fishnet bodysuit. Topped the outfit off with a curly tail, horns, and a ruby-studded pitchfork.

Typical bad-ass babe style, but perfect for that period of our lives. We had come out on that same day and visited the mall to celebrate by going on an official, totally-in-the-open date. We cruised through the neighboring shop plaza, tried on clothes in every shop, bought sale items at H&M and Zara, then headed into the main mall complex for lunch.

After plenty of wasabi-dipped sushi, we took the elevator up. It creaked and jerked. I cringed at the sounds, but Sachi laughed and squeezed my hand. "Watashi to ireba shinpai hitsuyo nai yo." She told me I didn't need to worry when I was with her, likely trying to comfort away my anxiety issues, but we had no idea then what was really lurking.

In the arcade, we sat in bloody red racing chairs and tossed shells at enemies. We posed dramatically in photo booths, then we popped in and out of stores, lingering over candy, toys, lingerie, and cosmetics. We bought costumes at Halloween Hallows, cosplay which we planned to wear the entire month in honor of our bravery to be queer and proud.

Sachi's parents had disowned her the moment she spoke up, weak ass bitches that they were. In a very Japanese, passive-aggressive, *maa maa maa* manner.

Mine applauded me for my honesty and invited more communication, though I spotted discomfort in their fidgeting fingers, hints of fearful conservative slipping in from strands of my Nigerian and Japanese heritage. "Sure this is what you want to be doing, my baby girl? If it is, then I'm feeling fine about it," said Mom. "Un," Dad grunted. "Shoganai na. Tanoshinde ne." He shrugged, downing another beer. At least he poured me one, too, for us to kanpai over.

I don't think my family fully appreciated the freedom I'd discovered. And I'm not sure they recognized my own fears. I hadn't shown them the hate lurking on our socials.

The elevator sat in clear view across the hall from the costume store entrance, between an aging, low-key, non-Starbucks coffee shop and the arcade rattling and sparkling with its UFO catchers and game machines.

Sachi poked the pitchfork at the elevator doors in jest.

I waved with a goth ghost dress in hand.

The ruby on her pitchfork flashed. "Hurry and put it on. That's gonna look so hot."

The elevator doors opened, empty of passengers. My stomach sloshed with unsettled sushi and shoyu. I pushed aside my anxiety, taking a step toward her, thinking I'd kiss her, tell her to wait, that I'd go with. But I stumbled. My sporadic symptoms of POTS lanced painfully through my leg. I leaned against a shelf and tried to wink at her. Probably looked like a wince.

"I'll be right back with the ice cream," Sachi said, and stepped inside the elevator. She put one high heel up on the elevator wall, calf muscles quivering, and flashed me. We had flirted like this all day, so in love and raised so high on hope and thrill now that we weren't hiding anything. I wouldn't have been surprised if she returned with a ring in the ice cream cone and a marriage proposal. As a live streamer, I was used to shutting down naughty attentions, but this was different. This was wholesome, erotic, and special rolled into a mind-blowing package. We had built toward this since childhood. It was so real.

I blew her a kiss and tossed my head back in mock orgasmic satisfaction.

To show her I was fine. To tell her to hurry back. To hide my unwarranted dread.

When I raised my head and looked at the elevator, the elevator doors thunked shut.

"Gone." I took a step onto the glossy tiles, as if to cross the hall and open the elevator up. I eyed the escalators two corridor turns away, as if I could race her downstairs to be sure she made it safely to the first floor.

A man cleared his throat from inside Halloween Hallows, and I jumped, yelping, "Yabai!"

"Sumimasen," the man said. He folded his arms across a gray button shirt with a pattern of recurring vampire bats below its collar. He wore a black leather mask with white fangs stitched on it.

I muttered to myself in English, certain the Japanese shop owner possessed zero language skills. "I sure hope you weren't watching us, prick."

He unfolded his arms and pointed at the ghost costume. Black leather gloves on his hands. "Kore de ii desu ka?" Gruff and to the point, he wanted to know if I was buying.

"Yeah. Hai. Kore de." This was the one. I passed it over.

He sniffed it, nodded, then pointed at the fake blood and webbing on a counter. Different scented varieties of makeup and accessories attracted my attention. I picked out a strawberry brand of blood to arouse Sachi. She loved strawberries. We had often bicycled past strawberry farms and bought ourselves baskets full.

SACHI NEVER CAME BACK from Thirty-One. She never exited that elevator again. They found her phone on the first-floor exit of the elevator, but nothing more. No shoes, no bloodstains, no hair when the police investigated. The mall closed for a week during investigations and resulted in nothing.

I hated that week. I wanted to go back and play the UFO catchers Sachi and I always played. Biking home from school alone, I avoided the crowds of other high schoolers. They whispered about me. I saw their furtive glances.

One pouty-eyed girl, Eriko, was brave or jaded enough to ask me out.

"Baka jyan," I said. "I am not a bitch's pity party. Sachi got eaten by a killer elevator and you think I want to chat over an ice cream with a rando?"

"Mari, she ditched you," Eriko said. "Ran away. Enough with the elevator. Let me—"

"Back off!"

After I rejected her, Eriko was like the rest, laughing at me, the one who lost her best friend to an elevator. The one who merely imagined it, right? Like she imagined her POTS. The one who made up all her pains and problems and needed more counseling.

THE MALL OPENED UP again with sales and promotions and respectful bunches of flowers in honor of the incident. Like when they celebrate the opening of a new restaurant. Seemed like misappropriation of her death when I thought of it that way.

But here I am, everyone. After a week of stopping by to stroke the steel frame of Sachi's bicycle, to remember cruising with her to the farms and freedom, to glower at the stained outer wall of that elevator, I've brought my own flowers. Added them to the hopeless collection, and now I'm looking for what took her. I'm staring at the elevator until my eyes hurt and passersby are asking if I'm okay.

Some evil shitty presence lurks in there. I know it. Just haven't spotted it yet. But you guys, my fans, maybe you can. I brought my gear: cams, mic, laptop, chargers. Whatever I need to maintain this live stream. Also, pepper spray, a knife, a baseball bat. Even salt and sharpened camping stakes. Three figurines for luck: fox, tanuki, cat. Just in case, I set it all up beside the elevator, then hit the button.

To the handheld cam, I'm giving you, my audience, a go-time, serious motherfucker gaze, but I'm fighting back tears. "Hey, thanks for watching as we do this. Whatever's in there is going to be seen. Whatever took Sachi is going to face me, and all of you keeping watch. If I don't make it, one of you carry the torch for us."

Hundreds of comments stream by while I wait for the elevator to arrive on the third floor.

Love: *OMG we got you Sachi and Mari! You both deserve better!*

Alongside the hate: *What a twisted, lying *****! What'd you really do to her?*

I salute the viewers and say, "Here goes."

A last-second message from Eriko: *Don't do it. I'm biking there now. Wait!*

Baka, I reply, adding eye-roll and sword-fencer emojis.

The elevator doors open, and I slide everything in. I check the camera feeds on the laptop. Elevator entrances on all four floors are covered. A fifth camera on the elevator wall, and a sixth lens attached to my forehead.

"Sprinkling salt round the area, people. Placing my figurines out for luck. Got my stakes ready. Let's nail this thing."

The doors close. I wait, listening. The walls creak and jerk. Static bursts on the camera feed. I raise my stake.

A yellow fog spirals from the walls, grabbing at me. It's slimy as mold.

I swing at it. The stake crunches. Useless. Stumbling, POTS pain spiking in my leg, I go to my knees and grab more supplies. Salt. I throw handfuls at it.

"Sizzling. Like it's burning. It's fucking burning! That's what we have to do."

The static on the camera feed turns violent and loud. Shit, the sizzling is my own damn skin bubbling like oil in a pan. Whatever this thing is, it's got me. I brush my arms to get it off and away, to give me time to run when the doors open, but I'm dissolving too fast and there's no way to stop it.

ERIKO ARRIVES AFTER I'VE already been sucked out of the metal box, so maybe she wasn't all bad, just late. I see her staring at the elevator. She tries calling.

My phone's just as dead as I am.

Mari takes my ethereal hand, and we hide before the elevator presence comes back. There's a lot of us ghosts hiding around the mall. I think maybe whatever the elevator presence is, it's here to play games. Deadly games.

Sachi says she saw the costume shop bat guy talking to the elevator, so if we can find some would-be savior to not freak out after reading the messages we lipstick onto bathroom mirrors, then maybe we can be the final girls. Another girl doesn't have to die.

Mari & Sachi killer = Hallows guy + elevator

The presence keeps smearing our messages into nonsense before anyone can read them, though. But we'll keep trying. Other surfaces, too: glass tables, coffee mugs, windshields in the parking lot.

It's almost Halloween, and the elevator opens hungrily. I can hear its stomach rumble through the walls of the mall as we pass through them.

I rattle our bicycles to warn the other high schoolers who park there.

Someone needs to listen. I don't think we have much time left before the next victim.

Like Velvet on His Neck

RYAN COLE

I heard the man running from two blocks away, his feet growing louder as he rounded the corner of Castro and Nineteenth Street, breath coming heavy in the chill San Francisco night. The thud of his over-worn sneakers on the pavement was all too familiar. It drowned in the car horns, the tires on asphalt, the oblivious chatter of the hundreds of people who acted as if they couldn't see him pushing past, couldn't bother with the men who were shouting from behind, chasing his heels as they had once chased me. To the city, the voice of his existence was a whisper. A minor inconvenience. A sound to be endured.

But to me—or the man I used to be—it was *everything*.

One block away, and I saw him lose his balance. I felt the crack of his knees as he fell on the sidewalk, hands scraped bloody, looking as lost as I had been in his place—before I'd been killed, and my soul repurposed, trading my flesh-and-blood body for concrete.

Over here! I desperately wanted to say. *Get up, get up! They're going to catch you!*

All of which died on the tip of my tongue. I knew what would happen if the man came towards me, knew I wouldn't be able to resist. So many nights of turning people away, so many dirt-streaked, disappointed faces, had led me to question the promise I had made to myself, and to my only friend left in this world. Had me willing to break it. No matter the cost.

Don't do it, said Cookie. *Wasn't last time bad enough?*

Her warning was a low-bass rumble in my scaffolding, as soft as the sweet dough baking in her ovens, pulsing the wood of the wall that we shared. It tickled my curtains, my purple felt carpet, the flickering marquee that hung on my face—so badly out of date—with *The Rocky Horror Picture Show Sing-along, tonight!* Half of the letters were either faded or missing. No one had seen *Rocky Horror* in months. All thanks to the padlock clapped on my doors.

One little mistake. One act of compassion. Now, I wasn't sure if I would ever re-open, would ever get the chance to serve the people I loved. If I opened my padlock, that chance might be gone. And with it, the scraps of my soul that remained.

Then Cookie again, her rumbling persistent. *He'll be fine on his own, Cas. Let him find his way.*

Easy for the soul of a bakery to say. Cookie, when alive, had a family to love her, a city that didn't try to make her feel invisible. Her voice, while small, was one people listened to, trading her time for full mouths and fuller stomachs. But for all of her kindness, she didn't understand. She didn't know the fear of a cold night alone, the sharp ache of not having eaten in days, the never-ending dread of where to sleep and what to wear, numb feet shivering in someone else's dirty blankets. Not like I did. The stares and the shame were carved into my skin, making me feel as if I were the problem, and this was all my fault.

Luckily, that was a lifetime away. My pain was in the past.

Or so I tried to believe.

Half a block away now, his breath coming ragged. The man's feet scraped on the trash-littered sidewalk, the hems of his ripped jeans covered in mud, and he came to a stop just a few feet away from the window of my ticket booth.

I cringed as he pressed cold hands into the glass, hungry eyes searching for a way to escape.

Keep going! I said, my windowpane rattling.

But the man didn't leave. He climbed on the ticket counter, knocked on the glass, and in the rapping of his knuckles, in the way his face crumpled up in defeat, I recognized his fear. Knew that if any of these men were to catch him, they wouldn't let him go, wouldn't let him live.

His was a fear I had felt many times. One I was determined to never feel again.

So, against my better judgment, in spite of the drawn-out sigh from next door and the inevitable *I told you so* lecture I would receive, I did the one thing I was not supposed to do. With a sharp, metallic click, I unfastened my padlock. I swung wide my doors.

And I let the man in.

I WASN'T BORN A theater. The days of my youth were still clear in my mind—when my mother still talked to me, and my father hadn't left, and the myth of our perfect family hadn't been shattered. Sometimes, I miss the simplicity of those days.

Sometimes, I wish I had been someone else. A person whose voice resonated with the city, a pitch so whittled that it didn't stand out.

But then, I'd remember what it was like to be *heard*.

I'd never forget—it was my third week alone, of sleeping by the sewer-shafts, of scrounging for just enough change to buy dinner. I wasn't used to the glares, the abrupt dismissals. The overwhelming fact of being nothing and nobody. That was what made the experience so special.

When the doors opened for me, and I walked under a marquee of bright, glowing letters, and the carpet seemed to guide me to a seat in the front row, walls thump-thumping with an eager hello, I felt, for the first time, that I was wanted. For once, I was someone who was worthy of attention.

After that day, I made the theater my home. Sleeping in the orchestra. Snacking on popcorn and nuts and cherry-cola. Hiding from the people and the voices and the city that had once spat me out and tried to grind me into dust. This was my place, where I was free to be me.

The theater agreed. Every night, it would unlock its wooden-panel doors, crank up the projector, and the two of us would sit in the comfort of each other.

It lasted for two months.

Until one day, my past caught up to me, and everything I had gained was ripped out of my hands.

BE QUIET, I SAID with a delicate rumble, the gaudy chandeliers on my ceiling starting to clink. *You're going to wake him.*

Cookie just huffed, a choppy release of the steam in her ovens, baking the sweet treats for which she was named. Ever since the man had barreled into my lobby, my friend had insisted on making me aware of every flaw in my decision. No matter that he was asleep, unarmed and barely clothed, his shirt missing half of its mismatched buttons. Every once in a while, he would flinch at the noise of our hushed conversation—the camouflaged words that only buildings can decipher, aside from those few lucky patrons we taught. But mostly, he sat there, his arms around his knees, his back to the wall and his eyes pressed shut.

I couldn't just leave him on the street, I said.

Yes, you could, said Cookie, her voice coming softly through the crawlspace connecting us, which allowed us to speak without the city overhearing. *You've done it many times over the last few months. What makes him so different?*

I shrugged, sending tremors through the cracks in my foundation. But deep down, I knew. The more I watched him, the more I liked him. The more of my once-human self I saw in him. *He needed me*, I said. *It was the right thing to do.*

Cookie grumbled at me, a well-practiced response. *You know what will happen. The Bars made it clear. If you keep housing vagrants, they'll shut you down for good.*

The memory of the threat made me clench my locked doors, sent a long-buried shiver up my brick-laden spine. *You don't belong here anymore*, the Bars had said to me and Cookie. They had rumbled from the corner of Castro and Market Street, tinny with the echo of the night's DJ track, their voices all sticky with the liquor on their floors. *You aren't any fun. And the riffraff you bring around only hurts our reputation.*

Fun—the Bars' lifeblood, the key to their existence. They acted as if it were the only thing that mattered—more than their patrons, or the lives we tried to save. So, I knew full-well they would carry out their threat. They had come at me before—both in life, and after.

Cookie's voice shifted from annoyed to concerned. *Once they find out, they'll send more than just the patrons. They'll call the police.*

We both knew the painful implication of that word. Of where it might lead: citations, inspections, or even worse, *demolition*. All of my hard work turned into nothing.

I have to help him, I said, trying hard to sound confident, to stifle the old fear seeping into my walls.

But of course, Cookie heard. *I know*, she whispered, a matronly smile coming through the vibrations. *Just promise me, Cas. Be careful this time.*

What was there to say? She knew the repercussions, knew the Bars would blame her too. Yet she welcomed the risk. She put her needs below mine. Just like the mother I never had and always wanted.

Walls quietly trembling, I whispered, *I promise.*

LATER THAT EVENING, THE man woke up. Bleary-eyed, he peered through the window on my door, presumably searching for the Bars' angry minions. But they were long gone. It was just the two of us now, with Cookie close by, pretending not to listen as she baked the next day's stock.

It's okay, I tried to tell him, my chandeliers clinking. *You're safe now, don't worry.*

The man glanced at my gently humming ceiling. There was no recognition in his wide green eyes. Not that I could blame him. The first time the theater had spoken to me, I hadn't heard it either. Regardless of the fact that we had wanted the same thing, its voice had been foreign. It had taken many nights for me to begin to understand.

I rippled the fibers of my purple felt carpet, trying to guide him, to lead him inside. But he quickly backed away.

Not how I wanted our relationship to start.

Come rest, I said. *Have something to eat.* I fired up the stove tucked behind the candy counter, bracing myself for the rush of hot air as the kernels started to crackle, the butter to melt. I filled up one of my buckets to the brim, and I wiggled the bottom onto the surface of the carpet, let it ride on the rippling threads across the room, only stopping when it tapped on the toe of the man's sneaker.

I kept my walls silent, my chandeliers still, hoping he'd see that I wasn't a threat. I knew he was hungry, even though he didn't show it. A symptom of never knowing when the next meal would come. Of hiding his pain from those who didn't want to see it.

But this time, hunger won. He tore through the popcorn, green eyes constantly looking over his shoulder for the nonexistent people who would try to steal his food. Seeing him do it made me think of myself. When I was his age, always one meal away from an ever-hollow stomach.

The man stared into the now-empty bucket. He held it out in front of him, eyes to the ceiling. *More?* that look said, hopeful, pleading.

And there was our truce.

With my rippling carpet, I led him to the counter, determined to do what I had never done before. I thumped on the glass near a carton of gumdrops, hard enough to send them all sprawling onto the surface. I jiggled the glass until each of the multicolored candies was arranged in a string of uneven, and oddly shaped, letters.

"Cas," said the man, under his breath. "Is that your name?"

I swelled with the excitement of the word on his lips. No one, besides Cookie, had spoken it in years. *That's right!* I tried to tell him, my walls starting to rumble.

He blinked in surprise, still wary, still hesitant. "I'm Charlie," he said, and he held out his hand, pressing the warmth of his fingers into my glass.

Later on, I led him into the heart of the theater—all the way to the front row, smack-dab in the center, to the seat I had sat in on my first night here. The seat I had slept in, and lived in, and dreamed in. The seat in which the theater had helped me find myself.

Charlie eased into the fuzzy red upholstery. His body felt warm, and when he leaned all the way back, his neck brushed delicately up against my fabric, as soft as a kiss.

We would sit there, like this, for many nights to come. He in my arms, and me in his eyes, watching the flickering screen on the wall as my projector in the back slowly put him to sleep. I fed him my candy, I poured him my soda, I made him believe that all his troubles were behind him.

Not everyone, however, was as happy as we were.

You're growing too attached, Cas, Cookie would say, her oven-racks hissing in their overprotective way. *You can't give him what he wants, what he needs to be happy.*

But couldn't she see? Charlie was special. My patrons only saw me for what I could give them, but with him, someone saw me for the man I truly was. A protector, a home for the ones who didn't have one. I needed him as much as he needed me.

I'm telling you, Cookie was fond of repeating. *This isn't a good idea.*

Somewhere, deep in the bowels of my foundation, I suspected she was right. And yet, I still didn't listen, didn't want to believe her, didn't want to break the best thing I had found in years.

Something had me caught.

Was it love? Maybe…

I WAS NINETEEN YEARS old when the Bars came for me. So sick of hiding, so sick of running my feet into the ground. Back then, the theater was still open to the public. It was only closed at night, those scant few hours when the world was a distant and existential threat. In the daylight hours, I was back on the street. Lurking and hoping that no one would see me.

And yet, they already had. I just didn't know it.

One of their patrons caught me just after dusk. He was waiting in the shadows of the alley out back, near the small, struggling bakery that always snuck me cookies. I didn't hear him behind me. Only felt his hot, liquor-slick breath on my ear, his muscular arm like a pipe around my neck. *You don't belong here,* he said as I squirmed in the darkness, his voice gone slurry with the echo of his employers.

And as I desperately tried to break free of his grip, my hands going numb, my head throb-throbbing with too much blood, I remembered, for the first time, thinking he was wrong.

THE MOVIE HAD JUST ended—a rerun of *Mary Poppins*, the sing-along version. I kept the lights dimmed as I shut off the projector. Charlie didn't move. He slept with his knees tucked up to his chest. I watched him as the theater had once watched me, before it had saved the broken pieces of my soul, catching me just as I untethered from my body. The latest iteration of a decades-long cycle.

Which made me think of Cookie. *This isn't a good idea.*

And why couldn't it be? We were good for each other. Why was that so hard for my friend to understand?

I softened my fabric to kiss him goodnight, and that was when I heard it: a tinkle of glass, the slap of heavy feet as they landed on my carpet.

Charlie heard it, too. His eyes snapped open and he jumped from his seat. "What was that?" he said, not waiting for an answer. He bolted down the aisle towards the door to the lobby.

I saw him clearly now—a man in my doorway, standing in the newly shattered glass of my window; he was pulling someone else through the hole he had created.

Don't! I said to Charlie, but of course, he didn't listen. He ran to my concession stand, grabbed a hot canister of butter from the stove, and he dumped it on the man who had broken my barrier.

The man began to shriek. He dropped the heavy arms of his friend in the window, who tumbled out onto the pavement. The skin on his neck had turned a cherry-syrup red, his eyes a blistering pink. "It's him!" he said, snarling. "Throw me the—"

Charlie's fist popped him in the jaw mid-sentence. But not quickly enough. I knew that voice. It was the last thing I heard on the night I had died.

Frantically, I rippled my carpet out in waves, causing the patron to stumble and fall. He landed on his back, underneath my chandelier, and with a well-timed *click*, I let one of the candelabras fall from its chain, cracking in half on the man's outstretched leg.

Then Charlie was on him. Punching him, knocking his face bruised and bloody. Bits of the man's teeth all around them on my carpet.

Let go of him! I said, my walls all a-rumble. No matter how much I wanted Charlie to win, I knew that if he killed the man, the Bars wouldn't stop. They would chase Charlie down, and there wouldn't be anything I could do to keep him safe.

Charlie seemed to notice. He looked at the blood all smeared on his knuckles, looked at the man underneath him on the floor, and he shuffled away to the back of the candy counter.

Which gave me my chance. I unfastened my padlock, I opened my doors, and I tossed the Bars' patron like the trash that he was out onto the sidewalk, slamming them shut before he could even stand up.

I watched as the two men ran up the street, limping, to the corner of Castro and Market.

Charlie slumped onto his knees on the floor, a smile on his lips, blind to the raging can of worms he had opened.

He may be alive. We may have won today's battle.

But there was no question. The men would be back.

THREE DAYS PASSED. THREE days of watching old movies in my theater, of desperately trying to forget what had happened. Charlie ate his popcorn, he guzzled his soda, but when he looked at me, eyes staring dully at my screen, their green didn't hold the same sparkle, the same joy. I noticed his mind was somewhere several blocks away. Somewhere I would very much rather it didn't go.

I knew it was only a matter of time. In the dozens of others I had helped over the years, I had seen this behavior—of holding a grudge, obsessed with the wrongs he could avenge beyond my walls, where I couldn't protect him. If Charlie were to go, he might never come back. A victim of the Bars like so many before him.

So silly of me to think he would leave them in the past.

"I want to leave," said Charlie, his face to the ceiling.

I froze, not willing to lose another friend. If I pretended not to hear, then maybe, just maybe, he would decide to change his mind. Charlie was different. *He was supposed to be different.*

Then he said it again. "I want to leave, Cas," his fingers digging into my upholstery, rough skin pulsing with pent-up anger. "I'm tired of running. I'm tired of hiding." I saw it in the way his lips began to quiver, heard it in the double-bass boom of his heartbeat—Charlie was scared. And yet, he didn't let that stop him.

I softened my fabric to help him relax, but he winced at my touch. "It's the only way," he said. "We have to fight back."

A dangerous way to think. If I relented, if I let Charlie do what he wanted, the Bars and their patrons would find him and end him, leaving me empty—both in body and soul.

I won't let you, I said, my walls quietly rumbling.

But Charlie didn't listen. He trudged resolutely to my wooden-panel doors, and he reached for the handle.

At that moment, I panicked. I clicked shut the deadbolt, locking him in.

My doorframe shook as he jiggled the handle. Pulled until his face turned red, veins bulging.

With a huff, he let go—but not in defeat. He scavenged my hallways, the breadth of my lobby, the dust-covered air vents and moldy broom closets, for another way out. Which he wouldn't ever find. I had intentionally kept my other exit a secret. Feverishly hoping this moment wouldn't come.

When he gave up, I exhaled in weary relief, safe in the knowledge I had done what was right—for me, and even though he didn't know it yet, for Charlie. He stood there, inspecting my door for several minutes. "Whatever," he said. "You win, Cas. I'll stay." Grumbling, he walked back into my theater, both of his hands balled up into fists. He passed by my seats and curled up on the floor.

We lay there together, in uncomfortable silence, for the rest of the night.

And I wondered if the two of us weren't so alike after all.

THEY CAME BACK THE next evening. And this time, they weren't alone.

Red lights flashing on the face of my marquee, I watched as a cop car parked at my doorstep. Four people emerged—three men and one woman. The woman and one of the men were in uniform, head-to-toe blue, with guns at their waists. Behind them were the disgruntled patrons from before. They waited by the car as the policewoman approached me.

Get up! I said to Charlie. *They're here! You have to hide!*

Charlie didn't move from his blanket on the floor. He picked at his fingernails, ignoring my rumbles, just as he had done since I had locked him inside. Couldn't he see? This wasn't a game. There was only so long I could keep the woman out.

If they find you, they'll arrest you, I said, my walls shaking.

That caught his attention. Or perhaps it was the rattle of the glass in my windows, the shouts from outside, the clink of the chain as the policewoman unwound the padlock from my handles.

Charlie sat up, shoulders tense, eyes wide.

Oh, no, I thought, as he started to run.

I caught him with my curtain in the door to the hallway, felt folds wrapping like rope around his ankles. He kicked at my fabric, but still I held onto him, didn't let him go. Didn't let him do the one thing that he shouldn't, that would send him to jail for the rest of his life.

I jolted as the padlock finally clicked open. Shuddered as the chain fell limp on the sidewalk. The policewoman kicked at my unguarded door. Yet I maintained the deadbolt, groaning as her boot chipped into my wood.

Distracted by the door, I let loose my curtain. Charlie kicked free. And as he ran past the candy counter into my lobby, my hinges gave in, glass flying everywhere.

The policewoman stepped, breathing hard, across my threshold. She coughed on the dust that was pluming from the floor. When she saw Charlie there, fists up in front of her, it felt like my disparate worlds had collided. The pain of my past and the joy of my present, mixing together like oil and water. Neither could live while the other existed.

She held up her gun, finger on the trigger.

Unthinking, I rippled my carpet at her feet, tugged with as much of my strength as remained.

Her bullet went wide, tearing through the thin, dusty glass of the concession stand. The woman fell over with a resonating thud.

Thankfully, Charlie seemed to realize his error. This was a fight he was not meant to win. Freedom or vengeance; he couldn't have both.

Scrambling, he dove past the curtains on the floor, into the hallway that led to the theater. He ran all the way to the front row, searching. But there was nowhere to hide.

Over here, said Cookie, her hot ovens hissing. Her thin walls rattled by the entrance to the crawlspace that connected our foundations, long boarded up. *Quickly, they're coming!*

I could hear the policewoman limping through the lobby. Stomping on my carpet, drawing ever closer.

Not much time. Not much of a choice. And despite my reluctance, despite the inevitable sorrow that would come, Charlie had to do the one thing I had feared: in order to survive, he couldn't hide. He had to leave.

I had to let him leave.

Carefully, I unhooked the latches on the crawlspace, using my carpet to guide him to the entrance. After Charlie crawled in, I refastened the door. Watched him as he scuffled to the hole in the alley, dirty clothes gradually fading into the darkness.

I imagined I heard him turn around as he left, imagined my name on his scruffy, perfect lips. "Thanks, Cas," a ghost of a whisper.

And then he was gone.

WE DIDN'T SEE EACH other for close to a year. I started to wonder if we ever would again, if the choice I had made had been right, was worth something. Cookie tried to soothe me in her usual way. *You did the right thing, Cas. I'm proud of you*, she'd say. But for all we knew, Charlie was dead or locked away in a jail cell. And while I was being renovated—thanks to an old, wealthy patron from downtown who had persuaded the city to overlook my crimes—I worried the worst had become of my friend. That my fate was his. That the cycle continued.

Then, on a chilly afternoon, he proved me wrong.

I heard his quiet footsteps as he walked up the street. His jeans weren't ripped, his sneakers were intact, his cheeks were shaved clean of their once messy stubble, green eyes scrubbed of their perpetual fear. He looked sure of himself, of where he belonged. He looked like a man who had been given another chance.

He purchased a ticket from the woman in my ticket booth, grinned at the bold blinking lights on my marquee. When he stepped on my carpet, and the voice of his existence gently sank into mine, it felt like before, like nothing had changed. But it had. I could hear it. All for the better.

He sat in his seat in the very front row, his skin on my fabric, so warm and familiar. And as the lights began to dim, and he sank into my arms, I cradled his neck with all the love I could hold, like a kiss of red velvet.

The Abyss and The Apex

J. DANIEL STONE

I listen for the voices because I don't want to see their bodies. Echoes and specters, apparent apparitions. They've been with me for quite some time now.

But to see them, I choose not.

To see them is to question reality.

"A SQUARE CAN NEVER fit a circle," Jocynda said over and over.

Her cheekbone drove into my shoulder like a knife, hand-rolled cigarette wriggling as would a worm between her lips. Nobody was stranger in my life than Jocynda. Thin as sidewalk chalk, funeral-chic clothing style, and Shoggoth hair. She made the ordinary freak seem normal, given that she looked as if she'd been drawn by Edward Gorey…but pumped full of blood.

"Just like *onion* can never be a palindrome," I said in a jocose manner.

"You making fun again, Ginny?" Jocynda curled one of her maroon lips.

Barely twenty-nine and Jocynda had already been pronounced dead twice, but somehow, she kept coming back. She was a purveyor of experimental drug use and addicted to the solace at the bottom of a liquor bottle. There had been jail time and rehab stints, but she walked out of those establishments, a ghost none the wiser. It seemed she was bored of life; nothing could satiate Jocynda's endless hunger for change, not even her failing health. Nothing scared her, nothing made her bat an eye.

"This nail polish sucks," Jocynda said, showing me her ugly-colored nails.

"Want me to get it off?"

"No. You stink like beer, Ginny."

I chinked the bottle of Magic Hat against my teeth. "So do you."

She got up and placed herself in an old rocking chair, occupying it like a schizophrenic on the run from demons. But that was what drew me to her. Jocynda was the love of my life. I could watch her for hours; she delighted me so. It didn't bother me how much she drank or how much she talked to herself, or how the cigarettes deepened her voice. All that mattered was that she was with me, sane or not, happy or not. I would take care of her forever.

"Piece of shit, filthy chair!" She smeared black lipstick on the headrest, deepening the level of spooky that naturally enticed me. "I can't smoke in this damn thing."

Moonlight illuminated our motel window, casting a bright ribbon across my hand as I opened the dusty curtains. A gasp left my lips at how terrifyingly empty downtown Detroit was. I watched the city with owl eyes. I've always found cities to be generally scary. Turn one corner and you don't know what you'll find. Enter a building and you might never find your way out. Every city has a voice, every city is hungry.

"Look at it out there."

"It's as cold and lonely as me," Jocynda snarled.

"Wide and empty, as I."

Jocynda's passion in life was to travel. Obviously, she was running from something she never wanted to talk about. This has led us to many places far and wide, sunny and cold, dusty and dirty. Miami was a shiny vampire's city, overcrowded and poisoned by too many pastels; the helter-skelter of San Francisco left me with liquor-laced nightmares, and Chicago's winds literally swirled my brain. We languished over buildings tall as the sky as much we did tenement housing that lay squat and crumbling.

But Detroit? The greatest culture shock of all. Ramshackle city with hardly a car on the street. It looked more dead than alive, even though I did not sense the presence of ghosts. There was only a brooding abandonment, as if the city was waiting for something. If I listened closely, I could hear the buildings sigh, crack and creak.

What the fuck went wrong with this city? I thought.

BEFORE JOCYNDA BECAME ADDICTED to avoiding her thoughts, she busied herself with making art. Those were the days when we were based between Manhattan and Brooklyn, which was a haven for people like us. But Jocynda never hung out with any clique or crowd; she was a natural-born loner, aside from my company. Creating took time and focus, and Jocynda never liked the idea of answering to other people. How lucky I was that she was into me!

Her art was never confined to a specific medium. The internal guide was *need* and self-expression was her calling. If she wasn't painting, then she was penning whiney poetry in the dark. If she wasn't scribbling, then she was making music with a beat-up guitar. If she wasn't sewing rags together, she was stretching her bones in ways that made modern dance seem ridiculous. And each time she completed a project, Jocynda would fall into a hypnotized state that left her lips so dry they cracked and bled once they formed words again.

"Is that a new dance?" I once asked.

"One day you'll get me, Ginny. One day you'll let me *breathe*."

Jocynda's back was against the wall, bare toe grazing Lana Del Rey's lips on the vinyl record slipcase cover. She'd smoked a Pall Mall down to the filter, and even then, she took a final drag. I'd caught her in a candid moment, disheveled hair, shirt pulled up so that I could smell her armpits, see the dark breasts and even darker nipples. I wanted to run my tongue across them for the taste of caramel, paint them with kisses. But she was at such an interesting angle I could do nothing but stare, abhorred that her spine hadn't yet snapped.

"I admire you."

Jocynda righted herself. "But you don't get me."

"I know you better than I know myself." I raised my cup of wine to her.

Jocynda rolled her dark eyes. "Wine this early?"

"It's five o'clock somewhere."

As drifters, we had to take whatever job came our way. I wasn't the type to beg in the street, but Jocynda didn't mind. I much preferred something stable, but finding a job in Manhattan was not as easy as it was in our parents' generation, especially when that person was a queer girl, had some tattoos, a lip ring, and gauges in her ears. Those folk had all migrated to Brooklyn.

Bushwick had become the melting pot of art and culture, and the small businesses lining the avenues sought people like me. Multitudinous windows displayed a *HELP WANTED* sign, so odd jobs were strangely plentiful, if you accepted that getting paid a small wage under the table would be offset by the tips. For me, the reality was that any income was good, so I took whatever work I could find.

But then came the third Sunday in August of last summer. Jocynda kept me up the entire night before my shift, so I was irritable and exhausted. Must have been why tips were so bad. Her diatribe raged as usual, overwrought with a thin anger and envy. A bad dream, a monster in the closet. She talked about how she was already a ghost, and then changed the subject to something cosmic and deep, or deeply comical. We drank until the sun warned me that if I fell asleep, I'd not make it to work. So, I spent my shift hung over.

That night, on my walk home, something happened. New York City summers are brutal and can be very wet even when it doesn't rain. The humidity becomes so heavy you can lose your breath. I lit a cigarette and noticed the zippo flame blew out before I had the chance to close it. Simultaneously, so did half the streetlights. I heard a series of snaps, crackles, and pops. When it's this hot out, blackouts are common.

Night rushed over me as the tide does land. I felt it go through my hair, sizzle like electricity on my skin. The world suddenly felt weighted, burrowing into me. The cigarette was gone before I knew it, leaving me with the taste of ash in my mouth. I heard someone talking, but it was muffled, so I shrugged it off.

"You don't get me."

The voice was not too far ahead. I flicked open my pocketknife and looked between the dark spaces, alas, finding no corporeal being. But then something fluttered across my vision. Just as a moth beats itself against a lightbulb until it fries, I too was tempting something I knew would hurt me, but I could not stop myself from finding out.

I walked in the direction of the voice. A car alarm went off, a young kid ran past me bouncing a basketball and I nearly sucker punched him. Above me, dozens of air conditioners dangled unsafely and sounded like dying motors. If one dropped on my head, I'd be done for. When I regained focus, my path devolved into utter black. I couldn't see the buildings or the road in front of me.

From my view, Manhattan was half dark. A rather queer sight for a city of gargoyles and spires that stabbed the sky in a grotesque manner. I set my sights on the east river to distract myself and control my thoughts. But something was happening. The water was rising way too high, splitting off into dark funnels that chewed the shoreline. It even made a gargling sound. Then there was only the outline of something vapid and shapeless.

That's when my phone rang. *Jocynda*. Spitfire. I barely understood her, and that confused me, being that I spoke her madness fluently. There was an inflection in her voice I'd never heard before. I thought maybe she was up to something stupid again, creating a new type of art, a twisted cut up not even William S. Burroughs could imagine; maybe she'd sniffed too much glue.

"Did you see it?" I heard her say before the line cut out.

See it? I thought to myself. *How could she have known?* The fear in her voice filled me with dread. But nothing prepared me for the whisper that I heard.

"Let me go."

And then the tall body made an awful sound, fully charging in my direction. I felt it embrace my bones as if it wanted to pull them out of my skin. I fell into an infantile state, cradling my knees to my chest, bruising my cheek as I rubbed it into the concrete. I bit my lip, forgetting about the piercing. Blood came fast, and I knew I would regret the pain later, but it alleviated the vision, so I welcomed the salty pain. It was four blocks of torture before I found the train, questioning myself.

When I got home, Jocynda had turned our apartment upside down. Now, you gotta realize that in Brooklyn, most places are trash to begin with. They can build new buildings or renovate firetraps, but for people with little money like Jocynda and I, we were subjugated to the shittiest of room and board.

At first, the twister of clothes and upturned furniture was nothing out of the ordinary. It stunk of Jocynda and showcased her usual oddities. I would never put it past her to lose her temper and destroy our home. But there were things I never expected her to ruin. Rare posters were torn to shreds, books were ripped in two and stomped on. There were blood spatters and illegible prose was written everywhere; even the lava lamp was shattered, and a sad green glob winked at me from the floor.

"You better let me go!" Jocynda scowled.

"What are you talking about?"

She crawled out of the kitchen, fast as a roach, as if something was controlling her. She wasn't the girl I was in love with, but an unnatural thing. Hair gripped her face like starfish do to rocks, nails bleeding against the cheap tile. I couldn't see her eyes, couldn't make out the sly curve of her mouth, but I knew her face wasn't right. It was as if she was looking into me, deep into me as her eyes burned and her teeth ground to powder.

And then she stood, turned on the kitchen light, scaring herself as if she'd not known how bright it would be. That's when I realized what was truly going on. She'd been painting something terrible. Maroon smudges polluted the walls, shaped very much like the body I had seen, and behind that a sea of endless black threaded with small points of light. Maybe she'd taken the drugs one step too far; maybe the dance routine she was teaching herself cut oxygen off to her brain.

"We're leaving," I told her firmly. "And we're never coming back."

Even as we departed, all I could think about was what happened to me.

"I MUST BE A ghost," Jocynda said. "Can't feel my fingers."

"Isn't that neuropathy?"

"Cyanosis, actually."

"So you *do* listen to the doctor every now and again."

"Only when I feel like it."

I took her hands in mine, hoping to transfer warmth to the skin that was now as blue as her nail polish. The contrast of our coloring looked unnatural. No human should have been that hue. I didn't know what to do other than hold her hand. But after a while, she grew bored with me and put gloves on.

"I think I'm dead."

"Will you stop that."

We'd been walking through the treacherous streets of Detroit. It was an arid place that wanted to be taken as seriously as New York or Chicago, but was nothing more than a sad blot of ink on the world map. Not even the gentrification efforts have made this place interesting. Detroit is a city that has been paralyzed by its own ruin.

Jocynda was the first to notice how night changed the look of the oncoming blocks. It flooded the pavement listlessly, licking anything in its path. Hardly a soul out here, but with the unbearable weather, it made sense. Cold like this would keep anybody inside, but the homeless were rampant. We walked past sad local dredges scrawling angry poetry, *NoT a MoNsTeR* and *THE D!* their skin grey as the grave and glowing jaundiced eyes. The sight deepened my understanding of this cemetery city.

We trotted through the snow-white streets looking at trinkets through store windows, trying to forget New York as if it was a wasted relationship. I never wanted to talk about what I saw, but Jocynda made me remember through poetry, portraits, and terrible songs. I asked her to stop throwing it in my face, but she would only shrug, as if she didn't care about my feelings.

The snow was coming down fast. Walls of grey swallowed the skyline; businesses were frozen, literally and figuratively, and would sadly remain that way until a greater power saved this city. I grabbed Jocynda by the waist, and for the first time in a long time, I kissed her. Not a squeamish peck, but a deep soul kiss, my tongue invading her mouth without resistance.

She breathed heavily. I felt her breast through her coat, thought about her nipples, ran my hand across the buttery slide of her neck. She always had such velvety skin. She kissed me back this time, ran her hand up the inside of my thigh and pressed her gloved hand over my vulva. For a split second, the world stopped; I thought I heard something trailing us before realizing that was my heart in my ears.

"What's wrong?" Jocynda asked. "Don't you like me?"

"Your kiss tastes like ash."

The wind picked up. There came a loud boom, like a bulldozer crushing a car. I covered Jocynda with my body, waiting for impact. The ringing inside my head grew louder and the heaviness in my chest pressed so hard against my lungs that I nearly passed out. It was the end of the world; I was sure of it.

And for one moment of madness, I saw them. No escaping them now. Dark bodies, nothing that could have been mammalian in any sense of the word. Jocynda pushed me aside and ran towards them. I screamed in protest, but she said that she needed to *see* clearly. Luckily, my feet became possessed by newfound power, propelling me past Jocynda to block her trajectory. She crashed into me, and we slid on ice until we hit a hard stop on an abandoned car.

"The fuck is wrong with you?" Jocynda said.

"You don't know what they are."

"Yes, I do," she said assuredly. "They're me!"

"What the hell do you mean?"

Now the snow came down fluffier and darker. Not snow. Ash. So much of it. I stood up and looked about the suburbs, a once white landscape now stained grey. Jocynda snarled. Her face was streaked with dark lines.

"I can't feel my hands."

"The doctor said—"

"Fuck the doctor!"

She bolted into a forgotten place. My phone said that we were in an area called Brush Park. The houses wilted cryptically, and the bare-bone trees seemed to rise straight out of the concrete. A Victorian tragedy. Brush Park's desolation was written in plain sight on its vacant mansions, words like *DECOLONIZE* and *PEAR DOMINATION* in bright aerosol. The city was so far away now, a smear of smog and ice. But Jocynda was suddenly a child in a candy shop. She ran and ran, turning on Adelaide Street, and nearly disappeared.

The house she stopped at had a spired roof and its edifice was mostly timeworn brick. Beautiful in its decay, but the way vines crawled through the boarded windows proved it had not been occupied for a long time. I caught an image out of my peripheral vision: a candelabra lit by the ghost of flame. Jocynda must have seen it as well, because she scaled the gate, kicked in the door, and let herself into absolute black.

"…AND AT THE BOTTOM of every abyss is the apex," Jocynda read from her book of poetry.

"What does that mean?"

"For me to know and you to find out, Ginny."

The house stunk of abandonment, as if loneliness could have its own smell. By the purity of moonlight, I focused my attention on the gutted foyer, peeling damask wallpaper, and the collapsing ceiling. Beneath my converses, a grand Chinese carpet curled into itself, and on the wall next to me intricate shadows spilled through lace curtains.

Jocynda planted herself onto a rocking chair. I was taken aback by the exquisite damage that had been done by weather and time as much as I was by the things that remained untouched. I lit a black pillar candle and moved my hand over the flame for warmth. The dampness of the temperature exchange reminded me of the special wetness between Jocynda's legs.

"Wanna warm up your hands?" I said.

"No." Jocynda's eyes were on me, hollowed, full of too much thought.

I walked into the next room, one that could only be considered the living quarters. There was Victorian ephemera everywhere. Pince-nez, brandy glasses, books, bonnets, and top hats. Antiquated bottles, pigeon feathers, and rat droppings. A deck of tarot was spread out. I noticed the Queen of Swords, The Devil, The Moon, Past, Present, and Future. A sardonic sign?

"It's warm in here," Jocynda said. "These old houses are insulated well."

"I'm freezing."

Jocynda lit a cigarette. "You're weird."

I lit one as well and inhaled, only to cough half of the smoke out. This sent my brain into a strange place, like reality lost itself somewhere between twilight zone and nightmare. A slow gurgling sound bellowed below me. I put my ear down onto the floor, hearing an old boiler, or frozen pipes, trying to pass water through them. Not that at all. *Voices*. But there were no vessels to house them. They were part of the house. Part of me.

I was hopelessly trapped.

Jocynda made sure of it.

The warped ceiling leaked a red fluid, like bloody bath water. It would not surprise me if this house had been a host for suicides and murders in all the years it had been around. There was too much history for that *not* to have happened.

"Every house has a story," Jocynda said.

Had she read my mind?

"Every city has a story."

She was babbling again.

"Every person has a story."

As the water crept down the walls, I made Jocynda look up, but she denied the sight. She was a bad listener. It was then I saw the bottle of beer in her hands—I'd no clue where she got it—and her breath instantly smelled of hops. It made my mouth water.

"I want some."

"Well, you can't have any."

Red dripped onto my face. I swallowed dryly, but my throat might as well have been stone. I had no more words. Neither did Jocynda. A full bar appeared before us, but in terrible disarray. Bottles of beer were knocked out of their holders and liquor spilled from ornate cabinetry. What should have been puddles became so much more. I saw the dreams that I thought had died back in New York. They infiltrated the skeleton of the house, bringing it to life, forcing it to molt. I wanted to scream. *Please, just let me scream*, I thought. *Scream and it will all be over.*

But there was no time. Jocynda had cried out for help. I ran into the other room to see that Jocynda had removed her gloves, her arms lifted above her head. The only thing I saw were stubs. Her hands were gone! *I can't feel them, Ginny…can't see them*, she whispered. I grabbed her and hauled ass so that we made an elaborate, but loud, escape through the front window. We landed on a pile of cardboard, our clothes sprinkled with glass and red snow. I carried her the rest of the way back to the motel.

HOURS LOST, DAYS INTO nights, each week blended into the other. The sky never changed, and the sun was never bright. Winter incapacitated Detroit. Temperatures reached record-breaking lows.

My dreams blended curiously with my nightmares. Being cooped up brought out the worst in me. I quickly burned out, mentally and physically. Jocynda only talked about the house, despite being nearly bed-ridden.

"We're not going back there," I said.

"As if I'd ever listen to you," Jocynda howled.

She threw up her hands, and they were as normal as they'd ever been. What had I seen? Had she seen it as well? We didn't talk about it; she had bigger fish to fry. Jocynda took her current frustration out on drawing. Our motel had become her literal studio, and she would not leave it until she was well and ready. I stapled the illustrations upon every wall, draped them across furniture, even piled them in the sink like dishes. Black and purple spirals twisting into red skies and orange terrains. Nothing made sense to me, much like the reality of our relationship. But I knew that if she didn't get whatever it was out of her head, she was going to snap.

"We must go see it again," Jocynda said after she came out of her cave with sage in her hand.

"See what?" I was playing dumb, focusing on my drink.

Jocynda sucked her teeth. "My house."

I winced, too afraid to ask what she meant.

REDUX. AN ADVENTURE I didn't want to go on. Jocynda led us on the mad hunt. The city was now covered in so much ice it looked glassy. In the sky, the sun refused to break through the clouds, but at times I caught a ray of light threading the wilted trees, warming the grass at our feet. Quite picturesque. There was no telling when this tundra would end.

As the gloomiest hour arrived, Jocynda's hair appeared frozen in place and her eyebrows were dusted in snow. The blue beanie she wore didn't cover her ears, and so they were an angry red. We'd spent the better part of the day riding the People Mover to and from various districts. It was a way to kill time and leave things like memory and fear at home. Jocynda never wasted time on trivial emotions, not when there was so much exploring to do.

"We're going back to Brush Park," Jocynda said.

I immediately tensed, and she could see it in my face.

"You really want to go back to that house?"

"I want to be where I belong."

I held my cup of coffee tight, took a sip, and then threw it away. The café we bought it from was small, artisan, and claimed to serve the best breakfast desserts in all suburban Detroit. I ate a blueberry muffin and Jocynda had a large chocolate cookie. If there was one thing we always agreed on, it was that sweets were in order.

Back outside, I lit a cigarette and stared at the ice. The café's reflection was limitless and threatening. The door opened and closed, welcoming a new world behind it, a new angle to the universe. I closed my eyes, inhaled as much smoke as I could and counted until the images no longer burned the backs of my eyes.

But like muscle memory, or wallowing in my own delusion, I envisioned the tall bodies and heard the voices that bellowed out of them. As I stepped back, they spoke, but I held my ears and closed my eyes, letting out a howl of my own. That's when Jocynda shook me so hard I almost lost consciousness.

"What are you doing?"

Blood starred the snow at my feet, and when I looked at my hands, I saw them wet with and red. I'd been scratching my face. But when Jocynda saw, I mean *truly saw*, what I'd done to myself, she bolted. I ran as fast as I could behind her, through a dozen empty avenues, sad streets, and past trees frozen as fossils. Jocynda was a good hundred feet ahead of me, but somehow, I heard her speak.

You are my guide.

To cross me over.

Somehow, I'd collapsed into the snow. I was so cold I thought all the nerves in my face had been obliterated, until I realized the twinkling was not snow at all, but glass. It had cut deep into my cheeks, my lips…eye sockets. When I stood, the world was watery red, but my head turned immediately toward the sound of a scream.

"Let me go already!"

Brush Park was as alive as a poltergeist, but without the plan for revenge. Each house was more haunting than the next. The roofs were falling apart and many of the windows were boarded. I watched silhouettes ascend the walls and darkness creep into the snow near my feet.

The scream ran through me again, forced me down into benediction as if my knees had been bashed with a baseball bat. But I ran. I had to save her. I shouldered through the old Victorian door and found Jocynda sprawled on the floor. Pale, sad and dried up as a dead rose. Her hands and feet were scaly, deprived of blood flow. Her dark lips drooped sluggishly, and her limbs fanned out lazily.

"Let me go," Jocynda whispered. "I'm your ghost."

And as the lights faded, I saw Jocynda's hands begin to recede into her wrists, her feet into her ankles. I laid myself next to her, picked up her head, and let it rest within the crook of my arm. That's when I saw the red wet frown that was carved from ear to ear and the skin of her face began to delineate, sliding slowly into my hands like chewed gum until I was met with only a skull to look at. I saw the knife that she used next to me. I wanted to use it on myself. I wanted to feel her blood touch mine, come closer to understanding the spiral of her philosophies.

But then I'd come to realize she was never running away from anything other than me. She'd been gone a long time, but I didn't have the courage to accept it. All I did was keep this insidious memory alive. And as I pulled Jocynda closer, my grip punched into her like a rotted vegetable bulb. If I had any power to wake her up, I certainly couldn't find it. That hope quickly died.

Still, I couldn't let her go. She was all I had.

What was left of her began peeling away. Layer by layer, Russian Doll, onionskin. She was leaving me by her own volition. All this time I had been holding onto her voice and her body, only to see her finally find her own way. But I would not let her become erased from my head. So long as I kept going, she would be with me. No matter how faded her voice would become, no matter how distant the touch of her body would be.

Detroit is a city that won't let anyone go.

The apex at the end of the abyss…

Phantom Limbs

M. EDUSA

Nights are hard now, for all the same reasons they used to be easy. I'm alone.

I lurch off the mattress, wheezing, and grasp at my throat. Thick black smoke crawls out of my lungs, forcing my teeth open with claw-like hands. It billows slowly into the darkness as I suffocate.

The room spins. I throw myself to the side and land hard on the floor, catching myself by instinct on my forearm with enough jarring force to shake my eyeballs in my skull. I hack and spit, my stomach muscles clenching in agony. There's nothing left to come up. There's no oxygen, either.

Maybe it's an hour, maybe it's thirty minutes later. Maybe a full day. I wake. I'm still on the floor, my right arm folded and cramping under my chest. Groaning, I roll slowly onto my back and huff out a breath. I stare at my barracks ceiling, slowly growing pale as my burning eyes adjust to the seeping safety lights from the poles outside.

My lungs are full of glass and blood. I wipe my lips, and it's somehow surprising to me that my hand comes away clean. No red.

Spitting out half-breaths, tasting sand and smoke, I sit up painfully. My body is mercilessly stiff from the abuse I've put it through over the past… however long it's been. A couple of hours, probably.

"Are you here?" I ask the empty shadows in the corner of the room where Stoll sometimes sits. Waiting for me to wake up. Stoll is silent. The room is empty.

I don't sleep for the rest of the night.

"I THINK THE CHAPLAIN'S in his office this morning," Jamie offers mildly, without looking directly at me. "I hear he takes walk-ins."

"Get fucked, Harris." I snap back at him with less venom than I intended and more than he deserves. This is primarily because he tried to get in my pants once when we were both drunk boots and I've never forgiven him for it. Forgiveness is a game for much younger, much healthier soldiers than I am now.

Jamie hums with infuriating good-nature and sips his iced coffee. He's well-aware that he's still paying penance for sins he committed when he was nineteen and plastered. He has the good grace I lack and never holds it against me.

We're standing on the running track in the middle of the Kuwaiti desert, both of us holding clipboards and coffee and nursing sleep-deprivation hangovers. In lines on the artificial turf, rows of new arrivals in black PT uniforms are struggling through morning exercises.

"Straighten your fucking back," I tell one of the young soldiers in the line. "You get one warning."

Jamie follows behind me, soothing my scalding tone with generic encouragement. "You're doing great, Allen. Almost there. Thirty seconds."

I have no empty platitudes in me. I have little these days, in fact, besides the rage and feral instinct of a dying animal, putting on a show of toughness and aggression for any potential predator that steps too close. It's a poor act, but the show must go on. It *has* to, or people throw around words like "chaplain."

Hey chaplain, I saw your door was open and decided to walk in. Sorry to bug you, I wanted to drop a couple of bombs on you real quick. I hate my life, kinda want to die, and I've been seeing my dead best friend since 2016. Anyway, how's your day going?

That's a quick way to get myself med-boarded out of a job, I think sourly. As far as I'm concerned, morale services exist not to help soldiers, but to trap them into saying something they can't un-say. Getting a label slapped on them that will never come off.

"His office hours start at zero eight-hundred," Jamie calls after me obnoxiously as I turn my back on him. "I'll tell him to expect you."

I pretend not to hear him.

I return to my barracks after dinner, where I sat alone, and I ate alone—speaking to no one and inviting no conversation. The chow hall food was always subpar at best, but thanks to my sleepless night, it tasted especially bad today.

I stomp into my building with no regard for noise because the room across from mine has been empty for the five months I've been in-country. Everyone else is still out and about, enjoying the start of their one-day weekend. I draw up short at my own door when I realize someone else is in the hallway after all.

A short woman in a uniform is shutting the door across from mine, her patrol cap hanging from one manicured hand. Her nails are short, shining, flawless.

"Hi," she says simply. "I'm your new roommate. Or, barracks-mate, I guess. I have the room across the hall." She gestures to the aforementioned door, as if I didn't watch her step out of it a moment ago.

"Hey," I manage to say flatly.

I'm momentarily taken aback by her, because nobody has had the gall to stand face-to-face with me and have a regular human conversation in… well. A long time. Avoidance and murmured greetings in passing seem to be the standard anymore. I only recognize that now, in this exact moment, by sheer contrast.

"Kashvi," she smiles with perfect white teeth and extends one of those manicured hands. "Kashvi Behl."

I stare at her hand. Women don't generally shake one another's hands, and I'm stunned once again.

I'm staring at her for too long and recognizing it too late.

"Are you okay?" She asks, her eyebrows drawing together. She pulls her hand back slowly, looking uncertain. Concerned.

"Yes." I snap it out like a whip, a clear lie, a clear dodge. "Sorry. I have to go."

I right-face to my door, my cheeks burning, and jam the key in. It takes three half-turns and a prayer before I can jiggle the damn thing open, and I shut it behind me quickly, without a look back, without another word.

I LOVED A MAN once. Not in the same way that you love a husband or a girlfriend or a partner. I loved him in the way you love something you were never meant to touch.

Mine were the dirty, calloused hands cradling a million-dollar diamond. I was the tourist who saved her last dime to stare at the Mona Lisa for a few seconds. I was a death-row inmate, watching a brilliant sunset through prison bars.

I loved him the way an abandoned animal loves the first hand that shows it kindness. Blindly, with immense gratitude and unwavering loyalty.

Every other man around was telling me I did not belong there. That I was not welcome, that I could never be a part of the life I had chosen. Worse, I started to believe them. I was angry. Bitter, stubborn. I'd heard all the usual names: I was a Pitbull, a porcupine, a cactus. A colorful litany of other, even less savory slurs men always use to label the women who will never sleep with them.

The hatred in me grew, a tiny little spark of a flame, fanned by everything that came too close. Every condescending name, every dirty look, every snide remark. The spark became a bonfire.

I was a raging inferno on the day I met Stoll in March 2014.

We were at the range, all of us caked in that fine desert dust that crawls into your throat and lodges into the corners of your eyes. I was laying in it with an M4 buttstock pressed against my cheek. Gunpowder in my nostrils. My lips pressed together in a hard line, trying, and failing, to keep the dust out. Frustrated, overheated. My skin was crawling off my bones and, to top it off, my rifle refused to cooperate with my ambitions.

We were living in an oven, comforted on that particular day by not even the slightest hint of a breeze. The sun overhead was relentless and scalding. My straining eyes relaxed for a moment as a shadow fell over my prone position, and I squinted as I looked up.

Stoll was standing above me, peering downrange at my target. The sun shone like a halo from behind his head, and I was momentarily blinded. Before this moment, I had only known him from afar. He was one of the company's golden boys, and he could do no wrong as far as the commanders were concerned. I'd always avoided him for precisely that reason.

"You're alright, kid," he said simply, with a nod of his sharp jaw. "Adjust your left hand. Get a good grip, try it again."

Uncertainty and nerves went to war in my gut as I settled back down into the dust, pressing my cheek hard against the buttstock. Breathing in through my nose, out through my mouth. Curling the pad of my finger around the trigger and squeezing slow.

My eyes stayed focused on my ACOG as the shot went off. I didn't look at my target downrange. I gazed at Stoll instead.

He smiled at me in a way no man has ever smiled at me before. Free of lust, or disgust, or condescension or begrudging admiration. I understood he was truly proud of me, and the ice around my heart chipped with a crack I could almost hear.

Stoll's eyes were the color of a blue sky. His hair golden, like the sun cracking through the clouds. To me, he was a god who came down from above to grace me with a smile when my life was in chaos. I was the ship. A storm was raging around me. My sails were ripped, my hull battered. I was one hard hit away from smashing to pieces entirely, and then there he was: smiling at me.

I spent the next two years chasing that high.

I was no one. A PFC with a chip on her shoulder and a man's haircut and a hard glint to her eye. I had been standing in the shadows for my entire life. Unseen.

Stoll saw me. He took me apart at the seams. With blue eyes. With kindness.

IN NOVEMBER 2016, I held Stoll in my lap. Smoke billowed around us, the color of reflected candlelight, the flavor of dust. I held pieces of his skull together with my bare hands and begged for something I couldn't name. A miracle, maybe. Some lightning bolt from the sky to undo it all. To knit bone fragments and brain matter back together like puzzle pieces and put that sparkle back in his blue eyes.

"Please, please, please," I begged the sky. I begged the smoke. I couldn't find a single other word to say.

Stoll lay in the dry dust, boneless. Strange noises were coming out of his throat. Blood was coming from his mouth, his nose, his ears. Bubbling and neon-bright.

I know now that blood isn't sticky or dark like it is on the big screen. It's slick. It makes things hard to hold on to. Like pieces of your best friend's skull. Like shit-eating grins and knowing eyes.

I couldn't hold him together. I tried. I pressed both my hands against the massive hole in his head and folded myself over him. My uniform was warm and soaked and slick. Pieces of bone moved wet and loose under my palms, like gravel in thick mud.

I think I screamed. I can't remember.

Hands pulled me off him, rough and disorienting. I fought them. There was a large hand in the back of my vest's carry handle, and I couldn't dislodge it. It was superhuman and relentless, dragging me straight backwards through the rubble. I left a trail of Stoll's blood in the sand behind me.

I was still watching his eyes. Bright blue eyes, staring up at an empty, smoke-clogged sky.

Stoll was still alive, still fighting, and the last thing he was going to see was a stranger's face. It wasn't right. I should be there with him. Everything was so goddamn wrong, and I couldn't sit there and let it all be wrong. I couldn't let this be it.

"Let me go!" I was screaming, thrashing wildly, kicking my boots out into the dust. I reached back with clumsy hands, trying to find that iron grip, to pull it away. "Fucker–let go of me!"

"Dawson!" A voice was close to my ear, but it sounded incredibly distant. Underwater. A hand landed heavy on my plate carrier, hitting me twice. "You're good. Stop fighting. You're okay."

I wasn't okay. In fact, after that day, I was never okay again.

IT WAS JAMIE HARRIS who had pulled me away from Stoll, which was for all practical reasons, the right course of action: the combat medics needed to move in and do their job, they needed space to work. They had the skills, equipment, and training I lacked, but they still couldn't save him.

All the Army's medics and all the Army's men couldn't put Stoll back together again.

I never forgave Jamie. I know it wasn't his fault. Of course it wasn't. Nothing that happened that day was his fault, or mine, or anyone's. Even so, it felt good to have someone to point my rage at like a rocket launcher.

Fire away. *Hasta la vista,* fucker. Take that.

I started feeding my bonfire of rage and pain and hate again, and I never stopped.

I WANDER INTO MY room in the dark. I don't turn the lights on. I sit heavily on the edge of my cot and yank the laces out of my boots. Kick them off one at a time and shove them under the bed. This is about as far as I make it. The gas tank of my energy is red-lined, and I suddenly find that I have nothing left.

My body falls sideways onto the mattress. It takes a lot of effort to swing my legs up, to roll onto my side facing the wall. I draw my knees to my chest and pull the pillow under my head. My arms weigh a hundred pounds apiece.

I listen to the air creak on somewhere in the night. I listen to the darkness.

Behind me, the thin mattress dips and creaks.

My eyes shutter. My breath catches in my chest.

An ice-cold hand lands on my shoulder. Not pushing, or pulling, or gripping. Simply resting. Even radiating that strange cold, it's familiar. Comforting in all the wrong ways. Something dead shouldn't be comforting. But it is.

"I miss you," I say into the cold.

"You're alright, kid," says Stoll's ghost.

Kid. I'm not a kid, I haven't been one since the day I was born. But I still like the way he says it. Like he's giving me that "kid" as an excuse for all my pettiness, pride, and rage. Slotting himself into the void, right there where it's always been empty. Somewhere between dad, brother, boss, best friend, deity.

If I'd been born right–born normal–I think I would have been madly in love with Stoll. I could have fallen in love with him the way a man and a woman fall in love in the movies. Effortlessly, magnetically. I think some nights that a part of me, deep down, might love him even still, even though I've never cared for a man that way in my life.

I know I miss him. The way I'd miss my leg if I had to saw it off. I'd feel it all the time, even when it was gone, a phantom limb in phantom pain.

Stoll stands next to me on the track when I grade the fitness test for the new batch of soldiers who landed in-country. He stands behind me in the chow line, a full foot taller than me, a genuine grin on his face I can always feel, even when I'm not looking at him. He lays in the thin dust beside me at the range, critiquing my shots with humor and expertise, and he sits beside me at the fire pit outside my barracks when 0300 strikes and sleep becomes a lost cause.

Stoll is my phantom limb.

He's the leg I chopped off, and nobody can see him but me. He still hurts like a motherfucker.

KASHVI FINDS ME AT the firepit. It's not quite one in the morning, and the NCO barracks are all quiet and still, like they should be in the middle of the night.

"God, unpacking is taking me forever," she announces. Without ceremony or invitation, she takes the seat across the fire from me, sighing as she gets comfortable.

I stare at her, the cigarette I'd been about to light hanging forgotten between my fingers.

"I really didn't feel like I brought that much shit. Three duffle bags; that's pretty good. Turns out I fit everything in there but the kitchen sink."

Listening, still adjusting to her presence, I finally light my cigarette. Looking up at her, I hesitate only a moment before offering her the pack. It surprises me when she beams out a smile and takes it. She shakes one out and lights it with her own lighter.

"I didn't want to ask, but thank you." She hands the pack back. "I needed this."

She takes a long breath, holds it. Sends it puffing out into the night in little white wisps. My absolute silence doesn't seem to bother her in the slightest.

"I'm calling it for the night," she hums. "The unpacking anyway. Not the smoking."

"I fucking hate packing," I say around my cigarette, surprising myself. I hadn't planned to say anything, really. It slipped out.

Still surprised by the sound of my own voice, I glance up. My eyes seeking the cement block where Stoll had been sitting a foot or two to my left. He's gone.

It's only me at the fire. Me and Kashvi, who is beautiful. Who is still talking to me, real and easy, like normal people talk to one another on any normal night.

For the first time in a long time, I talk, too. For a few hours, I'm not a social pariah or a self-isolated storm of rage roaming around base, ready and willing to steamroll anyone in my path. I'm a human, and I can laugh, tell stories, ask questions, and make lingering eye contact with another human, who sits across from me with her face shining in the firelight.

Kashvi tells me I look like Ruby Rose, and I tell her she looks like Princess Jasmine. We both laugh about it, flattered, and I avoid making eye contact for a few minutes after that. She asks me about my tattoos. She shows me hers, a delicate bit of script on her collarbone that gives me a funny fluttering feeling in my stomach. We smoke halfway through my pack of Camels without noticing.

It's nearly three in the morning when we head back inside, and it's only the sudden rain, spitting big angry drops out of the sky without warning, which ends our firepit peace.

SHE JOINS ME AGAIN the next night, and I try to act casual, like I hadn't been sitting out there for two hours hoping she'd show up. This time, she brings her own cigarettes and shares them with me.

A group of NCOs walk by, on their way to or from somewhere I don't go, and they shoot me a strange look. I know exactly why. Nobody has sat with me by this firepit in a long time. Nobody but Stoll, who is conspicuously absent.

Kashvi notices and waves at them with raised eyebrows, her hand transforming from a friendly wave to a middle finger as soon as their backs were turned.

I snort. She makes fun of me for that for the rest of the night.

We fall into this routine easily, sometimes trading cigarettes for coffee, or the disgusting zero-alcohol beer they sell out of coolers down at the PX.

"You seem different," Harris remarks, peering at me with suspicion when I show early to the track one morning. I brought him a coffee that required neither coercion nor pleading, and he stares down at it as I hold it out to him like he thinks it might be poisoned.

"Do you want it or not?" There's no real venom in my voice. I'm daydreaming about chocolate-brown eyes and full lips wrapped around cigarettes in the firelight.

He grunts and takes it, reluctant, but he's still staring at me with narrowed eyes. "Yeah. Something's different. What's wrong with you?"

I don't explain myself, but there's a little part of me that wants to smile as I hit the astroturf to stretch out.

Deep down, I think he's right. Something is different.

THAT NIGHT, KASHVI DIDN'T come to the firepit.

Stoll is sitting with me in the dark, making no comment as I spend too much time poking the shattered chunks of wood pallet into the wire-mesh.

"Where is she?" I ask under my breath. I look at Stoll and watch the fire reflected in his eyes.

Stoll smiles like he knows a secret I never told him. "Why don't you go find out?"

I consider this and find it to be tempting. I can't think of a clever way to talk myself out of it, in fact. I blink, and I'm standing in front of her door. I'm knocking, and breathing as if I just ran a marathon, because my bravery, my plan, extended no further than this.

When Kashvi appears, the room behind her is dark. She holds her wallet and phone like she has been about to walk out the door.

"Did you wanna…" I trail off, jerking one thumb over my shoulder, forgetting how to speak.

Something in her star-deep eyes chokes up my throat. I'm still trying to figure out what it is, exactly, when she throws her phone onto the chair next to the door. Reaches and grabs the back of my neck.

She kisses me.

I fall into her, into the room. Kicking the door shut behind me, my mind gone blessedly silent. I sink both my hands into her silky hair, like part of me has been thinking about doing all week, and kiss her back like I mean it.

"I think there's something really wrong with me," I tell her without meaning to as we lay in bed together at midnight, our legs tangled under the sheets, our sweat drying on our skin.

I'm staring at the bunk across the room, dark and empty. Thinking that in the room across the hall, Stoll is sitting on that same empty bunk, waiting for me.

Kashvi wraps her arms around me and kisses me on the jaw. Her lips are soft, her breath warm.

"Me too," she whispers back.

TWO NIGHTS LATER, I turn my head when I hear footsteps, expecting Kashvi. Instead, it's Jamie, trudging closer with his hands in his pockets from the long sidewalk that runs between the buildings.

"I come in peace," Harris jokes, holding up both hands. "Look, uh. Don't stab me or anything, but I see you out here a lot. And some of the guys told me they've seen you sitting out here a lot, too. Like, every night."

I feel my jaw clench. "Sounds to me like some of the guys need to mind their own fucking business."

Jamie helps himself to a seat and sighs, a long breath out through his nose. Gathering his infinite patience like a shield against my infinite sarcasm.

"Am I allowed to be worried about you?" Jamie smiles mirthlessly. "Actually, don't answer that. I'll tell you. I *am* allowed. Sorry, not sorry."

"I'm fine."

"Is there…" Jamie's shoulders pull up, his hands moving helplessly in a half-shrug. "I don't know. Anything you need to talk about? Or want to?"

I clench my teeth. "No."

I stare at him. Willing him to stand and walk away.

"You're always isolated. You've been in a good mood." Jamie, who is apparently not done with me, holds up one big hand as he counts off his points one finger at a time. "You even bought me a goddamn coffee, like, out of the blue. You've been sitting out here all night, every night, talking to yourself. What does that sound like to you?"

He looks at me intently, and a part of me knew exactly where he was going with this all along.

"Because to me it sounds like some classic red-flag bullshit, okay? And I'm not gonna be the one who saw all the signs and didn't say anything."

I say nothing to ease Jamie's mind. My own is racing.

"Goddamit, Dawson." His bravado fully exhausted, Jamie sits forward, resting his elbow on his knee and scrubbing a hand across his eyes harshly. "Say something."

"I'm fine," is what comes out of my mouth. Inwardly, I cringe at the sound of it.

Still practicing all the patience of a saint, Jamie sits there. He says nothing, and stares at me while I stare at the fire.

"Go inside. Go to sleep." He speaks eventually, conceding defeat as he stands, looking older than I've ever seen him look. "I'll check in on you tomorrow, I guess."

I don't answer, and I don't return his goodnight as he disappears into the darkness.

I look at the empty place where Jamie had been sitting for a long, long time. My brain turning his words over and over like a Rubik's Cube. Without conscious thought, I reach down and let my hand trail in the sand, in the remains of the little bits of stone and gravel that have been worn down to nothing by time and foot traffic. That's a mistake.

I shake my fingers off quickly, rubbing them on my jeans. My throat feels clogged with dust and smoke all over again. My hands feel slick.

I stand abruptly, knocking over my folding chair. I leave it right where it is and trudge up the three short steps into my barracks.

My heart is pounding as I knock on Kashvi's door. I think I already knew nobody was going to answer it, but I go through the motions, anyway. Eventually, I try the doorknob myself. It opens.

I step into the dark. The door shuts behind me.

When my eyes adjust to the shadows, I see Kashvi sitting on the bench underneath the single window. She stands slowly and steps forward to meet me.

I wait, just looking at her. Thinking that she looks more real than anything I've seen in years. Thinking too, that I haven't been able to tell what's real and what's a nightmare in a long, long time.

"I was going to tell you," she says softly. Something in her voice is broken. She looks devastated.

What I have to say—what I have to ask—must be written all over my face.

You've been sitting out here all night, every night, talking to yourself.

I want to ask her how she died. I want to ask her how I can see her, why she chose me, of all people, to torment this way. Why me? Why now?

I think that the moment my eyes land on her, I changed my mind.

Instead, I cross the room and touch her face. Letting the slide of her soft hair wipe the feeling of blood off my fingers.

I kiss her and taste cigarettes, and something sweet that doesn't remind me of sand at all.

THE NEXT MORNING, I'M standing in front of an unfamiliar door.

My hands are shaking as I reach up and knock on the wood with none of my usual strength. The sound is weak to my ears, and for a terrifying moment I think it might not have been loud enough. Maybe I'll have to knock again, and I don't know if I have the strength in me to do it. I don't think I do.

Kashvi's warm hand finds mine and I jump at the contact. I turn, and her brown eyes are by my right shoulder, warm and encouraging. Drowning in my own nerves, I almost forgot she was there. Her hair is in a loose ponytail, chocolate-black strands falling around her face. She's beautiful.

I grip her hand back and squeeze hard.

On the other side of me, sun-hot and ice-cold all at once, Stoll's ghost presses his shoulder against mine.

"You're alright, kid." The first words he ever spoke to me. The ones I hear without rhyme or reason every night, every hour, knocking around in my head like a bowling ball made of glass.

My eyes burn.

Taking a deep breath in through my nose, I steel myself. I set my spine. Remind myself to breathe. I'm almost prepared to knock again, but I don't need to. The door opens.

"Dawson," the chaplain greets me with a genuine smile. He's tall, wrinkles forming around perpetually smiling eyes. "I'm really glad you came. Want to come in?"

"Do you want me to come with you?" Kashvi asks me quietly, her hand still in mine.

My eyes drift away from hers to the bright blue ones that have been smiling at me for eight years. Stoll grins. The sun breaking from behind my storm clouds. He nods at me once and takes my other hand. Squeezes hard.

Smoke is heavy on my tongue. Sand grinds between my teeth.

"Yeah," I say to them both. "I do."

The Scold's Bridle

AMANDA NEVADA DEMEL

They put this mask on me for the sole purpose of humiliation. It's successful. The public maskings always disgusted me — the very idea that a grown woman with preferences and desires needs correcting makes my body tense — but never did I think I would be the one on display. After all, so many years had passed since the last one. Only rumors of that woman's depraved deeds remain, in both the town's memory and my own.

The shame boiling within me is strong, so much stronger than even the rage I felt when I first learned of my punishment. The only good thing about this mask is that no one can see my reddened face. The face that they do see has been crudely painted onto the metal. It shows a feminine visage, with plump, scarlet lips spread wide into a jubilant smile. It is repulsive, brimming with the trapper's cheer.

It is the first day of my punishment, and I already feel my resolve crumbling. I can't fathom spending a month behind this cold sheet of metal. The only time I look forward to is the evening, when they will so graciously allow me to eat supper and sleep without the mask, or so they say. Even then, I will be kept apart from my husband. They fear that I will harm him in some way, and he must be kept alive, of course. He can produce more children with more women, which our town will count on him to do. I would be expected to produce a baby every nine months if I were to subject myself to that torture. A slave to the law is a worthy man; a woman of will is wicked. I always knew the nature of a woman's expected conduct, but I never imagined that my husband would enforce the decrees so strictly, especially not in our own home. Perhaps I should have held my tongue when they announced the new law. Perhaps I should have agreed with my husband that the Nine Month Edict was a brilliant idea. I could have lied, asserted excitement about having a horde of children at last. But I was fooled into a sense of ease by my husband's history. After all, a past knave must hold some disapproval of the law, I thought. It turned out that his court service had wiped away all ideas of freedom and compassion.

Justice is a myth. I am disgusted that I once believed in it. I am even more disgusted that I married a servant of the courts. I was blind to the warning signs because of the tenderness he once showed me. I did not believe that I was worthy of love, and then he came into my life. Well, some love that turned out to be. He never hid his jealousy. In fact, I used to find it charming, how much he wanted me for himself. Now, if I could, I would embrace a stranger. I would make a true display of obscene affection. Yet no one in town will approach me, let alone allow me to embrace them. My own mother looks at me with disdain.

My thoughts stretch and flex and knot themselves as I toil throughout the day, hauling water from the river to the village. But what else can I do? I must do my penance, or I'll be cast out like that woman from so long ago. Even so, my mind rages. Not to mention the scorching drought in my throat, the terrible need to moisten my lips, to take a meager sip of the water I bring to town.

My husband has been warped by the company he keeps. The court and council, so holy and important, took him in and raised him up. Our lives seemed to improve as he climbed the ranks: we built a new, spacious house, we were never hungry or lonely, and even my mother graced us with smiles. Her smile could have been beautiful once, but I only saw it stained with selfishness. As for my husband, I should have seen the changes in him sooner. He stopped giving bread and water to the poor, the unskilled, the downtrodden people of our village. Soon enough, he stopped greeting them, and then he pretended not to hear their pleas and moans. What a fool I was, assuming that he was simply occupied with his court duties. He had been accepted by the privileged and had been living in their style. Why should he sacrifice those newfound luxuries?

I can't stop my thoughts from storming or my body from bringing water to town from the stream. My thoughts temporarily fill with idyllic pictures of nighttime. Without the mask, I could breathe deeply, I could take large gulps of water, I could eat and sleep. However, those hopes fade and sour. I consider all the possibilities of the evening and see that even the best of them are dreadful. The respite from the mask will only be temporary. My meal will be spent in solitude, my rest will take place in a dank sepulcher of the Church. The most vivid image, the vision that freezes my blood, is of my husband. Such a minion of the court, he must obey their edict. Eventually, he will be sent to come into my dreary chamber, fit in a wall of catacombs, adorned only with a cot and a chamber pot, and he will gladly fulfill his marital duty while I lie still, powerless, abhorrent. Imagining his hands on me, acting on a service that is expected of us, makes my lungs contract. The cold hand of icy malice wraps itself around my chest.

When I wake, the process will start again. An officer will wake me, drag me to the town square, ceremoniously place the bridle on my head while the townsfolk take in the sight. Just like this morning, when I was first made an example of, the parents will tell their daughters, "That's why you must never disobey your husband." The daughters will see me as an embodiment of failure, a warning tale for their potentially rebellious tendencies. Such a display instilled fear in me for years. Although I do not recall the ceremony of the bridle for the previous pariah, I remember the lesson quite clearly. Where did that woman go? I suppose, as time goes on, that the memory of an outcast ebbs, therefore, requiring the flow of a new one.

My protests against the Nine Month Edict have only strengthened over the months since its announcement, and though I had aired them only in confidentiality, I dare not give voice to them ever again. I can't bear the possibility of rearing a boy into this world, sowing ideals of superiority in his malleable mind. I can't merely stand at the edge of his vision as my husband instills his wisdom of the world. I can't support that wisdom with my silence. And then to pair him off with an innocent, young girl, to watch him spawn his own children, to continue the cycle of inequity. Could I bring myself to love such a creature? Could I sleep at night, knowing I contribute so directly to the misery of the choiceless and voiceless? And raising a little girl — I cannot put words to the flames that this thought stokes.

Tomorrow, with the bridle secured over my head and the bit in my mouth once again, I will walk to the stream, retrieve water, bring it to the town, and watch them all benefit from my labor. The townsfolk will do their washing, cook, drink, and gods know what else with the water. But I will partake in none of these privileges. At night, my husband will return to the little cot in the Church to perform his holy duties. And in nine months . . .

If I stay here, I will surely commit worse deeds than I have already done. I don't care for the townsfolk, who mindlessly support anything the Church spews at them. I don't care for my betraying husband, who informed the courts of my discontent. I don't care for my weak mother, who hardly raised me. I care only for myself, only for my liberty.

That woman from long ago did the right thing, I'm sure, even if I don't know what her crime was.

They will not escort me to the Church tonight. My husband will not find me waiting. I must leave my birthplace, my history, my heritage. No one or thing is worth the cost of staying here.

The sky begins to darken, and my heart starts to gallop. I survey the woods around the stream. I am well acquainted with my surroundings. In the distance, smoke rises from the chimneys of the town. I used to play around these tall, old trees, climbing their branches, hiding behind their thick trunks, sitting in their shade. This is where my husband first courted me, but those memories are now colored by the dark ink of regret and rage. Where there once was warmth, there is now a bitter chill in my chest.

Five years ago, I found him emerging from the thicket. I had been washing my mother's clothing in the stream. Then I heard heavy footsteps. Thinking it was a guard of the Church at best and a large bear at worst, I began to gather the water-logged garments in a frenzy. An unfamiliar, deep voice asked me to wait. I turned to see that the source of the voice was a panting, sweating young man. It was obvious that he needed help, that he was on the run. His clothes were tattered and dirty, and his face was hidden behind a bush of facial hair. I didn't ask why or from what he was escaping, but instead offered him refuge and a hot meal. In those distant days, I fancied myself a believer in good will and intention. The look he gave me, wide-eyed with a subtle smile, showed tenderness and gratitude. Such expressions had never been directed at me before. I was immediately enraptured.

In the weeks following, he showered me in compliments, bathed me in his affection like no other man had done. Being the ugly youngest daughter, I never expected to capture anyone's attention. He didn't care about my looks or lack of dowry. He seemed to care for me. I had fallen for the ruse. He saw me as nothing but a pawn in his scheme to establish himself. I was the first object for him to own. Only four years later, he has at last gained an occupation, a home, and a steady ring of contacts. Now he only needs a son. May the gods strike me dead if I give one to him.

I now see that all I knew was infatuation. If he ever felt any sincere emotions, which I doubt, then he must have tired of me soon after our first meeting. My position as the daughter of a slain knight, though not ideal, still gave him advantages over his crooked past. He saw the future, he saw beyond me, he saw power. Had I always been his inferior?

My jaw clenches around the bit with so much force that my skull vibrates. I will never go back to him. This is the final bucket of water that I will bring to town. The water sloshes around as I heave it uphill, splashing on my already-wet dress. The humid heat of the evening makes the clinging garment even more uncomfortable. I stop at the top of the hill to catch my breath. Looking down at the village, my chest tightens. I am trapped in a harness of emotion. All the bitterness of my world wraps around me and tightens like the laces of a bodice. I have lost everything. The weak ties I once held to the community have been brutally torn to pieces. That little town was once my home. It is where I was born, where my mother and her mother were born. Seeing my neighbors go about their mundane lives sparks a strange envy in me. Why could I never accept my lowly place? I spent my oblivious childhood in that village, among those selfish people, and I found my husband hiding in those woods only five years ago.

My eyes latch onto a group of young girls. They can't be much older than ten years. Their thoughts of love and commitment are yet unsoiled by reality. Their nights are devoid of marital duty. If only I could warn them, plant seeds of freedom in their fertile minds! Yet, at the same time, I hope that they never experience the hoe of rebellion raking at them. If there is any chance of the girls living happily within a cage, then I wish them speedy weddings. May they always succumb to their fears of being outcast from their families, unlike that strange woman had done so many generations ago.

When I reach town at last, I want to dump the water on the hot earth. I want to see the dirt absorb the fruit of my labor. Even more so, I want to pour it over my head and feel it cascading over my body. I know, however, that I need to play the role of subservience if I am to escape.

Bringing the bucket into the Church, I set it down between the separated men's and women's pews. The pastor looks up when the wood hits the floor. A slight smirk creeps across his lips, but he makes no further movement.

"You have finished your deliveries, Marta?" he asks.

"Yes, Father," I say, my words obstructed by the bit in my mouth. "Now I must get my nightclothes. I will return."

"You need not leave." His smile grows. "We will supply you with a modest dressing gown. Allow me to summon the guards."

I hadn't considered that they would supply me with clothing, that they would strip me of my own belongings. I knew there would be guards, but I didn't expect them until it was time to be shoved into the night room. I will have to make a more obvious escape now, one in the waning sunlight, one with less planning.

"May I say goodbye to my mother?" Surely, he would give in to such a simple, innocent plea. Surely, the quiver in my voice could be mistaken for an emotional connection and would not expose my lie.

He thinks for a moment, then concedes. "You may, but you must return promptly. I will send someone to follow you."

I babble my false thanks and hurry out of the Church. Hastening to my mother's house, I take in the village for the last time. Near the Church is the chapel, over there is the courthouse, and farther down is the butcher's home. I recall when my mother tried to push me toward marrying the gruff butcher. However, I was already smitten with the man who would betray me. Would living with one brute have been better than the other? Could I have been happy, or at least content, with the butcher? Could I have tolerated the blows of his fists and feet? Perhaps he would have sold me for good favor or fortune, like the traitor and my mother did. It's too late to know for certain.

The windows of my mother's house are dark. She is probably at the tavern, her favorite place. She always found comfort in its unruly squalor and rowdy patrons. The Church always saw these visits as her method of coping with my father's death. But I remember when I was a child and my mother came home late at night, crashing into doors and cupboards, laughing with some lewd man. I can still smell the bitter stench of liquor on them. Her drunken habits used to bother me, though I am now neither surprised nor irritated. She is likely drinking away the memories of her daughter right now. Her blind acceptance of the story of my crime and the verdict for my punishment baffles me. She acts as if she had always been the paragon of virtue, as if she had never expressed discontent with the Church. She acts as if my shame is wholly unrelated to her parenting. But I know better. I vowed long ago never to poison a life as she poisoned mine, never to bring a life into this world with the certainty of my shortcomings.

The fact that I can't bid her a bitter farewell makes my shoulders tense, but upon further consideration, I realize that it gives me more time to outrun the guards. I must seize this final chance to run free, even if I can't fully escape the clutches of the law.

My only opportunity is now. A brief glance behind me shows no one closing in. Even so, I pretend to examine the flower beds as I walk to the far side of the house. I can't risk the slightest suspicion. After one more furtive glance and one more deep breath, I bolt toward the woods, making sure to stomp on the delicate flowers as I run. The noise of tall grass shifting around my feet almost drowns out my heartbeat. I'm certain someone will hear me escaping, but that only spurs me to run faster. Dried weeds and flora crunch under my feet.

At last, I reach the edge of the woods. Passing that first line of trees feels like entering the river. There are the dangers of getting swept away and being lost in the darkness, yet there is a delightful chill. Stepping into the woods on this sweltering day brings a sense of relief, however short lived.

The metal bridle is heavy. It jostles on my head as I sprint, and the sharp edges cut into my scalp and the top of my ears. The thick material hinders my ability to breathe, and saliva trails down my jaw as my teeth clamp on the bit. The slats in front of my eyes don't allow enough light to come in; I believe that I may trip in the overgrowth any second. Sweat gathers at the creases of my eyes, threatening to slip in and blind me. My chest is tight, and my limbs are on fire. I continue running.

In the distance I hear one of the Church's henchmen call after me, but I don't hear the heavy plodding of boots nearby. As my feet pummel onward, I try to keep track of the sounds around me. Birds chirp from branches. Blood pumps in my ears. Leaves are crushed under my footfalls. Shouts come from somewhere behind me. Though I try to hone in on the shouts, there is too much happening. I am in a whirlpool of noise, and it swirls me around, preventing me from feeling grounded. When will it be safe to stop?

My entire body aches and burns. Where there was once one voice, there are now at least four. I hear them call to each other, reporting my location and how far they are.

Far out in the woods stands a large, square structure. Although I don't know who resides there, if anyone does, I pour all my hope into a kind soul letting me enter. A faint warning bell tolls in my head, but it is likely just the throbbing of blood in my ears. I need to catch my breath. I need to be free of this mask. I need solace.

The distance is closing in between me and the henchmen, but I don't stop until I reach the house. I crash into the brick wall and bile rises in my throat. I try to pull the mask off, even though I know it won't budge without the key. I can't breathe. I can't scream for help or mercy, either.

The door to the building creaks open. A fleeting thought arises: can this be the home of that shamed woman from all those years ago? I turn toward the door and swallow the contents of my throat.

"Come inside," a soft, high-pitched voice offers. She is calm and unaffected by my panic, as if she expected a stranger's arrival.

I spare a glance behind me. I can't see their faces, but I can see the undulation of their broad shoulders as they run toward me. Disregarding every warning I've ever heard about the house in the woods, I rush past the doorway.

"And take off that ridiculous trap," she says, pointing to the bridle.

The back of the mask suddenly clicks and loosens. With trembling arms, I reach up and pull apart the two sides of the strap. The air is blessedly cool as it hits my neck. Elation sprawls from the exposed skin. I push the mask up and off my head and inhale, finally free from the wooden bit in my mouth, but the sensation is too much too fast. It's as if I suck in the mighty winds of a storm, which are much too wild for my frail human form to contain. My body constricts as I vomit.

"I'm so sorry," I gush, trying to catch my breath. "If you have a rag, I'll clean that up. I'm so sorr—"

"Look up."

I do as I am told. An old woman stands in front of me. She wears a majestic black cloak over a white, dirt-stained dress without a bodice. She is surprisingly tall for a woman with so many wrinkles, and she looks steady and strong. She must be an apothecary, judging by the copious jars and books behind her and the prevalent, acrid smell.

Still catching my breath, I listen for any sounds from outside. There are no birds, no rustling leaves, and most importantly, no footsteps. I only hear the hissing and boiling of hot liquids, the cracking licks of a large fire. I let my head hang down again, and I catch sight of the mask in my hands. Bile once more bubbles in my throat. I tilt up my head and swallow. On the ceiling, I notice a bizarre pattern of circles and five-pointed stars. My thoughts briefly wander toward their meaning and order, but then the woman speaks. I look at her and a new danger dawns on me. I don't know this woman, though I have an inkling of who she is. She must have freed me from the bridle, I realize. But what does she expect in return?

"Destroy it," she says, gesturing toward a mighty fireplace.

Without speaking, I walk to the fire and spit on the bridle. I throw it into the flames with such strength that it scrapes against the wall of the hearth. The painted face soon curls up and chips off. Then the color of the dense metal quickly changes to a glowing orange, as if it were but a thin scrap. The orange is surrounded by yellows and reds, all twisting and waving on the mask, looking like a stream in Hell. Instead of blending into the fire, the mask ignites. The flames grow and snap. I can't look away, and I don't want to. The miraculous sight brings tears to my eyes.

"You have done well," she says, breaking me out of the reverie.

Remembering where I am, I stand up, give my thanks, and scramble toward the door. Before I get there, the woman extends her arm to stop me. Her face remains calm.

"It is not safe for you out there," she reminds me. "Not yet." There is a gentle smile on her face. It is the first smile I have seen without obvious ill-will behind it. "Stay here, Marta. I can teach you how to protect yourself. More than that, I can teach you how to enact your revenge."

I am silent, shocked by her apparent knowledge of my situation. Too many questions flood my mind. However, I don't feel the need to ask anything. After all, I am in no position to refuse help, and I know she must be the one who released me from the mask. I am in her debt.

"Wouldn't you like to see them suffer?" she asks. "Your husband, your neighbors, those self-righteous clergymen—they need to face the consequences of their actions. Even your mother is not without sin." I feel the corners of my lips perk up, but I try to stop it. "You can smile now that you are free. You are the master of your actions."

"Thank you," I whisper.

Can she truly be encouraging me? Does she really see me as a person, valid with thought, worthy of free will? Her promises of retribution may very well be empty, but I haven't anything to lose. I am homeless, without money, without skill, without any worldly ties. Any course of action is favorable to going back, including a lifetime of servitude to this woman. Freedom always comes at a cost. I will gladly substitute my old master for a new one, especially one who acknowledges my humanity.

"I want—I need—they must never know impunity again. Please," I say, "let me be your pupil. I want to learn."

"And you will, my child. Come here."

She leads me to a far corner of the room. We pass long tables covered with open books, vials, candles, and jars of roots and animal parts. All the drawers under the tables are closed. A thick, leather-bound book sits on its own table in the corner. A mirror hangs on each wall that the table touches. I catch a glimpse of my reflection, red and shining, puffy and hideous, but quickly flick my eyes back to the tome. The woman flips through the thick pages, revealing crowded illustrations in dark red ink, none of which I can parse. Eventually, she stops at a page only half-filled with scribbles.

"You may learn by my hand if you will give yours," she says. "This page will bind us together. Your signature will open your mind to the beauty of truth. Only after you sign can I teach you the way."

Once more, the blood rushes to my face. This shame is not furious but instead defeated. I dare not voice my shortcoming.

"Do not worry," the woman says, wrapping her long, calloused fingers around my wrist. "I will guide your hand."

I look up at her in awe, and she stares down at me. Hope flutters in my chest. Turning my hand, I reveal my palm. She places a quill in my grasp and instructs me to close my fingers. She then guides my hand in swirling motions on the page. With each subtle movement, I feel sharp pricks on my palm. I grip the quill tighter, squeezing out blood, letting it trickle down and smear on the page. The pain pales next to the enchanting sight of my dark blood sinking into the parchment.

"Welcome, Marta."

The voice that booms from the woman's mouth is light, loud, beautiful. It cradles me in security. The fire crackles as the wind howls in the fireplace. My dizziness has dissipated, and I feel as if I am a mighty, ancient oak, prepared to weather the elements and the woodsmen who dare try to defile me. I stand tall, beaming with accomplishment, staring into the mirror. That is my reflection, my self, and I will never hide or be hidden again. Tears roll down my cheeks. I don't know for how long I will be an apprentice, but one day I will rise. One day I will go back to that town. One day, they will all beg for my forgiveness. But they shall have none.

Need to Know

DARRELL Z. GRIZZLE

Jubal Sanders looked around at the abandoned buildings. There were only a few. A saloon, a boarding house, a general store with post office, and a church, in a small clearing surrounded by trees. A row of small clapboard houses was up the hill, behind the church.

Jubal pulled the reins on his horse as his men, Thurman and Shaw, also on horseback, came up behind him.

"I've heard of ghost towns," said Private Sam Thurman, "but I've never seen one."

"It's an old mining town," said Private Thomas Shaw. "When the mine taps out, the people pack up and move on to the next one."

"And we're supposed to find an escaped prisoner here?"

"Those are our orders," said Jubal. "He's said to be armed and dangerous, so best to ready your revolvers as well as your rifles. He could be in one of these empty buildings, or he might be hiding among the trees. And be sure to use the special heavy-duty bullets the Major General issued to us."

"This prisoner must be someone important, for the Major General to get involved," said Thurman. "I had never actually met him till yesterday."

"My guess is the prisoner is someone important, or someone especially dangerous," said Jubal.

"There's a hitchin' post where we can tie up our horses," Shaw pointed. "Although it looks pretty rickety."

"Everything in this town looks rickety." The stillness of the town raised goosebumps along Jubal's arms. He was trying not to let his nervousness show. This was the first mission he had led, and he was only a corporal, just one step up from the privates under his command.

"OK, let's split up. You take the saloon," Jubal said, nodding at Shaw, "and you take the old church," pointing at Thurman. "I'll take the general store."

THE SHELVES OF THE general store had been ransacked. Bags of food and grain had been ripped open and cans thrown to the floor, where they were gathering dust. There was a moldy, sour smell in the air. Jubal wondered how long this ghost town had been abandoned. Their orders had been simple but lacking in detail. *Find the escaped prisoner. He could be hiding in any of the abandoned buildings. Bring him back alive if possible, dead if not. If you have to, shoot him before he shoots you.*

Jubal was about to open the door to a back room in the store when he heard a muffled scream coming from outside of the building. He ran out and saw Thurman trembling with fear in the center of the ghost town.

The sky had suddenly gone dark. Eerie, crescent-shaped shadows were moving along the ground.

"What—what's happening?" asked Thurman. He sounded like he was about to cry.

"This must be an eclipse," said Jubal. "It's nothing to worry about."

"Something is terribly wrong! Look at these shadows!" The shadows looked alive, crawling along the ground.

"No," said Shaw, who had come running when he heard Thurman's shout. "It just means the moon is passing between the earth and the sun. It's a perfectly natural event."

"If it's perfectly natural, how come I've never seen it before?" Thurman's voice was shaking.

"It doesn't happen very often. But it does happen," said Jubal. "Just calm down."

"Is this the end of days? The Bible says there will be signs and wonders in the sky!"

"Tell you what," said Jubal, lowering his voice as he placed his free hand on Thurman's shoulder. "Let's go over to the church building and you can sit in the pews till you calm down."

"The church. That's a good idea," said Thurman, heading over to the abandoned church. "Probably the best place for us to be."

Jubal looked over at Shaw and they exchanged smiles. "All these shadows, they *are* kinda spooky," said Shaw. "But oddly beautiful."

"Like you, Thomas," whispered Jubal, low enough for Shaw to hear but not Thurman, who was already running up the steps of the small wooden church. Shaw gave Jubal a discrete wink.

When they entered the church, they almost bumped into Thurman, who was frozen in place. They followed his gaze to the pulpit area at the other end of the church. A huge wolf was on the floor behind the altar rail, suckling three wolf pups. The wolf was growling at them.

"I've never seen a wolf that big," whispered Shaw.

"No sudden moves," said Jubal. Shaw was right. The wolf was every bit as big as a person. And while she was continuing to growl at them, she looked each of the three soldiers in the face, in turn. She made eye contact with Jubal last, and he gasped when he saw that she almost looked human in the face.

The late-morning light was starting to shine again. A single beam of sunlight shone through one of the broken church windows, illuminating the dust in the old church and giving the whole scene a dreamlike quality. "I think we should slowly back out," Shaw said, his voice low. "Don't turn around."

A gun shot fired, narrowly missing the wolf. Jubal glanced over at Thurman and saw him lowering his firearm. "Thurman!" he shouted. The wolf sprang into action and Thurman ran out the door. The wolf went straight for Shaw, knocking him to the floor as it ripped out his throat. Blood spewed out of Shaw's ruined neck. The wolf ran out the door.

Jubal knelt down and cradled Shaw in his arms. "Tom!" he cried out desperately. "Don't die, Tom. Please. Don't die." He tried to press his hands against Shaw's throat to stop the bleeding, but it was a hopeless task. He could hear the abandoned wolf pups yowling behind the altar rail.

Thomas looked up at Jubal. He was still alive but gasping for breath. "That you be my poem," he wheezed, each word punctuated with blood. "I whisper with my lips close to your ear." He smiled weakly at Jubal.

Jubal recognized the line by Walt Whitman. Shaw had given him a first edition of *Leaves of Grass* for his birthday the year before. He knew that line ended with, "I love none better than you." Jubal whispered those words, but Thomas Shaw was already gone. A single tear streamed down Jubal's face as he held Thomas in his arms. Shaw's blood was soaking through both of their uniforms.

Outside the church, he could hear Thurman's screams and Jubal knew the wolf had found the frightened Private.

"THERE NEVER WAS AN escaped prisoner," said the Major General, taking a sip of his brandy. "The target was the werewolf you reported."

Jubal swallowed his brandy hard. "Werewolf?"

The light from the fireplace danced on the brandy snifters. "Yes. We've had run-ins in the past in that area, and we're trying to get rid of them before they move into more populated locations. Also, the railroad has expressed interest in laying track, maybe reviving the old town. Can't do that if werewolves are prowling about."

"With all due respect, the wolf we encountered was very large, but it did not seem like a werewolf to me. Do werewolves even exist?"

"Yes, that's why we issued the special bullets that have a silver core. They have also been blessed with holy water by the territory's Catholic bishop, who has experience with these matters. Not that I'm a damn Catholic, but we've lost several soldiers to the werewolves before, and we don't want to take any chances."

For a moment Jubal thought he must be dreaming. What the Major General was saying sounded crazy. His hand moved to the medal on his chest, and he grabbed it as a way of grounding himself. "So, the medal you awarded me is for werewolf hunting?"

The Major General chuckled. "No, Corporal, the medal is for bravery. Your bravery in the face of danger, and your valiant efforts to save the lives of your men. The Army does not officially recognize the existence of werewolves, or any other supernatural creatures, for that matter. But we do have to deal with them from time to time."

"You said 'other supernatural creatures.' What do you mean?"

The Major General chuckled again. "There are more things in heaven and earth, Horatio…"

Jubal finished the quote. "…than are dreamt of in your philosophy."

"You know Shakespeare?" The Major General seemed surprised.

"Yes sir. I've read many of the classics."

"Good for you." He poured more brandy into both of their glasses. Jubal heard a note of condescension in his voice. He was curious to know what other supernatural creatures the Major General had dealt with. But he decided to risk asking a bolder question.

"Is there a reason we weren't told exactly who – or what – we were hunting? I can't help but think that if we had been better prepared…" Jubal didn't finish the sentence. He didn't want to come across as blaming the Major General's orders for the deaths of Shaw and Thurman.

The Major General bristled. "That," he said stiffly, "was on a need-to-know basis."

"SO BASICALLY, WE WERE human fodder. Others lost their lives before us on the same type of mission."

Jubal nodded yes. The ghost of Thomas Shaw, floating in the ether beside Jubal's bed, scowled.

"Hey," said Jubal. "When you get angry, you become more solid. I can still see through you, but not as much."

"That," said Tom, "gives me an idea."

JUBAL KNEW THE MEMORY. Tom had shown him once, but only after Jubal had asked him repeatedly. The memory of the wolf lunging at him, the gouts of blood everywhere, the intense pain as the wolf's teeth shredded his throat. The gasping for breath. Jubal could *feel* the pain Tom had felt. He found himself gasping for breath. Jubal knew it was only a memory, but it felt like he was actually dying.

And then the parting words, whispered through blood, as Jubal held him in his arms.

The memory was so real. It frightened him with its vividness. It was like a magic lantern show behind his eyes, but the images were moving. Jubal never asked Tom to share that memory again. Only that one time.

There were other memories Tom shared on the evenings he spent by Tom's bed, much more pleasant memories. But that memory of dying, from Tom's point of view, was by far the most intense.

THE TRAIN RIDE WAS long. Jubal was carrying his beloved copy of *Leaves of Grass*, but he found himself staring blankly out the train window, watching the countryside go past, unable to read. He did not know why the Major General had summoned him this time. He had no desire to see the man again. He was still grieving, and he felt nothing but anger at the man who had, in essence, ordered Tom's death and the death of Private Sam Thurman.

Jubal was wearing the medal of bravery around his neck, as a sign of respect. But he wanted to rip it off. He leaned against the window and tried to sleep. He could see the ghost of Tom in the seat across from him, and he could feel Tom's love.

IT HAD ONLY BEEN a month, but the Major General looked very different. The strong, confident man who had sipped brandy by the fireplace was gone. In his place was a weak, sickly man, lying in a hospital bed.

"Do you know why I called you here?" The Major General decided to skip all pleasantries. His voice was weak. He sounded exhausted.

"No sir, I don't. Can I get you anything? Water?" Jubal sat down beside the bed, near the pitcher of water on the night table.

The Major General waved his hand dismissively. "I don't need *water*. What I need is for you to make it stop."

"Make what stop, sir?"

The Major General stared at him. He couldn't decide whether Jubal was truly ignorant of the situation, or he was being insubordinate. He glanced over at the door to make sure it was shut and the two were alone. He took as deep a breath as he could. "I have not had a full night's sleep since I saw you last. I get thirty, forty minutes of sleep a night, if that. My heart has been weakened, and the doctors say I cannot go on like this."

"I am truly sorry to hear that, sir," said Jubal, and to his own surprise he meant it sincerely. "But what has that to do with me?"

"It has to do with your," – the Major General scowled – "with your *friend*, Private Thomas Shaw. The only thing I can figure is that Shaw is haunting me."

The look of surprise on Jubal's face was genuine. Tom had not told him about haunting the Major General.

"Every night, ten or eleven times a night, I relive the experience of Shaw's death. I see the wolf and the blood, I feel the pain, I wake up gasping for breath. My heart stopped beating once, and the medics here revived me. I don't know how long I can continue. Please," he said, reaching out and weakly grabbing Jubal's hand. "Please make it stop."

Jubal looked down at his hand. "I can't make it stop. Tom has always been his own person. I have no control over his ghost."

The Major General withdrew his hand. "Apparently, you have control over very little. Including your own lusts."

Jubal recoiled. "What the hell does that mean?"

Anger flashed in the Major General's eyes. "You will address me with respect while I'm still alive. I have relived your parting exchange with Shaw, as he lay dying. I know his last words to you, and yours to him. I know that you loved Private Shaw in a way that scandalizes common decency. I could have you prosecuted in criminal court for buggery. Or at the very least, horsewhipped."

Jubal glared at the Major General before responding in a firm, even tone. "Based on the testimony of a ghost? Based on the delusions of a dying man who thinks he is haunted? I will not insult you, sir, by pretending to have a respect you have not earned. Yes, you could follow through on your threats, but if you do so, the hauntings will get worse."

The Major General actually trembled at that. He closed his eyes. "I had no idea," he murmured. "I knew that werewolves existed, but I had no idea that ghosts are real. I had no idea that hauntings can be so intense that they threaten a man's life. And I had no idea…"

Jubal waited.

The Major General opened his eyes and raised his head to look at Jubal. "I had no idea that a man could love another man so strongly. So purely." He closed his eyes, and his head fell back down on his pillow.

"All those things," said Jubal, "were on a need-to-know basis."

JUBAL WAS ALONE WHEN he rode back into the ghost town. In one of the rooms of the abandoned boarding house, on the ground floor near the back, he found the wolf and her pups, scrambling over each other on a mattress he had pulled from a bed and put on the floor. The wolf came over to Jubal and gently rubbed up against him, like a friendly dog.

And there, fussing over them, was the ghost of his beloved Tom.

Tom smiled to see him. "It's been three months. She's getting ready to take the pups out and show them how to hunt. There's plenty of game around here and no humans for miles. It's a good home for them. For us."

"I'm glad you're all doing well," said Jubal.

"I've named her Althea," said Tom. "She shared her real name with me, but it's a werewolf name that humans cannot pronounce."

Jubal laughed. "Althea is a pretty name."

"I found out that an eclipse can induce labor prematurely in werewolves who are pregnant. Or at least that's what she's been told."

Jubal cleared his throat. "I wanted to let you know the Major General has died. He passed away in his sleep last night."

Tom did not seem surprised at all. "I know," he said.

"I thought you might. You never told me that you planned to haunt him."

Tom smiled. "That, my love, was on a need-to-know basis."

The Bitter Unthreading

SARA TANTLINGER

You are lore; a myth from the internet
morphed into flesh and blood, standing
half-dressed in a bathroom with bleach
and strawberry hair dye—bursting
crimson and blinking doe eyes, watching
waiting, always daring me, and do I dare?

Have I disturbed your universe enough, yet?
My galaxies grow combat-worn
from your charmed tongue spilling
our secrets like birdseed across
broken star topography, but no birds
come to sing for us any longer.

We're twin flames destined to outburn,
named problems to be solved by people
who were supposed to love us, and it's

stunningly sad how you slipped phantom-like
across the ocean to wait out all these years.

Time compresses, blunders onward; I wonder
if the world has broken you, shaped your feral
feminine into tame, withered pouts, but your lips
still summon me, even as your family wraps you
in luxury and buys your trust, but money
can't make alligator tears taste any less bitter, babe.

All our unforgiven days, forgiven in the end—
the scorch of us lingering beneath your cold
temperament as you seek warm fingertips to thaw
us out into the wild, where we grew electric, and I
can only remind you of the we were, not what we are.

What are we capable of feeling after
the blinking stretch of years yawn into
dizzy days unthreading dreams
until memory scars fade into salted fog,
until isolation creates a heartbeat mantra of
what if, what if, what if

and

we were, we were, we were.

About the Authors

CHRISTINA BERGLING has been writing since childhood. More than anything, she is a horror author, crafting creepy stories anywhere from psychological to horror-comedy. By day, Christina works in IT. In 2009, she traveled to Iraq to work as a contractor, training military groups on software. Christina has five books published (*Savages, The Waning, The Rest Will Come, Screechers,* and *Followers*). She also has works in over 20 anthologies, including *Collected Christmas Horror Shorts, Demonic Wildlife, Colorado's Emerging Authors,* and *Graveyard Girls.* Christinabergling.com

RYAN COLE is a speculative fiction writer who lives in Virginia with his husband and snuggly pug child. He is a winner of the Writers of the Future Contest, and his recent work has appeared in Clarkesworld, PodCastle, MetaStellar, Factor Four, Gallery of Curiosities, and Voyage YA by Uncharted, among others. Find out more at ryancolewrites.com.

AMANDA NEVADA DEMEL is an emerging speculative fiction author. Her favorite genre is horror, thanks to careful cultivation from her father. She especially appreciates media that can simultaneously scare her and make her cry. She is a recent MFA graduate from the University of New Hampshire, where she also worked as the fiction editor at *Barnstorm Journal.* Additionally, she loves reptiles, musicals, and breakfast foods.

AMANDA DIER is an emergency dispatcher by day. She has been previously published by *The Magazine of Fantasy and Science Fiction*, *Abyss & Apex*, and other markets. Amanda lives in Florida with her partner and dog in a carefully curated orchid and carnivorous plant forest.

SEAN EADS is a gay writer and librarian living in Denver, CO. His first novel, *The Survivors*, was a finalist for the Lambda Literary Award, and his third novel, *Lord Byron's Prophecy*, was a finalist for the Shirley Jackson Award and the Colorado Book Award. His latest novel, *Confessions*, was a finalist for the Colorado Book Award. His next novel, *Lost Story*, will be released in 2025 by Hex Publishers and Crystal Lake Publishing will be bringing out a novel and a short story collection in 2025 as well. Updates can be found at seaneadswriter.com.

M. EDUSA (she/her) is a Kansas City transplant who enjoys writing in the fantasy and horror genres, especially when she gets to feature queer and marginalized characters. Her professional background is in law enforcement and the military. She is currently writing short horror stories (and plugging away at a novel) from the Middle East where she is stationed with the U.S. Army.

MICHAEL THOMAS FORD is the author of numerous books for both young readers and adults. His novels for teenagers include

Every Star That Falls, Love & Other Curses, and *Suicide Notes*, while his books for younger readers include *The Headless Doll* and *The Lonely Ghost*. His short fiction appears regularly in *Weird Fiction Quarterly* and is included in the recent anthologies *We Mostly Come Out At Night, Other Terrors*, and *Unspeakable Horror 3: Dark Rainbow Rising*.

A five-time winner of the Lambda Literary Award for LGBTQ books, Michael has also been a finalist for the Shirley Jackson Award, the Bram Stoker® Award, the Ignyte Award, and the Firecracker Alternative Book Award. He lives in rural Ohio with his husband and dogs, where he gardens, collects flannel shirts, and waits impatiently for Mothman to pay him a visit. Find out more at michaelthomasford.com.

MAXWELL I. GOLD is a Jewish-American cosmic horror poet and editor, with an extensive body of work comprising over 300 poems since 2017. His writings have earned a place alongside many literary luminaries in the speculative fiction genre. His work has appeared in numerous literary journals, magazines, and anthologies. Maxwell's work has been recognized with multiple nominations, including the Eric Hoffer Award, Pushcart Prize, and Bram Stoker® Awards. Find him and his work at thewellsoftheweird.com.

DARRELL Z. GRIZZLE (he/him) is a horror, dark fantasy, and thriller writer. He is the author of *I Never Meant to Start a Murder Cult*. His story "Moonlight Sonata, with Scissors" was adapted into a short film by award-winning indie filmmaker Chris Ethridge. Darrell is featured in *Pink Triangle Rhapsody*, a book of pulp fiction by gay writers. His queer Lovecraftian story "Incantation on a Summer Night" is in the folk horror anthology *Lonely*

Hollows. Darrell lives in shadow-haunted Kennesaw, Georgia, with a murdercat and way too many books. His home on the web is ShadowHaunted.com.

JOHN GROVER is a multi-genre fiction author residing in Massachusetts. John grew up watching creature double feature with his brother on Saturday afternoons. This fueled his love of monsters, ghosts and the supernatural. He never missed an episode. In his spare time, he loves to cook, garden, go to the theater to watch horror movies with his friends, read, talk about food, bake amazing desserts, play with his dogs and draw-badly.

John's short fiction has appeared in anthologies and magazines such as *Wicked Creatures by* The New England Horror Writers, *Jersey Pines Crypto-Gnats Anthology, Best New Zombie Tales 1* by Books of the Dead Press, *The Vermin Anthology, The Northern Haunts Anthology* by Shroud Publishing, *The Zombology Series* by Library of the Living Dead Press, *Dark Recesses Press, Crimson Streets, Flesh and Blood Magazine, Underbelly Zine, Silver Blade, Morpheus Tales, Wrong World, The Willows, Alien Skin Magazine, Aurora Wolf* and more. Find out more at shadowtales.com.

TOSHIYA KAMEI (she/they) takes inspiration from fairy tales, folklore, and mythology. She attempts to reimagine the past, present, and future while shifting between various perspectives and points of view. Many of her characters are outsiders living on the margins of society. Her short stories have appeared in *Daily Science Fiction, Galaxy's Edge,* and elsewhere. Her piece "Hungry Moon" won *Apex Magazine*'s October 2022 Microfiction Contest.

BENJAMIN LARNED (he/they) is a queer horror writer and filmmaker. Their work is featured in Vastarien, Apocalypse Confidential, Creepy Podcast, and Seize the Press, among others. "What Scares a Ghost?", their story in Coffin Bell, was nominated for the Best Small Fictions 2023. Their short film "Payment" is streaming on ALTER. They hold an MFA from The New School.

R.J.K. LEE is a queer father born in Oregon, USA, and in 2005, immigrated to Japan, where he writes stories on trains and balconies while juggling work as a teacher, proofreader, and voice narrator. His fiction has previously appeared in such publications as Tales & Feathers, DreamForge, and the Clamour & Mischief anthology. Find him at his website rjklee.com.

G.B. LINDSEY's most salacious and long-term affair is with the horror genre, but she also writes sci-fi, romance, and historical fiction. By day, she works in kidney and liver transplant; by night she reads voraciously, rocks out to metal, and bothers her cat. She earned her Master's in Creative Writing in Newcastle Upon Tyne, and participates regularly in live readings and book sales through the Queer Sacramento Authors Collective, as well as acting as their events coordinator. She is proud to have been a featured writer in September 2021 for MITA's ongoing project, Madwomen in the Attic, during which she explored her experiences with chronic depression and clinical OCD. She was recently published in Ghost Orchid Press's eco-horror anthology, *Chlorophobia*, and in the Sapphic horror anthology *Moonflowers and Nightshade*. Follow more of her writing journey at gblindsey.com.

ROOK RILEY (she/they) is a former U.S. Army linguist and neurospicy nonbinary horror author, game writer, developmental editor, and former middle-school teacher. They are a member of the Horror Writers Association, The Red Herring Society, The Texas Center for the Missing, and the Cold Case Coalition. Binge-watching horror and collecting tattoos are their current hobbies. Will fight you for the love and affection of Walton Goggins, Pedro Pascal, and Eliza Dushku. NOTE: Matthew Lillard may sub in as a love interest at any time. To learn more about Rook, go to authorrookriley.com.

ERIC DAVID ROMAN is a serious writer, which you can tell by the fact he uses all three names. While not a noteworthy mathematician in any regard, he is the author of the queer horror novella Long Night at Lake Never, the raucous comedy Despicable People, and the short story, Clamshell, which was published with the online imprint, Roi Fainéant Press.

A would-be recluse, if not so annoyingly popular, Eric lives in a small town in Virginia with his husband of 25 years and their spoiled fur babies. "In my next life, I too want to come back as the cat of a gay couple and you should as well." He avoids social media (except for thirst traps), is beginning to have a slight disdain for technology, and continues to write stories focused on strong and diverse queer main characters, while navigating a world that's constantly trying to silence those voices.

SUMIKO SAULSON (ze/hir/hirs) is a Bram Stoker® Nominated poet for their 2022 collection *The Rat King: A Book of Dark Poetry* (*Dooky Zines*), and an award-winning author of Afrosurrealist and multicultural sci-fi and horror whose latest novel *Happiness and Other Diseases* is available on Mocha Memoirs Press.

Winner of the HWA Scholarship from Hell (2016) BCC Voice "Reframing the Other" contest (2017), Mixy Award (2017), Afrosurrealist Writer Award (2018), HWA Diversity Grant (2020), HWA Richard Laymon Presidents Award (2021), Ladies of Horror Fiction Readers Choice Award (2021). Sumiko has an AA in English from Berkeley City College, writes a column called "Writing While Black" for a national Black Newspaper, the San Francisco BayView is the host of the SOMA Leather and LGBT Cultural District's "Erotic Storytelling Hour," and teaches courses at the Speculative Fiction Academy. To stay abreast of Sumiko's work, go to SumikoSaulson.com.

J. DANIEL STONE is NYC born and raised, and writes urban horror with a queer focus. He sold his first story when he was 22 years old and has since written four novels, *The Absence of Light*, *Blood Kiss*, *Stations of Shadow*, and *Daubed in Darkness*, as well as a short story collection, *Lovebites & Razorlines*. His work has been selected for "Best Of" by Grey Matter Press. He writes under a pseudonym to keep the wolves at bay. Visit him at SolitarySpiral.com.

SARA TANTLINGER is the author of the Bram Stoker Award®-winning poetry collection, *The Devil's Dreamland: Poetry Inspired by H.H. Holmes,* and the Stoker-nominated works *To Be Devoured* and *Cradleland of Parasites.* She has also edited *Not All Monsters* and *Chromophobia.* She is an active HWA member and participates in the HWA Pittsburgh Chapter. She embraces all things macabre and can be found lurking in graveyards or at saratantlinger.com and on Instagram @inkychaotics.

MAY WALKER (she/her) is a fiction writer and former teacher residing in the Pittsburgh area. While her work has not previously been published, she is hard at work on several short stories and a novel. She is an active member of Penn Writers and the HWA. You can find her on Instagram @maywalkerwrites.

About the Editors

VINCE A. LIAGUNO is an award-winning writer, anthologist, critic, and poet. He is the Bram Stoker Award®-winning editor of *Unspeakable Horror: From the Shadows of the Closet* (co-edited with Chad Helder) and the acclaimed *Other Terrors: An Inclusive Anthology* (co-edited with Rena Mason), which was a finalist for both the prestigious Shirley Jackson and World Fantasy Awards. His debut novel, 2006's *The Literary Six,* was a tribute to the slasher films of the eighties and won an Independent Publisher Award (IPPY). His debut poetry collection, *Demo Reels and Arthouse Madness,* was released in February 2025 by Raw Dog Screaming Press.

Healthcare administrator by day, pop culture enthusiast by night, his jam: books, slasher films, and Jamie Lee Curtis. He is a member—and former Secretary—of the Horror Writers Association, International Thriller Writers (ITW) and the National Book Critics Circle (NBCC). Vince currently resides in the mitten-shaped state of Michigan with his husband and dogs. Visit his website to learn more www.VinceLiaguno.com.

ABOUT THE AUTHORS

Sirrah Medeiros is an award-winning author, editor, and anthologist, and the Editor-in-Chief of Tundra Swan Press. She is a Marine Corps veteran, staunch LGBTQ+ ally, and began writing horror, poetry, and dark fantasy while a member of the Vicious Writers consortium in 2009. Her latest works include The BookFest award-winning anthology, *The Haunted Zone: A Horror Anthology by Women Military Veterans,* and *The Malediction Plague*, a zombie novella published in 2024. Her debut novel, *Secrets of Mother*, from the Cristiane Bradford series, won the National Association of Book Entrepreneur's Pinnacle Book Achievement Award for Best in Fantasy.

She lives in Northern Virginia with her husband and two energetic, playful rescue dogs. She takes pleasure in supporting causes, mentoring writers, hiking with her pups, drawing on occasion, and uniting experienced authors with new voices in genre fiction.

Sirrah's short fiction and poetry are found in numerous anthologies. Visit her websites to learn more at TundraSwanPress.com and SirrahMedeiros.com.

Acknowledgments

A huge thanks to everyone who backed our
Don't Ask, Ghosts Tell Kickstarter campaign.

Jacob H Joseph

Zack Fissel

Davy Van Obbergen

Randy "Sherpa" Brown

Colleen Feeney

Kristina Meschi

Paul & Laura Trinies

Darrell Z. Grizzle

Em Wagner

Olivia Montoya

Terra M.

Jennifer L. Pierce

Christina Bergling

Blair Foster

Emily Wagoner

Ed Abbott

Richard O'Shea

Rachel Clements

KICKSTARTER BACKERS

Craig Esser

David Edmonds

Paige

Emily Pitner

Zen Hance

Kristi Hutson

Nancy Stroer

Susanna Miller

Nellie Cole

Dino Hicks

Rachel Branaman

Lisa Bergling

Kristina Reich

AlaskanBrat

Taylor Travis

Melissa Yi

Ryan Cole

James Stewart

Leslie Twitchell

Tara King

Vulpine

Josie Angel

Summer Dawn Smith

Prof Brown

Lane Blevins

Patrice Sarath

Jon Smith

Laura Bennett

Thomas Johnson

Steve Pattee

Ophelia Grace

Jill Lee

Joshua Hair

I. Smith

Caroline Coriell

Elena Medeiros

William P Davis

R. Alan Cloud

Christina M Fernandez

Anonymous

Rebecca Hale

Lisa Morton

Remington Marsh

Bona Books

Rosy

DON'T ASK, GHOSTS TELL

Thank you for reading our collection.

We hope you enjoyed your visit with us. If the journeys traveled linger in your soul and your mind rests on the hauntings within these pages, would you honor us by disclosing your experience with others?

Share your views, whether they are lengthy orations or short sound bites where you purchased the book, or on Goodreads and Amazon.

We will see you soon!

Our list of titles expands as our small press grows. To stay in touch, please join our Facebook group or sign up for our newsletter through our website TundraSwanPress.com.

Tundra Swan Press

TUNDRA SWAN PRESS is a micro-press of dark fiction, fantasy, and thrillers. Woman-veteran owned and operated.

Our mission is to travel to shadowy corners and deep recesses of genre fiction to share compelling tales that captivate your senses and pull you into a visceral entanglement of feelings and instinctive emotions.

If you liked *Don't Ask, Ghosts Tell*, you may also enjoy:

Other Titles from Tundra Swan Press

The Haunted Zone: A Horror Anthology by Women Military Veterans

The Malediction Plague

Secrets of Mother

Content Warning

Don't Ask, Ghosts Tell handles sensitive subjects with a gentle approach while remaining true to the horror genre. However, some stories and poems explore mature topics including substance abuse, grief, prejudice, psychological trauma, PTSD, the horrors of war, and physical abuse.

www.ingramcontent.com/pod-product-compliance
Lightning Source LLC
Chambersburg PA
CBHW061340310726

48974CB00001B/131